THE ENTREPRENEUR'S NURSE

By

Rose Fresquez

---

1. https://www.myidentifiers.com/title_registration?is-bn=978-1-961159-01-3&icon_type=New

To Joel, Isaiah, Caleb, Abigail and Micah. I love you so much and I'm so blessed to laugh and cry with you every day.

To my Mom Harriet, now in Heaven, thank you for being the Proverb 31 woman. To my Dad, James Mudoba—while several girls spent time working on the farm so that they could train to be wives, my siblings and I were in boarding school. Thank you for the sacrifices you made, the cows you sold so that I could go to school.

This story is for you. Thanks for the Inspiration.

ACKNOWLEDGEMENTS

I want to thank the Lord, my Savior. Without you, Father, there's no point in trying to do anything at all. It's my prayer that I can honor you with my words. I thank you for connecting me with an amazing group of people who helped support me in accomplishing this novel.

To my husband, Joel, who works so hard to provide for our family so I can stay home and take care of the kids. I'm so blessed we get to journey through life together.

To my children, Isaiah, Caleb, Abigail, and Micah, you fill my heart with joy. Thanks for the giggles, laughter, and encouragement.

Unending thanks to my editor, Deirdre Lockhart. Your insights and wisdom have helped shape this story.

To my insider team, thanks for always suggesting the coolest ideas.

To Nicole, Deb, Katherine, Elizabeth, and Trudy. You ladies are so amazing for the time you invested to brainstorm, beta read, and critique my manuscript. Thank you from the bottom of my heart.

CHAPTER 1

"African time!" Brady Sharp mumbled the receptionist's words as he strode out of the hotel lobby. Where was his driver? His muscles stiffened and his heart raced as he paced on the cobblestone court.

Humidity hung thick in the air. It wasn't even seven a.m. and sweat already trickled down his forehead and dampened his shirt, leaving his neck sticky. He stretched his arms to shrug out of his dress coat. The button-down by itself would have to do.

With minimal activity at the hotel entrance, most guests must be on vacation and still sleeping. He glanced at his Apple watch for probably the twentieth time.

Six ten. Ten minutes late. Enough to throw Brady off his A game. By hustling all day, he'd made it this far in business. He'd failed several times, yes, but he'd celebrated more deals gone right. Time management never hindered his prosperity, and it wouldn't start now—not when he'd flown thousands of miles from home.

Needing a distraction, he strode to the manicured lawn and retrieved the iPhone he'd bought after his plane landed. How irresponsible of him to rely on the hotel to communicate with his driver instead of saving the number himself.

When he'd arrived in Uganda yesterday, he'd scoped out a successful resort in one of Kampala's suburbs. It made more sense to stay the night in Kampala, twenty-five miles away from the Entebbe resort he was about to buy—well, lease, because he was a new foreigner.

He checked his watch again. What were the odds his property lawyer made it on time? He blew out a breath to relax his nerves.

Think positive.

Based on his assistant's calculations, he needed an hour to reach Entebbe. That is, if he missed the morning rush hour. All the more reason he'd given himself the extra hour cushion.

If he hadn't already checked out of the hotel, he'd return to his room and type a few emails to his regional managers, or go over his proposal for the investor meeting in Manhattan—a meeting a mere thirty-four hours away.

With a packed week of meetings ahead, he shouldn't be traveling overseas, but the resort sellers preferred a face-to-face meeting over a virtual meeting. And this wasn't a deal he'd blow.

He shook his head to brush off the creeping doubt. He'd better succeed to make his time count. If something went wrong and he didn't make it on time, the other eager buyer would end up as the new owner.

Failure was not an option.

He clenched and unclenched his fist. With four of his forty-five resorts not doing well, Sharp Resorts could lose some investors if Brady didn't pull through to the next income bracket in the upcoming financial year. Ten figures was so close, he could almost taste it.

Regardless, he could always do something to gain leverage over the competitors.

He ducked when a bee buzzed over his ear and landed on one of the many pink bougainvillea shrubs creeping along the metal fence.

Yesterday's familiar Volvo pulled in front of the hotel, and the same driver, Nsanji, stepped out. Brady barreled past the vibrant flower gardens to take a shortcut into the lobby for his luggage.

"I will get that." Nsanji met him outside the revolving door and put his hand out to take Brady's luggage.

His suitcase held only the outfit he'd worn yesterday, and he didn't need to be waited on. "I got it."

The dark-skinned man hurried back to the car and held the passenger door. The man's smile was as bright as his yellow button-down.

"Thank you, Nsanji."

Nsanji inclined his head, oblivious to his tardiness. "Good morning, Mr. Sharp."

Brady forced his lips to fold into something like a smile. He'd save the time-management speech for his employees back in the States. He blew out a soft breath and gave a nod. "A good morning to you, too." He then buckled himself in as the tension loosened from his shoulders. They were on their way. If his assistant's calculations proved correct, he had forty-five minutes to spare.

"Did you sleep well?" A thick accent lilted his question as Nsanji started the car.

Brady nodded, the man's politeness making him at ease. Remembering the envelope of shillings left over, he retrieved it and handed it over. "I won't need Uganda currency anymore." Beth—his assistant—had already paid the airport taxi to pick him up from the resort at one. Plenty of time to roam the property after the meeting. "I paid the hotel for your work and tip. That's what I was told, I pay them." He wanted to make sure the man was being paid.

Another grin widened Nsanji's face when he peeked at the bills in the envelope. "Thank you very much, sir. The hotel pay me after they take their share for finding me customer."

When they drove through the gate, Nsanji waved at the two guards sitting in the gatehouse.

Relieved that the car was on the move, Brady tossed his bag in the back seat, loosened his tie, and folded his dress coat across his lap. He could relax and enjoy the orange and pink sky.

Horns honked and engines rattled as traffic came to a standstill when they approached a roundabout. Police in neon-green vests gestured to stop cars on one side and directed Brady's lane to move, but they barely had space to inch forward. Only the motorcycles were moving, cutting in front of slow-moving cars, swerving with no regard to their safety.

He'd need a miracle to reach the resort today. He wiped perspiration from his forehead with the back of his hand. Why was it so hot? He could've done without an undershirt. He squinted as he searched the dashboard buttons. "Is it okay if I turn on the AC?"

"AC don't work."

Brady lowered his window instead.

A soft breeze stirred scents of fried foods from street vendors carrying large trays and baskets of golden pastries along the sidewalk. The palm trees lining the sidewalk made him miss his beachfront house in San Diego.

He needed to do something besides stress about getting to his meeting. Now might be a good time to learn a thing or two in Uganda. "What does African time mean?" The receptionist muttered that when Brady had asked why Nsanji was running late.

Nsanji cleared his throat, another of his smiles unfolding. "Well... we Africans take things easy. If you want someone to meet you at six, you have to tell them five o'clock."

In other words, it was a cultural tendency for tardiness. "We don't operate like that in business."

"Work never end." His words thoughtful, Nsanji spoke the same way he had when he'd driven Brady across town to the competing resort yesterday. "You're go-go man. Try to look around Kampala before you return to America."

"I'll look around next time." Since he started the resort business thirteen years ago, relaxing wasn't an option. One had to operate by the mindset that the minute they thought they'd made it was the moment of failure.

A motorcycle with a passenger squeezed between the Volvo and a white minibus.

Brady shifted in his seat, gripping his coat when a car almost ran over the motorcycle.

Nsanji didn't waver.

"That man almost got hit," Brady said. Had Nsanji not seen it?

"That's how boda bodas drive. Very mad..." Nsanji talked about motorcyclists. Most of them rented the bikes and needed to transport a certain number of people before they made any profit in a given day. "Even if it means running over pedestrians, drivers will do whatever it takes to get customers to their destination as fast as possible."

"Who would be crazy enough to ride on those?"

With his chin, Nsanji motioned to all the cars surrounding them. More a parking lot without designated spots than a roadway. "People who don't want to sit in traffic."

While Nsanji talked about the traffic they might be sitting in for another hour, Brady's heart rate shot up. He checked his watch. They'd only moved one mile in fifteen minutes. He bounced his feet as if to push the car forward.

By the time they got out of the jammed traffic and ascended the hill on Entebbe Road, the car gave a little gurgle. Nsanji frowned as he pressed his foot on the gas pedal.

"Out of gas?" With no gas stations in sight, that could be a major issue.

"Uh... I..."

The engine sputtered and lost speed. Nsanji turned the key, but only a clicking noise drifted up.

"This is not good." The man gripped the steering wheel, his forehead glistening, and smashed his fist into it when the engine died. "No!"

Brady should respond with, "It's okay." Really, he should. But it wasn't in him. He hid his fisted hand beneath his coat. Yelling or growling wouldn't fix anything.

Desperate to get moving, he swung open the door. "I'll get out and push." To the side of the road, at least.

They pushed the Volvo to a paint-chipped building. Trash littered the ground where street vendors had temporary booths on display.

White minibuses drove past, and Brady scrunched his nose at the powerful diesel fumes now mingling with fried-food scents. He pressed a hand to his queasy stomach.

Of all the things he'd tinkered with as a child, cars had never interested him. Standing feet away, he tossed his coat on his shoulder and planted a hand on his hip.

Nsanji opened the smoke-filled engine.

People walked along. Those who greeted him in broken English smiled while street peddlers presented their items.

A teenage boy tried to slide a necklace around his neck, and Brady ducked—turning when another man threw a shirt over his shoulder while asking him to pay for it.

Talk about high-pressure sales tactics. He shook his head and lifted his hands. "No, thanks. I don't need anything." Supporting their businesses would be nice, but right now, he needed to get back to his own. Plus, he'd gotten rid of his money. He burrowed through the tangle of arms and legs to Nsanji.

Ouch! Pain jolted through him at a tight grip on his wrist. When he looked at his hand to assess the pain, a boy not much older than ten sprinted off with his watch.

"Hey!" He pointed in the kid's direction. A couple of guys tried to chase the kid but gave up as the boy disappeared up a path between two buildings.

Brady needed to get out of here. It would be safe to assume all the people around him were thieves. Except for Nsanji.

With his height advantage, Brady peered over people's heads to keep a steady gaze on Nsanji, the only familiar face.

The driver's frown as he closed the hood depleted Brady's remaining hope. He rubbed at his throbbing temples.

"I need to see a mechanic." Nsanji brushed his blackened hands together.

The rapid blood circulation through his system left Brady's shirt damp. There went that deal! He'd be hard-pressed to make it to the resort, but he had to try.

"Any chance you can find me another cab—special taxi," he corrected when he remembered how Nsanji called himself. "Do you think I'll make it?"

"Not unless you take a boda boda."

No way! Motorcyclists within earshot rolled their bikes, and soon, options surrounded him.

"Mzungu, take mine!" one of them shouted. Mzungu, he'd learned, was the nickname the natives used for Caucasians.

"Mine has a new seat," said another.

He rubbed his temples again. What choice did he have? Take a taxi and show up three hours late, or make it on time with disheveled hair from the wind whipping at him on a motorcycle?

The motorcyclists spoke over each other as they argued why Brady should ride on their bike.

Despite the tension in his shoulders, he forced a smile at their enthusiasm. They reminded him of himself. Even as a ten-year-old Boy Scout selling popcorn, he never took no for an answer. That skill still came in handy when he had to throw investors a convincing pitch.

Nsanji urged the eager businessmen to step back. Wiping his brow with a handkerchief, he addressed Brady. "Can I get you a boda boda, Mr. Sharp?"

The men flashed hopeful smiles. Going back home with a failed mission was worse than shutting down one of his branches. "Sure."

Nsanji handled the negotiations in their language. Then in English, Brady asked, "Who can speak English?"

With only two motorcyclists left, Nsanji pulled out different colored bills and handed money to the short man who would be Brady's driver. That was thoughtful of him. Brady would have to make sure he got reimbursed later.

Karim's smile was as kind as Nsanji's. And the throbbing slowed in Brady's temple. He'd make it on time, and this man wouldn't drive as crazy as the bikers he'd seen earlier.

Likely sensing Brady's fear, Nsanji pointed a warning finger. "Be very careful with mzungu. Don't drive too fast."

Brady's tense nerves eased, but he had another bigger problem. He'd never ridden a motorcycle. "So, what do I do?"

"Hold onto the driver's waist or the handles." Nsanji handed Brady his bag. "You will be fine."

He had to be. Karim steadied the small motorcycle for Brady to climb on.

"Keep your feet on the pedals," Nsanji reminded Brady, then told the driver their destination.

Moments later, Brady was perched high up on a flimsy pad resembling a seat. This was not safe, but backing out wasn't an option. "Do you offer your passengers helmets?"

The man stifled a laugh. He probably assumed Brady was teasing, and one look at all the bikers hovering with nothing on their heads meant a helmet was a foreign word in their vocabulary. "Never mind."

With the grab rails practically nonexistent, Brady clung on as the driver accelerated the uphill. In all the years he'd sought adventure through scuba diving and parasailing, he'd never feared for his life as he did when Karim squeezed through the traffic and weaved between cars. Brady's knee brushed against a minibus on his left.

He shouted over the honking horns for the driver to slow down, but how could Karim hear him? He closed his eyes, not wanting to watch a car hit them any minute.

Traffic died down the further they drove from the city. He kept his eyes half-open so the dirt didn't sting them. He still managed to see the tall grass between residential homes spaced acres apart along the highway's far side.

The stirring breeze flapped his dampened shirt. He'd need to fix his hair before his meeting. Speaking of cool air, where was his coat? He patted his bag. Wait, he had it on his lap in the car. Did he leave it there? No, he'd tossed it over his shoulder during the chaos. "They stole my coat!"

"What?"

There was no sense in talking to Karim. Why would he hear anything when he was driving so fast? "Never mind!"

Brady moved his hand from the rail and gripped his bag onto his lap. At this speed, it would be falling anytime.

Just as he leaned out, the man gunned the motor. Unprepared for the sudden acceleration, Brady flew off the bike, thudding to the grainy ground.

Someone groaned. It was him. Something sharp sliced the side of his jaw or forehead or both.

"Help!" He struggled to keep his eyes open as the tall grass around him started to blur. Sticks poked through his shirt, scratching his neck. The whooshing cars seemed more distant with each passing second.

Where was his driver? Did he fall, too? Brady opened his mouth to call him. No...what was his name again?

He rubbed at his eye. Something was in it. He tried to force his body to stand, but his feet felt heavy. Battered and bruised, he groaned. "God, why am I here?"

He should've stayed in the States where everything was safe and familiar.

CHAPTER 2

There were moments when Ruth Kirabo was grateful for her job as an RN—moments like now when she swaddled a wiggly baby in a blanket and handed her to the grinning dad.

The spring bed squeaked when Sajid moved to take the baby. Not far from him, his wife lay there, staring at the metal ceiling as she rubbed a hand over swollen eyes.

Ruth's eyes tingled, and she blinked back joyous tears. She'd had another successful delivery with less medical equipment.

"We're naming the baby after you, Musawo." Namase's lopsided wig almost fell off her head when she shifted to look at her husband and child.

Musawo was Ruth's nickname, her job title.

"Ruth." Sajid gently swayed the bundle in his arms, his smile wide. "You will be as smart as Musawo."

Sajid's compliment warmed her heart. This would be the fifth baby in the community named after her. Maybe sixth, she'd lost count. "I'm honored to be her namesake." Did her tone hide the twinge of sadness engulfing her?

"Ruth is a powerful Bible name." She turned to the window and slid open the dark curtains. She needed to keep her hands busy rather than reveal sadness in front of the happy family. Natural light now filled the bedroom. "My grandmom named me after the biblical character."

"Ruth," Sajid whispered the name as he gazed at his baby. Although a Muslim, Sajid didn't seem bent on sticking to names in his religion.

With her work done, Ruth grabbed her bag of medical supplies. She had to head back to the clinic, which doubled as her house. "When you're ready to talk about family planning, let me know."

She looked down to the yawning mom of seven kids. Namase was five years younger than Ruth's thirty. Most women Ruth's age were married and had kids, although several of them were ignorant about family planning.

"Chacha!" Sajid called after the maid as she walked out of the room with bloodstained bedsheets in the basin. "Get Ruth some breakfast."

Ruth winced, hating to turn down their food for more reasons than the obvious. "I have to get back to my patient, but I will stay next time."

She'd received a text at three a.m. when Namase's labor pains intensified. Although Sajid was her landlord, he lived five kilometers from his rental property.

"Take some mandazi, at least." Sajid eased the now fussing baby into Namase's arms. "Don't forget to add this bill to last month's."

Ruth stopped in the doorway. "I will do so as soon as I get to the clinic." Like all the other times she met her landlord's family needs, she wrote it off from her rent. With twenty-some kids and three wives, Sajid was always in need of medicine for a sick child. At times, Ruth or her colleague delivered one of his wives' babies. So she managed to keep her rent low, and most months, she didn't need to pay. "Should I add Asim's medical bills to yours?"

Sajid narrowed his eyes, his gaze sweeping over her as he nodded and dismissed her question. "If your *mzungu* dreams don't work out, you will make a good wife for my son. Asim will feed you, and you will be fat in a month."

Despite her average size, Ruth was considered skinny by the Ugandan standard. Being overweight was a symbol of wealth, but she was content with how she looked. Plus, it would be a long time before she gained more weight—not when she barely had time to eat two meals a day.

She stifled a chuckle. She didn't want to sound proud if she spoke her mind. So she stuck to her usual response whenever his son came up in their conversation. "God will drop a mzungu on my lap one of these days."

Sajid laughed heartily as he rubbed his bald head. She got the same reaction from him and many of her friends whenever she used a mzungu to brush off their matchmaking with their husbands' friends—friends who were already married but wanted a second or third wife.

The few single men who'd shown interest in her were threatened by her career, and she had no intention of quitting. Although she wasn't a doctor, her clinic was the closest thing to a hospital within the entire sixty-kilometer radius. Most people couldn't afford to pay for a hospital. So she was needed full time. Maybe a man didn't need her, but this community and her home village needed her—her family needed her too.

"Asim will be waiting whenever you're ready." Sajid jolted her out of her thoughts.

"I think his wife and two kids are keeping him happy." Time to make her escape. "I'll see you later." She spoke over her shoulder as she disappeared through the door and hitched for the first boda boda she spotted.

RUTH'S CLINIC WAS A separate building from the three shops lined next to each other across from hers. Walking across the veranda of her closed clinic, she greeted the tailor, who was rolling his sewing machine in front of his shop.

"Olyotya, Musawo!" the butcher bellowed a cheerful greeting, setting up a scale below a hook that hung with a chunk of meat.

Ruth responded, breathing in the samosas' pleasant smell wafting from the charcoal stove.

Jamila greeted her, ladling a handful of golden triangle pastries from the pan and setting them on a flat tray.

"I'll stop by your shop later to buy some samosas for dinner," Ruth said, assuming Jamila would have any samosas left by the end of the day.

"I'll save you some."

Ruth thanked her, then walked around the building to enter the back door. From the single-room apartments, people opened their windows and swung aside floral curtains in their doors.

Inside, she put the fried bread on her coffee table. A white lace curtain divided the bed from the living space. Sajid's mandazi would make a perfect breakfast for her patient. She rubbed the back of her neck, grateful not to have to light a charcoal stove to cook one meal. Then she opened the wooden door to her clinic to check on Ivan, and draped the curtain across the clinic's spare room.

The seventy-year-old man had had a rough night too. The twin spring bed creaked when he turned to the side. With his breathing heavy and graying eyebrows still, he looked so peaceful. She wouldn't wake him yet. The EKG and breakfast could wait for another hour. She'd checked him before she left to deliver the baby, and his heart's electrical activity had been stable, the way it had been since he'd shown up with chest pain two days ago.

She kept him on the EKG for forty-eight hours after he showed up this time—his fourth time this year. The blood tests, X-rays, and EKG hadn't shown anything of concern, but she'd started a hospital fund for him since his MRI didn't reveal anything. The doctor recommended an angiogram in case Ivan had a blockage an X-ray and MRI couldn't detect.

Since it was her only emergency patient bed, she could only hope no one else would need it today.

She took the next thirty minutes to shower and pray, since the day always got away from her once she started. Which was why she'd designated Tuesdays to fast, so she could be diligent to pray on that given day.

With the Bible on the table and her prayer diary in hand, her thoughts wandered to her conversation with Sajid. The mzungu conversation brought to mind her prayers from two years ago.

She flipped through the pages of the diary she reserved for special prayers. The pastor had taught a sermon about faith. He'd challenged the congregation to write three things that seemed impossible to man—things only God could do.

She traced her finger over the lines she'd written.

1: Start a clinic on the city's outskirts to accumulate funds
to help people in my village and family.

2. Start a clinic in the village.

Her finger paused, then tapped against the last word. This was underway since she went to the village once every two months and set up a temporary clinic for three to four days depending on how long the medicine lasted. She still dreamed of a permanent clinic with full-time doctors and nurses, but she was thankful for the first steps.

She let her finger drop down to the next line.

3. A white man who loved God.

Somewhere along the way, she'd stopped praying for a mzungu. A slight part of her doubted she'd ever meet one.

Her previous relationship attempts with a pastor and a doctor she'd met in college failed—both left her for full-time housewives. Those experiences had shaken her, and the legalization of polygamy... well, the idea of sharing her husband with another woman terrified her. Those two reasons brought Ruth to a place of praying for a white man.

She and Eunice used to watch an American soap opera in college, and the white men seemed to marry one woman. Even if they broke up with their spouses, at least it was then that they moved on to someone else. That last part was why she wanted a white man who believed in the Bible and till death do us part.

But she was never going to find one if she kept herself tucked away in a suburb treating locals. No wonder her neighbors thought she was a dreamer. She needed to frequent where tourists hung out. Which would never happen because she didn't have the time.

With God, anything is possible. It was high time she resumed those prayers.

She knelt and closed her eyes, pleading with God to bring comfort and healing to the kids in her home village, and the widows and widowers who'd lost their spouses to AIDS. And for God's will in her life if she was ever to get married—which she longed to at times. "Drop a mzungu on my lap, one who loves You more than anything." If a man put God first, he'd love and respect her as well.

The wooden door dividing the clinic from her room opened.

"I got your text this morning." Eunice, Ruth's best friend and colleague, hung her handbag on the hook in the corner. "How did the delivery go?"

"Not as long as yours yesterday." Ruth covered her Bible and set it back on the table as she gave Eunice a rundown of the four hours at Sajid's house.

Besides their RN certifications, Ruth and Eunice had taken maternity training because it was critical for their community's needs.

Ruth stood. Since Eunice was here, she needed to get to the central pharmacy. "Ivan is still sleeping." Ruth requested Eunice check the vitals and make his tea when he woke up. "I hope he won't mind having percolator tea."

Eunice pursed her red lips. "The man is probably back because you cook for him. Who wouldn't want to stay in a clinic where they got fed?"

Ivan lived with his brother and sister-in-law. Even if their relationship was rocky most of the time, Ruth doubted he faked chest pains for a free meal. "What if he's really sick?"

He should be in a hospital. But, without money, they'd stop him at the front desk and send him home. Most people stayed at home and dealt with their pain until it was too late to do anything about it. "It's best to not take any chances."

After retrieving a slip of paper from the clinic's glass counter, she skimmed the long list written on both sides of a copy paper. "Did I forget anything to add?"

Eunice was now scratching her temple. The tight cornrows she'd braided two days ago were probably still throbbing. "Medicine envelopes."

"I have those down." Ruth needed plenty of envelopes for when she divided medicine for each family in the village. "Rashida will be an hour late. I hope you won't be too busy until she gets here."

"Quit stressing about everything." Eunice waved a hand. "People don't mind waiting."

True. They didn't have a choice whenever the clinic got busy.

Ruth hoisted her blue handbag to her shoulder before walking through the back door.

Dongo's red washcloth dangled when he waved his greeting before turning to wipe down his 2012 Corona. He serviced as a private taxi.

Gnarled branches stuck out on the narrow dirt path, slapping dew on her legs and feet. Her skirt and flat sandals weren't the best attire for taking a shortcut, but wearing anything past the knees wouldn't be the best option once the midmorning heat kicked in.

The highway came into view when she emerged from the path. Two taxis wheezed past. If they were half-empty, the driver would stop when they saw a pedestrian.

Catching a taxi this early was always a challenge, but she had a better chance finding the medicine on her list if she got to the pharmacy right as it opened. Although she was tempted to hire Dongo's private taxi, it would cost her a fortune. It was best she waited for the public minibus.

She jerked at the sound of faint moaning. Tall grass rustled. Movement and a hint of something blue caught her eye. It couldn't be a person, and surely not an animal.

She shuffled back through the grass, shoving it out of her face and almost tripping over a black bag meters away from—Oh my!

A white man lay on the ground, his brown hair rumpled.

Her heart constricting, Ruth gasped and pressed a hand against her chest. What? How? Questions crowded her mind, but only one answer arose. He was dressed like a businessman or a tourist on his way somewhere.

She dropped her purse and knelt beside him. No doubt he fell off a boda boda. It had happened to her sister. She'd fallen off a motorcycle, and the driver had taken off so they didn't have to be held responsible.

"Hello?" She placed two fingers on his neck. A faint pulse throbbed beneath them. *Thank You, Lord. He's alive.*

Bruises discolored his face. Blood dripped from the cut on his forehead. The corner of his lip was swollen and he mumbled nonsensical words.

She touched his face and his neck.

His hand gripped hers. "Ama…" He rolled his eyes, squeezing her hand. When she leaned closer to catch a sense of his words, he stopped talking.

"I'm Ruth." She squeezed his hand, and with her other, she brushed the dust from his forehead, frowning at the blood tracing along his square jaw. The open road rash required stitches, and she eased her hand from his to check his feet for any sign of broken bones.

"Don…t." He tried to pull her back. His eyes filled with fear, intent on her.

"I'm not leaving you." She patted his shoulder for reassurance. "Let me just check your feet."

After she explained why it was necessary, he let go of her hand.

She slid off his dress shoes and lifted his right foot, then his left, asking him to wiggle his toes, which he barely managed. Some of the tension loosened from her shoulders. He didn't have any broken bones or joint swelling. She took his hand to assure him he was going to be all right. "I'm a nurse, and I'm going to take care of you."

He opened his mouth as if to speak, but he didn't.

"What's your name?"

"Ug…"

Getting him to the hospital would take forever, and she had no guarantee they'd skip a two-hour waiting line before the doctor tended to him. How was she going to get him back to the clinic for a thorough examination?

He was in no shape to walk the unstable trail. Maybe she could sight somebody to ask for help. But not many people left for town earlier than nine unless they had jobs. Even if they did, rarely did anyone take the shortcut.

Dongo. The name came to mind. If he hadn't left for his taxi services… She retrieved her cell phone in her bag and called her neighbor. He answered at the second ring. "I need your help." Once she explained, Dongo said he'd be over right away.

The man groaned, and she returned to his side, "Help is on the way."

She stood as tires crunched through the grass, and soon, Dongo parked and sprang out toward them. How his car managed to trespass the bumpy ground, she had no idea.

"How are we going to do this?"

Dongo was already crouched and his strong arms hoisting the man on his shoulder. Panting, he carried him to his Corona's open back door. Well, that was one way of answering her question.

At the clinic, Dongo laid him on the examining table. While Ruth gathered the antibiotic and equipment needed to clean and stitch him up, Eunice tended to the other patients.

Since he kept swiping his tongue on his lips, Ruth asked Dongo to borrow bottled water from Jamila's shop. She would pay her later. As soon as Dongo returned, Ruth tilted the water bottle to the man's lips for him to take little sips.

Sweet cologne wafted from his dusty shirt when she worked the buttons to strip it off. Broad shoulders stretched beneath the white undershirt when she lifted it to inspect the scratched area on his shoulder. His skin was red and slightly bruised.

She numbed the injury with antiseptic before using a soapy washcloth to clean his bruised shoulder and face. He frowned and gasped when she cleaned the open wound above his left eye.

"Sorry." Cringing, she tried to be careful. "I'm almost done."

Although he was still incoherent, she expected a nod when she asked, "Have you had a tetanus immunization yet?"

He mumbled something about his bag. Did he mean he had it in his bag? She didn't feel comfortable rummaging through his items, but if he was a tourist, he must have had a tetanus shot before coming to Uganda.

After a thorough check, his skin revealed no loose tendons—or any fat, for that matter. She numbed his face and proceeded with the needle.

He winced and mumbled as she threaded the needle through his forehead. Nine stitches later, she was done.

The hushed whispers on the veranda reminded her that her neighbors waited for Mzungu to step out of the clinic. She didn't blame their curiosity. Never did they get a white man in their area. Most of them, like Ruth, had never seen one this close. He looked more handsome than the ones she'd seen on TV.

With Ivan still occupying the clinic bed and the exam table needed when they got more patients throughout the day, Ruth requested Eunice to administer pain medicine to the tourist while she changed her bedsheets. If he slept for a few hours, he'd feel better before he left for wherever he needed to go.

Moments later, she held one of his elbows and Eunice held the other as they led him to the back room. While her colleague returned to the clinic, Ruth drew aside the bed curtains so she could keep an eye on him. She'd forgotten to put back the pillow when she changed the bedsheets. She reached for it from the love seat and eased it beneath his head.

As she moved his head, he opened his eyes—eyes the color of clear skies in her village. They bore deeply into her own. His hand cupped her cheek as if studying her. She swallowed, and her breath caught under his scrutiny. The man might have brain damage. Now, she doubted she should let him sleep.

The corners of his lips folded. "Thank you." He then dropped his hand back to his chest.

She smiled in return, her tongue already tied. Before she could form a response, he closed his eyes. She stood, her body warm as his chest rose and fell until his breathing grew shallow.

Even though it wasn't mosquito season, she untangled the net from the knot and spread it over him just in case one snuck in her house.

She then opened the curtains. If he was waking up in a strange place, a bright room might help him ease into his new surroundings.

The clinic seemed busier than most days, making her grateful to have Rashida, the temporary nurse, around. More people were getting measles and polio vaccinations. Malaria patients had come in, as had those who came to stock up malaria medicine before the rainy season next month.

Ruth checked on the tourist from time to time, and when the line in the clinic slowed down, she walked to Jamila's shop to buy some vegetable samosas and bottled water. She'd read well water wasn't safe for tourists to drink.

She set the water on the table when she found her patient still sleeping, then headed to check on Ivan.

He sat up when he saw Ruth, and his face crinkled into a smile. "Ruth, my child."

"How are you feeling?" Eunice had already checked his blood pressure, and the EKG results were still normal, which was a good sign.

"A little bit better." His shoulders sagged. "Looks like you'll need your bed back."

He could go home today, but his brother had no time to take care of him. "Mzungu should be well and on his way when he wakes."

Ivan smiled. "I'm glad he's okay."

So was Ruth. "I ordered chapati with the eggs wrapped in it—a rolex—for your lunch. Jamila will bring it over soon." A perk from treating Jamila's kids when they were sick. Ruth traded groceries for medical services with the shop owner.

When she left Ivan, she met Eunice at the counter measuring a patient's prescription. "God has finally answered your prayer. There's a mzungu dropped on your lap."

"I don't think he's the one." He'd said something about a meeting. Did he live here, or was he on a business trip? Either way, he was on Entebbe Road and probably headed for the airport. "My prayer was for one who will marry me, not one who's leaving the country."

"The man is in your house," Eunice mouthed as she counted the pills before sliding them into a tiny envelope. "It's your chance to show him you're single and searching."

Ruth laughed as Eunice waggled her brows. "You want me to take advantage of an incoherent man."

"He won't be when he wakes up."

No reason to tell Eunice he'd touched her face and she'd somehow been affected by the feel of his soft fingers. After all, he wasn't in his right state of mind at the time.

With everything under control in the clinic, Ruth left to keep an eye on Mzungu. She needed some time to catch up on praying and reading her Bible while she waited for him to wake up.

She shook her head and smiled when she glanced at the man on her bed before she flopped down on the love seat. *I have a white man in my clinic—my house—and he's sleeping in my bed.*

She had no idea where his spiritual stand was, but he was white. She'd find out more details later. It was like a dream, yet everything in her house was real.

CHAPTER 3

*R*uth... The name tasted like honey to his lips. A refreshing and tender voice that he could still hear echoing in his mind kept repeating, "I'm not leaving you."

Then terror replaced the warmth and comfort as he flew midair and thudded into sharp shrubs. He groaned, struggling to open his eyes and escape the nightmare.

He stirred. It wasn't shrubs but fabric underneath his back. The throbbing headache resurfaced earlier memories.

Warm hands soothed his forehead, and kind brown eyes probed his terror. "What's your name?"

He tried to open his mouth to speak, but he couldn't get the words out.

"It's okay." Feminine and gentle, her words floated over him. Her hands glided along his neck and feet when she asked him to wiggle his toe. "I don't think you've broken any bones, so that's good."

When her hand touched his jaw, he grabbed it, clung to it, not wanting to let go. Soft reassurance curved into his palm, as if he could hold onto something so intangible.

Stitches. He strained at the memory of the pain, yet the comforting voice had driven away his fear. "I'm sorry. Sometimes the numbing doesn't work," she'd said.

Through fragmented images, he remembered cupping her face, and its soft curves somehow remained engraved in his mind. Heat burned the back of his neck. He'd never done such a thing before—not to a stranger, anyway.

He shifted, and pain shot up his leg. His lips tasted like salt when he slid his tongue over them. Why? He opened his eyes to the reality of his dream.

A net floated above him, and hard boards supported him beneath a thin mattress. Bright light streamed through the windows. A breeze fluttered the white curtains drawn aside. Where was he?

After squinting at the metal ceiling, he turned to the side. A medium-sized portable closet rested at the foot of the bed, which made sense because the room was smaller than his hotel room last night.

What was he doing here?

A soft song playing in a foreign language relaxed him, and a wooden frame on the right wall drew his focus. Bold red letters proclaimed: *But as for me and my house, we will serve the Lord.* Joshua 24:15

The one next to it read: *We can make our plans, but the Lord determines our steps.* Proverbs 16:9

The words pierced his soul with a daunting familiarity. Before his business was successful, he'd kneel and pray and read the Bible for guidance. He'd stopped going to church when he started working after hours, including Sundays. Those peaceful times praying and reading the Bible ended once work occupied every moment of his day.

His gaze swept the rest of the room. A camping stove hunkered on the floor near the far corner. A pan warmed on a slow fire.

Two inches from him was a small wooden table and beyond that, a love seat... a figure. He blinked to clear the fog.

The figure sitting there possessed the familiar face with clear-as-glass ebony skin. Her long eyelashes swept over in concentration as she read a black book with gold edges on it. A Bible. A book Brady owned but had tucked away decades ago. The clock above her showed three forty-five.

Oh no! He was supposed to be on his way home. He jerked up. "My flight!" The words rasped his throat, and he winced when a sharp pain shot through his head, his face, and his shoulder. Everything hurt. Groaning, he fell back to the pillow and gritted his teeth.

The woman appeared at his side, kneeling. "Can I get you some pain medicine?"

The soothing voice from his dream now blanketed him, calming the turmoil tightening his muscles. Warm hands pressed against his forehead, skimming the patched area he assumed was bandaged. "I'll get you some water and medicine."

Like water and medicine, her voice was calm. Refreshing.

Medicine was far from his problems. Yet he would need something to ease the pain if he was going anywhere soon.

She returned with bottled water that she uncapped, tipped to pour in a glass, and set on the burgundy rug by the bed. She must have noticed his struggle to sit up when she eased his head up before handing him a couple of round brown pills. "Tylenol."

Water soothed his parched throat, and he gulped the rest of it after downing the pills. He stared at her while she reached for the glass. He wanted to apologize for touching her cheek, but the words died in his mouth when their eyes met and held. The air left his lungs at the questions filling her doe-like brown eyes. If she was wondering why he'd touched her, he had no answers.

Introductions were a good place to rid this awkwardness he'd created. He cleared his throat. "Ruth?"

"Oh!" She squared her shoulders, then pushed dark curls from her face, a warm smile lifting the corners of her lips. "You remember?"

He gave a curt nod and cringed at the foolish motion as the pain in his head intensified. But, really, how could he forget the eyes that had been his final thread of hope?

She set the glass on the rug where she knelt. "I found you on the road and brought you here." She told him how many stitches he'd gotten, and he tried not to think of the meeting he'd missed or wonder how he was supposed to call his property lawyer when he didn't have the man's number memorized. The investor's meeting in less than twenty-four hours and several other appointments would have to be pushed back should he not reach Manhattan by morning.

He dragged in a breath before meeting Ruth's brown eyes. She was waiting for him to say something about himself. An introduction. Yes, he could do that after everything she'd done for him. "I'm Brady... Sharp."

"Nice to meet you."

He took a sharp inhale of breath, as if needing it to get him through the next few hours. "How can I get to the airport? I missed my flight, but..." He could only hope they had an empty seat on the flights departing that night.

She stood, and her eyes swept over his forehead—at the injury, he assumed. His heart quickened when those eyes locked with his again.

She moved her gaze to his head, her lips parting as if to say something, but she clamped them closed before picking up the glass. "I'll call a boda boda for you."

"No way!" He couldn't risk putting his life in danger again. Did he even have his passport? His stomach tightened. Without it, he was stuck here for a while. "You didn't by chance find me with a bag?"

"It's over there." She tilted her chin to the wooden bookshelf.

His shoulders loosened, and the knots gave way in his stomach. Yes, that was his luggage on the bottom shelf. "I need to pay you, but I don't have cash."

"Don't worry. I'm glad you're okay."

Regardless, he'd need to pay for the taxi to the airport. "Where can I find an ATM?"

She tapped a hand on her chin. "In Kampala, but with rush-hour traffic, unless you take a boda boda, I doubt the banks will be open by the time you get there."

He'd witnessed what their traffic was like that morning, and a motorcycle was not an option. "Aren't ATMs open for twenty-four hours?"

"No, they're not."

As his luck would have it, of course, they wouldn't be. That explained why ninety percent of businesses dealt only in cash transactions. He closed his eyes and fisted his hand so tight his palm burned. What was he going to do?

"Let me first call the airport and see if they have a flight leaving tonight." He opened his eyes to listen to her promising suggestion. "If they do, I will call my neighbor, Dongo. He's a taxi driver, and he can take you to the airport."

How was he going to pay him?

As if reading his mind, she said, "I will take care of Dongo." She walked toward the table and set the glass down. "If I help you, you will help someone else, and the chain goes on."

Grateful for her kindness, he relaxed. "Like paying it forward?"

She shrugged and smiled—a smile that warmed his entire body. "Something like that."

His head throbbed like something sharp jabbed it. The medicine he'd taken hadn't kicked in yet. He rubbed at heavy eyes, feeling the effects of jet lag.

Even though he couldn't understand what Ruth was saying on the phone in her language, her frown as she scribbled on the notebook couldn't be good news.

Soon she was back. Her knit forehead drained the hope out of him. "The airport doesn't schedule flights." She leaned against the wall and crossed her arms. "They said, if you missed your flight, you have to go to the airline's office." She flicked the paper in her hand. "I didn't know which airline you used, but they gave me a list of all four airlines' addresses and office hours—"

"British Airways."

Her frown deepened. "Unfortunately, they said both the British Airways and United Arab Emirates offices are closed today. They open tomorrow at nine."

Pain exploded in his head. He had to call his assistant. He also had to call the resort and see if they could reschedule his appointment. Being the CEO, he always had everything he needed, and he wasn't used to asking for help. But now, he wasn't a boss—not when he was lying on a mattress pad and covered with pink floral bedsheets and a Mickey Mouse blanket. "Is it okay if I borrow your phone?"

"Of course." She knelt and handed him the phone. He wasn't comfortable with her kneeling for him, but he'd deal with that later. "If you're making an international call, the airtime might not be enough."

Oh, he'd forgotten the phones operated on pay as you go. "I'll pay for your airtime." This was an emergency. "Do you, by some miracle, know how I can find the Entebbe resort's number?"

She reached for a newspaper from her bookshelf and returned, taking the phone from him. She then punched in the numbers she read off the paper and handed back the phone with the resort's number on dial. "I'll give you some privacy." She left the room and entered another, where he could hear muted voices.

Each call to the resort went to voicemail. No wonder the place was going out of business. When he hung up, he dialed Beth's cell. Having no clue what time it was in New York, he hated that he could be waking her up. She answered on the first ring, far before he could end the call.

"Beth, it's Brady."

"Brady? What number is—Shouldn't you be on the plane right now?" She'd long ago become like a second mom. "Brady, *where* are you?"

"Uganda." With the limited airtime. "I missed my flight and need you to reschedule all my meetings."

"Slow down, Brady. I got everything under control." No doubt she did. He'd hired her as his personal assistant because she was detail-oriented and knowledgeable. That, and she'd worked for the same company for fifteen years—with not a single sick day or leave on her record. "Don't give yourself a heart attack. Sometimes, we must be stopped in our tracks to slow down."

"But..."

Beep... beep... The phone crackled. "Beth!" He looked at the screen, now only portraying the time and day. *Slow down?* He threw back his head. *I can't afford to slow down.* He clenched his jaw and raked his fingers through his hair. *Ouch.* He needed to remember the stupid wound on his forehead before he tampered with his head.

When Ruth returned, he told her about his debacle and the appointment he'd missed.

"I'm so sorry." The sympathy in her eyes matched her tone. "Call tomorrow and see if they can meet with you."

Tomorrow was too far away, but he needed to find a place to stay tonight, which made him grateful when she spoke. "Stay here tonight, and my neighbor will drive you to the British Airways office first thing in the morning."

"I can't believe I missed that meeting." He slapped his forehead, then groaned when he hit near his wound.

"Try to put today behind you," she soothed as she settled him back on the pillow. "Tomorrow will be better."

He hoped so. A compelling simplicity about her made him want to believe tomorrow *would* be better. *Is this how You're getting my attention, God?*

He told her about his stolen watch and coat with his iPhone in it. "I'm grateful to be rescued by someone nice." Someone who wasn't stealing from him.

Whoa. She may not be a thief, but her smile held him captive. "The kids in the city... most of them are Sudanese refugees who have no place to live, and that's how they get money." She told him it'd happened to her once when they snatched her purse. "It's terrible that they have to live by making others' lives miserable."

"So they weren't just picking on me?"

She laughed. "Sometimes they might pick on you, but the street kids are just surviving."

She offered him a late lunch, but with his body more exhausted than hungry, he declined, yawning and struggling to keep his eyes open.

When the wooden door swung open and a lady called after Ruth, she introduced her as her colleague, Eunice, before she nodded to him. "I'll let you get some rest. I have a patient to tend to, but I'll change your bandages when you wake up."

"Thank you." He winked and closed his eyes. It didn't take long for sleep to claim him.

HE WOKE TO SUCH A WONDERFUL aroma his stomach growled.

To the far end, at a makeshift utility table, Ruth was stirring something in the pot nestled on the camping-size stove.

As she walked to the table and glanced toward the bed, he smiled to let her know he was awake.

She smiled back, wiping her hands over her round skirt. "Are you ready to have some dinner?" When his stomach growled again, she giggled. "I'll take that as a yes."

Brady chuckled. As much as he should be embarrassed for his stomach giving him away, he wasn't. Not with Ruth. "Guilty as charged." His bladder was full, but he'd surveyed the one room and hadn't seen any doors except for the one leading to the clinic. "I might need to use the bathroom first."

"Of course." She asked if he wanted to shower, but he'd been sleeping all day, not enough to make him need a shower.

"Maybe tomorrow morning." Before he left.

He winced at the throbbing sensation from his shoulder when he sat up and swung his feet out of the bed.

Ruth returned with blue sandals and knelt before him. A jolt shot through him when her fingers brushed his toes as she eased the sandals onto his feet. His heel almost hit the cool cement in the house and the dirt when he walked through a compound to get to an outer house.

The day was giving way to darkness, and the porch lights illuminated the charcoal stoves lining the long veranda. As people crouched around the pans, some waved in greeting, and he waved back.

Kids hopped, playing something resembling hopscotch. Others jumped rope, stirring the dirt in the air. With their happy squeals thrilling him, Brady found himself taking a moment to watch. They paused their game when they saw him and smiled as they waved. He waved back before heading to the toilet, where Ruth had set out a basin of water for him to wash his hands afterward.

The toilet smelled of lemon and disinfectant. It had been ages since he'd used a pit latrine, when he'd camped with the Boy Scouts.

As he walked back, he was grateful Ruth's building was separate from the many tenants' doorways. Otherwise, he'd be entering the wrong house.

Inside, something smelled good, and the naked bulb above the coffee table showcased an array of steaming food dishes. Ruth was kneeling before a graying man as she handed him a brown glass bottle.

She stood and tugged at her floral skirt, then faced Brady. "We have company." She guided him to the empty space next to the dark-skinned man. "This is one of my patients, Ivan."

"Brady." He shook Ivan's callused hands before he sat. "Nice to meet you."

The man looked up at Brady's forehead. He still hadn't seen a mirror around to assess his wound.

"Good that you didn't lose your eye." Ivan reached for his bottle from the table. "You would be blind."

"I'm glad Ruth saved my life."

"God did." She reminded him that Dongo had carried him to the car and driven him back to the clinic.

"I'll have to thank Dongo tomorrow." And God.

She left for her makeshift kitchen and returned with the bottle to kneel before him. She popped off the cap with a bottle opener. "I thought you might be familiar with rice and meat."

"Why do you kneel?" He didn't like it.

"It's sign of respect," Ivan said in his chipped English.

"For guests and elderly people you respect." Ruth handed him the serving plate and stood.

She looked younger than him, probably by seven or eight years, but he was no king or hero. "You don't have to kneel for me." When she tried to protest, he held up a hand. "It makes me feel like I'm better than you when I'm not." She'd just saved his life, for crying out loud.

"Oh..." She sat on the stool across from the love seat. "I didn't think of it like that." Collapsing her fingers together, she asked, "Are you comfortable if I pray for our food?"

"Yes, please." He needed a refresher course with prayers.

Her accent resembled the British English. Her prayer reached to his core when she thanked God for the food and for Brady's safety.

"Amen," he and Ivan said after her.

Brady's mouth watered when he poured a generous serving onto his plate, then spooned some rice soaked in beef stew and took his first bite. It melted in his mouth. "Hmm!"

"I'm glad you like it." She raised water to her lips.

"Beef stew, right?"

"Yes." Ivan spoke over a mouthful before digging his fingers back into his plate and filling them with a generous portion that he stuffed in his mouth.

Brady lifted the soda and sipped through the straw. Cold and refreshing, with a stingy taste that made him cough. Like ginger ale minus the extreme ginger flavor. He turned the bottle to read the kind of soda. "Stoney?"

"It has ginger in it." Ruth scrunched her face, apologetically. "I wanted to get you Fanta, but they only had Stoney left."

How sweet that she cared about his needs. "I've never tried Stoney before." The label showed the Coca-Cola brand. "When I go back home, I'll say I tried something new... foreign."

During their conversations, he learned Ivan had had chest pain for the last six months. It didn't hinder his appetite, since he kept filling his plate with more food.

"Nice to have Ruth's clinic. It's the only hospital helping people in the community."

"It's not a hospital." Ruth settled her half-eaten plate on her lap.

"The closest hospital is sixty kilometers away, and no one will treat me without money."

In other words, Ruth did charity work, too. Brady was benefiting from her grace as well.

It seemed the main hospital wasn't too reliable if you had an emergency, which made him grateful for home with its wealth of hospitals and emergency vehicles to come to the rescue.

"Let's hope it's nothing serious." He wasn't a doctor, but chest pains weren't a symptom you ignored. Ruth, however, had taken measures, as Ivan mentioned her taking him to the hospital for further tests.

"I'm hoping our next tests will help us figure out what's causing the pain," she said.

Spoons clanked against porcelain as they ate before he asked about her clinic. "I'm guessing since you stay at your work, you don't get a break."

"Yes and no." She sipped her water and set the glass down. "People knock when there's an emergency, but I like not having to pay for transport to get to work."

He could relate. At times, he got so busy he stayed the night in his office.

"Ivan said you stock up the clinic once a week? Where do you get your medicine?"

"I go to the main pharmacy at Kampala." Her brown eyes danced beneath the light. "I was on my way to catch a taxi when I found you."

He had no idea how long he'd lain in the grass, and what would've happened if she hadn't rescued him. "Thank you for saving me." He owed her more than money. The extra night in the country would be an opportunity for him to withdraw money from the ATM. He'd have to send it with the taxi driver, Dongo. Was he honest?

Nsanji had been nice until he'd hired a biker who'd run off and left Brady on the roadside. Ruth had explained the driver was afraid of liability and getting fired.

In the small house, he should be uncomfortable, yet just looking into Ruth's eyes made him feel at home. She was the only safe thing after being robbed in the city and left to die on the roadside.

When they finished eating, he let his gaze follow Ruth as she carried the dishes to her makeshift kitchen. Dark leggings showcased her curves and slim waist.

"She's not courting anyone." Ivan spoke for Brady's ears alone.

His cheeks flamed, and he gripped the back of his neck. Even if he wasn't searching, he was pleased to know she was single. Was it wrong... him thinking like that? He parted his lips to tell Ivan he was leaving tomorrow, but Ruth's return ended their conversation.

She motioned for Brady to follow her to the clinic. "Let's get your wound changed."

Once he settled on the exam table, she removed the gauze from his forehead and wiped the wound with a wet cloth. His heart raced as awareness of her buzzed through his veins.

"Let me know if I'm hurting you." She applied fresh gauze.

"You're doing great." He wasn't concerned about being hurt while he had major issues figuring what part of her face to look at. He closed his eyes instead and breathed in her sweet scent. Her soft fingers sent shockwaves to his entire body while she applied the antibiotic to his battered face and bruised shoulder.

He almost felt dizzy when he saw the blood-soaked gauze before Ruth tossed it in the trash can.

Ivan's breathing was labored as they walked back into Ruth's house. His head was tilted back on the edge of the love seat.

"I hate to wake him up, but he will be more comfortable in the bed." The careful way she tapped the man's shoulder to wake him pulled Brady in.

Then the room went dark when the power died. Ruth got the lamp, struck the match, and lit up the glass lantern with practiced ease, and the smell of paraffin replaced the savory dinner scents as she set the lamp on the table.

"A blackout." Ivan yawned, stretching his arms.

"Does this happen often?" Brady sat next to Ivan when Ruth sat on the rug by the table.

"Three to four times a week." The lamp's glow danced over her flawless skin and sparkled in her bottomless eyes. Wisps of her dark hair fell on her forehead, and a contemplative curve smoothed her lips. "It's always good to have paraffin on hand."

After Ivan yawned again, she handed him a flashlight and bid him good night. Brady held the man's hand and walked him to the wooden door when he almost lost balance.

"Thank you," Ivan said, closing the door behind him.

"Do you keep your door unlocked whenever you have a patient stay the night?" That could be dangerous if she had the wrong kind of patient.

"The door has a lock on it." She rolled out a mat next to the table. "I don't lock it when Ivan is here. With some other patients, I do."

She seemed trusting. Goodness, he was a stranger, too, and she was letting him stay in her house? "Many times sick people are not looking for trouble, but they're in need of healing."

Like him. He yawned, jet lag and exhaustion from long days at work now catching up to him.

"You better get some rest." She gestured to the bed.

Something in him balked. He didn't want to take her bed, and the short love seat couldn't fit anybody but a child. "Where are you going to sleep?"

She patted the mat. "Right here."

On a cement floor. Not even padding, worse than camping. "I will take that. You take the bed."

She ignored him, walked to the edge of the bed, and opened the plastic tub. Then she pulled out a blanket. Taking the cushion from the love seat as her pillow, she laid herself down, which left no room for him to argue. "I don't have a wounded arm or leg. Will it be okay if I pray?"

"Of course." He lumbered to the bed as she prayed for his plans to be successful the next day, for God to move heaven and earth so he could get the resort deal, and then for, above all else, God's will to be done. "Amen."

God's will. He stared at the dimmed lantern on the table. Was it God's will for his business to succeed? Was he self-centered to want a better life than Ruth's? One more resort, one more step to the next income bracket, always tempted him.

He shifted, turning to the side so he could see her. Was she smiling? Hard to tell in the dim light.

"Would you like the light on or off? I can sleep either way."

Yes, she was smiling, but he didn't want to pry by asking why.

"If you don't mind keeping it, that'll be great." Being in a new place, recovering from a bad experience, he might have nightmares.

In the silence of the night, he closed his eyes. Images of him flying midair flashed in his mind. He could've died. Ruth's kind eyes were all he could see. What were her plans for the future? Was she content with her simple life?

When he returned home, he'd send her money. Perhaps she would buy a house and not have to sleep in her clinic. She could separate work from homelife. Based on the home prices from his property lawyer, houses were much more affordable in Uganda than in Manhattan.

Ruth... Such a simple name. Lovely. It suited her, yet "Ruthie?" seemed perfect.

"Hmm?"

That was meant for his mind, but since she'd heard, he might as well utter the rest. "If you had a lot of money, what would you do with it?"

She chuckled. Unable to see her face, he could only imagine her smile. "Depends how much."

"Any amount." He wanted to know her plans either way.

"I'd build a clinic in my home village…. If I still had more money, I'd hire a doctor and some nurses to run the clinic while I ran this one."

What did she want to do for herself? "What else?"

"A better clinic here with an MRI and all the equipment we could use."

Whoa! She didn't want a bigger house or shopping money. Maybe he was chasing the wrong dream. No, he had a great life.

"Good night, Brady." Ruth spoke with a yawn.

"'Night."

Just like his future plans were in America, Ruth's future was in Uganda. Except, while her plans involved helping people, his involved building a legacy—for whom? For the first time, he wondered if he had any idea.

HE WOKE UP WELL RESTED—SOMETHING he hadn't done in months. His head didn't hurt as much, although a sharp pang twinged in his shoulder. He scratched his scruffy jaw. He'd shave when he got home in front of a mirror.

He didn't even want to *think* about all the hours he'd slept yesterday. But he'd been pushing himself all week, skimping by on a couple hours of sleep so he could wrap things up in the States before taking this trip. He'd worked on the plane and again that night after he reached his hotel room. It took some major jet lag and a head injury to make him listen to his body.

Ruth boiled water on the charcoal stove for him to have a warm shower. She was pampering him, but he had no idea how to use a basin to take a shower. So he let her pour the water in the basin and carry it for him to the bathhouse.

When he returned in his undershirt and pants, she had a set of new underwear and a button-down shirt. "My neighbor is a tailor. Since you didn't have any clean clothes, I hope these can work until you buy a suit or something."

No wonder she was a nurse. If he wasn't taking up her bed, he'd almost feel tempted to forget his flight and spend another day in her company.

She sat, and they talked while he savored the chai tea and the vegetable fried pastry she gave him for breakfast. After he ate the samosas, Ruth handed him two Tylenol, and he swallowed them with the remaining tea before she walked him out to the awaiting Corona.

"I'll never forget you, Ruth." And he meant it as he said goodbye.

"Me, too." Her response was almost a whisper. "Remember to get the stitches out in no longer than seven days."

"I will." He needed to leave because he was thinking about pulling her close for an embrace, but he'd already made a scene when he'd cupped her face yesterday. That, and a million other reasons pushed him toward the car. He lifted his hand to wave before sliding into the passenger seat where Dongo held the door open.

Brady thanked the muscular man for coming to his rescue. How the guy had managed to carry Brady, even though Dongo didn't seem to weigh much more than he did, Brady had no idea.

Settling in, he unzipped the side pocket of his luggage to retrieve his passport in case he needed it at the office.

A card? Frowning, he retrieved an envelope with his name on it and smiled at the script that seemed to bounce across the page like her vibrant curls.

May the Lord grant you your heart's desires and make your plans succeed. May He answer all your prayers. Prayer taken from Psalm 20.

Have a safe trip.

Ruth

He reread the passage until they approached the airline office.

With the minimal airlines, the next available flight was in five days, and it wasn't even first class. Standing there, he rubbed the throbbing point under his bandaged head and thought of Ruth and what he could make of the five days. When had he taken a vacation? He was way overdue.

"Sir? What do you want to do?" The service attendant peered up at him, her polite smile somewhat strained.

He drummed his fingers against his thigh. If he was taking five days, he might as well take ten. First class would be available by then.

Actually... ten days would give him time to hit the resort or maybe scout out another in the country. After watching the serene scenery on the tourist channel, he'd discovered property here wasn't only affordable, but it also offered great tourism potential.

When they left the airlines, he asked Dongo to drive him to the bank, where he withdrew money from the ATM. Then they stopped at a boutique by the hotel where he'd stayed. He bought a phone and a suit, just in case he rescheduled the resort meeting.

Dongo was willing to be his taxi driver for the day and ended up being Brady's tour guide. His English was minimal, but he seemed to understand what Brady asked. "Where can I find a computer?"

"Just around the corner." Dongo drove Brady to the internet café, and he typed his email to Beth, filling her in on his reason for an extended trip. He requested she reschedule his calendar for the next ten days. With access to his email, he found the number for his property lawyer.

He'd need the lawyer when he finagled another meeting at the resort. He dialed him when he was back in the car Dongo had parked along the street.

"What happened?" the man asked in a thick but understandable accent. Brady told him about his accident. "Did your taxi driver know the man?"

After what Ruth told him, the man's job could be in danger. It wasn't worth it to contact the hotel for Nsanji's phone number. "I'm fine now." Thanks to Ruth.

"They're considering the other buyer."

He winced as the lawyer's words pummeled him. "Did they tell you this?"

"No…"

"There's still hope, then." He had to cling to that. After promising to call if he succeeded in finding the resort owner, Brady hung up.

What better place to stay than the resort itself? A good way to scope out the premises in hopes the manager could point him to the people in charge. He dialed the resort's accommodation line, and they had a suite available. "I will be there in less than two hours."

Whew! He let out a breath. It felt like it had been a whole day. A glance at the clock on Dongo's dashboard showed 1:23. "You must be hungry." He hadn't thought of the driver.

"I'm good. I bought a rolex from the street when you went to the café."

Brady wasn't hungry. Not when he had so much to do. And he definitely wasn't eating a Rolex, even though he was pretty sure the guy wasn't referencing the watch brand. "How about you take me to the resort so I can check in?"

"Ye, ssebo… I mean, yes, sir." Just like Nsanji, Dongo was polite.

At times, Brady forgot the traffic stayed left instead of right. Good thing he wasn't driving.

Ruth's place was along the road to the resort, but he needed a real shower first. "After I check in, can you drive me back to Ruth's?"

Dongo nodded.

Brady needed to pay her for taking care of him. Thanking her over dinner would be even better. He doubted she ever went out to eat. Ivan's words about Ruth being single tempted him. "Is there somewhere I can buy flowers?"

"There's a flower shop in Entebbe, not far from the resort."

Brady eased back in his seat, buckling in as Dongo drove the familiar road he'd taken in this direction yesterday. Unlike yesterday morning, this afternoon's traffic was mild. Despite the tension he should feel for missing his flight, a sense of peace, exhilaration even, warmed him. He couldn't help wondering if extending his trip had nothing to do with business, and his heart quickened when Ruth came to mind. He could still smell her scented soap he'd used that morning. Could she be the reason behind his sudden vacation?

CHAPTER 4

Ruth finally had a moment to sip water. Today had been a long day. Prenatal care, malaria, and all sorts of walk-ins stopped in to buy medicine. Then Eunice had to go to someone's home to deliver a baby.

Ruth fingered through her hair, glad to have canceled her hair-braiding appointment. She'd hoped to use the cancellation to go shopping for medicine, but the day had escaped from her. Shopping would have to wait until tomorrow.

The busy day had also left her no room to think about Brady. After she'd said goodbye that morning, her heart had squeezed and filled with sadness over never seeing him again.

"It's five thirty already." Ivan's scruffy voice jolted her from her thoughts when he emerged from the patient room. "I better get home before they plan dinner without me."

A motorcycle engine rumbled outside. "Perfect timing." She'd called one of the tenants who was a boda boda driver to take Ivan home.

She grabbed the bag of food and blood thinners she'd packed. Although Ivan had no diagnosis yet, the blood thinners seemed to have helped ease his pain.

All the money she'd saved up was going toward the village, to buy nonperishable items for her family and medicine for the villagers.

In another month, she'd have Ivan's fund ready to take him back to the hospital. She handed over the bag after he perched on the motorcycle's passenger seat.

"Thank you for everything, Musawo. You're an angel."

"God provides. Don't forget that."

"How can I when you keep reminding me?" He gave her a thumbs-up.

Heat radiated through her chest. It was great to see him smile.

Although she wasn't financially prosperous, she still had more than most people who had little to nothing. She handed the motorcyclist two thousand shillings. She didn't need to remind the driver to be careful driving Ivan. Since she was his neighbor and family nurse, the boda boda had good reason to drive carefully.

Lifting a hand, she waved to Ivan while the motorcycle left dust behind, and she walked back to the clinic.

"Let's call it a day." She stifled a yawn as she approached Eunice, resting her elbow on the glass counter. "Even nurses need a break."

"That includes you. You need a break." Eunice stood. "I can stay longer to keep you company if you want."

Perhaps Ruth's sadness had been evident upon Brady's departure, but she was used to being alone whenever she wasn't working—or at least she had to tell herself so.

"Go home and make dinner for your husband." Somehow, Eunice had found one of the few men okay with a career woman.

Eunice shrugged. "That's what I pay the maid for."

Even so, Ruth still encouraged her friend to go home and rest. "I need to shower, wash my clothes, and get to bed early. Long day tomorrow."

"Maybe you can call Mzungu and see if he made it to America already."

She might have entertained the idea if she had his number. But she'd never asked, and he'd never offered it. "Call him and say what? Hi?"

"You were his nurse." Eunice rested a warm hand on Ruth's shoulder. "If I were you, I'd call him every day to see how he's fairing." She wiggled her penciled eyebrows. "That would be a good time to spice up those words you write in cards. Words can get him on the first flight back to Uganda."

Ruth laughed. She loved writing her patients notes of encouragement, but she didn't do it to woo men. By the time Brady found the note she'd snuck in his luggage, he'd be in America. "Is that what you did for your husband?"

"Phew!" Eunice waved Ruth off. "You already know I married him to save my nieces from having a monstrous stepmom." After Eunice's sister died, Eunice's brother-in-law's parents found him a wife Eunice feared to be a gold digger. So she'd taken matters into her hands—a usual tactic for women to ask a man out. She'd gone and cooked his little family dinner and asked him to go for evening walks. Not long after, he'd asked her to marry him. "Plus, Africans don't need notes to pamper them into a relationship. We get married and hope for the best."

Partially true. Her sisters got married, not for love, but because they found husbands in the city rather than ones on the farm in the village. Her dad was considered rich because he married five of his daughters to city men. In a way, he was wealthy, since he got bridewealth from all their husbands. Farmers in the village couldn't afford much bridewealth.

Before she parted with Eunice, she reminded her to call Rashida for tomorrow. She'd need their extra helper to fill in while Ruth went shopping for medical supplies.

Ruth rarely closed before six, but having the clinic open or closed didn't stop people from knocking at her door in an emergency. That was the main disadvantage of having her home at work.

She reached for the pen when she remembered to add one more item to her supply list. Then she toyed with the pen, sketching five letters across the bottom of her list and deepening them to bold print—B–R–A–D–Y.

"Brady." She smiled, imagining and testing his name to see how it rolled off her tongue. What would it be like if she married a white man? She set the pen on the counter, making sure it didn't roll away like her imagination was. "It would give the neighbors and my family something to talk about."

Then she walked around the glass counter to close the double doors. Two more hours of daylight. She could get a lot done. Wash laundry and head across to Jamila's shop to buy chapati. Flatbread and tea would make a decent dinner.

Her hand stilled at the door handle. What on earth? Excited screams ricocheted through the veranda as kids darted toward her building. Across the way, shoppers were staring at something. Then a kid called, "Mzungu!" And she followed the onlookers' focus to Brady!

A little gasp slid from her lips, and she closed her mouth as he stepped out of Dongo's Corona. A wide smile crinkled up the skin around his eyes while he strode forward focused on her. The bouquet he held occupied most of his broad chest.

Her vision wavered, and her heart thundered. She wasn't used to staring at a man, especially when she felt butterflies flapping in her stomach.

Hushed voices murmured across the veranda. Half the housewives and tenants were pushed against the edge of her building, their necks craning for a good look. When she waved at them, some responded with giggles.

The kids continued to shout "mzungu" as they clamored around Brady. Yeah, she'd join them in excitement, because there was never a mzungu at this side of town—not in her community, anyway.

A rush of adrenaline tingled through her body when his gaze captured hers as he climbed the veranda steps.

He offered her the flowers. Nobody ever gave her flowers. She loved them but could never prioritize buying some. "These are for you. Thank you for taking care of me."

Hearing his voice flooded her with warmth. He mustn't have gotten a flight—unless he was waiting for a midnight flight and came to say goodbye.

"You're back?" The words exited in a breathless rush as she dropped her hand from the door.

He shrugged his shoulders. "No flights today nor tomorrow. Lucky for me. I get to take you out to dinner if you're free tonight."

Her gaze flitted back to the glass vase in his hands, and she remembered to take it. Not trusting her shaky hands, she set it on the counter as his words sank in. *Take you out to dinner.* Is that what he'd said? That would be an evening outing with a mzungu. In the TV soaps, when they took someone out to dinner, they were interested in them. Was he interested in her, or had he said it was a thank-you supper?

Men liked a woman who could cook. "I can cook something...."

She finally met his warm blue eyes. Matooke and peanut sauce. Chicken and beef would take at least two hours if she wanted it cooked to perfection. Hmm! Peanut sauce wasn't a meal you made for a fancy guest—unless it was for breakfast or lunch. "I–I have some rice." Fifteen minutes to start the charcoal stove. Did he even have that much time? Was he headed to the resort for a late meeting afterward? Her mind was all over the place. "Did you, uh... call the resort?"

Something briefly crumpled his expression. "I guess it wasn't God's will for me to get the resort after all."

Small dark-brown hands creeped against Brady's arms. A couple of little boys wove their tiny fingers into Brady's, but he didn't seem bothered by their fascination with the hair on his arms. Ruth reminded them not to yank his hair when one of the kids assessed a strand from his hairy hands.

They were curious. Thankfully, Brady was smiling. He crouched to their level and patted their heads. Soon more kids squeezed through, shoving each other out of the way so a mzungu could pat their heads too.

"My turn," asserted six-year-old Prossy.

"Me too," said Abel.

With them all thrilled by his presence, Ruth hated to end their fun, but this was her only chance to claim the man she'd spent two years praying for. Not consistently, but yes... praying.

She sent the kids away and ushered Brady inside before she closed the door. Then she guided him to the love seat and pulled out a stool for herself.

"I don't want you to cook." He leaned back and sprawled out his arms across the love seat's back, making it appear smaller than it was. "I'm taking you out to dinner. Now that I have ten days in Uganda, I hope we can hang out. Maybe you can show me around Kampala for a few days."

Her shoulders fell, and her heart panged at the missed opportunity. All the days she'd imagined and dreamed of what it would be like to have a mzungu on her doorstep, she now had one, and he had to show when she was leaving for the village? *Really, God?*

She couldn't let the villagers down by postponing her arrival. Several of them had to rearrange their day to skip their farming obligations so they could come and get medicine or have their medical examination.

At least, she could enjoy dinner tonight. She raised her face to meet his waiting gaze. "Unfortunately, I can't show you around this week."

His blue eyes lost their spark. Had her disappointment shown, or was she seeing his? Lowering his hands to his sides, he seemed to stiffen as he pressed his lips together. "Why's that?"

He might need a drink as she explained. So she stood and walked to the utility table, then grabbed a mineral water and handed it to him.

"I have to go shopping for medical supplies tomorrow, and I will be going to the village for five days." So they wouldn't see each other after tonight. Unless his offer still stood? "Maybe I can show you around when I—"

"What do you do in the village?"

She told him how the patients awaited her there once every two months.

"I'll go with you." A firm nod dipping his chin, he twisted off the bottle cap. It wasn't a question. Did he know what he was getting himself into? "If you can use my help, that is."

She had to blink twice, or maybe more. She always needed help. Her mind envisioned their arrival and all the villagers staring at him like he'd been dropped on the planet. There were sleeping arrangements to worry about. Her grandparents had moved in with Mom and Dad, and they all slept on the floor in one room. If she showed up with a man, they'd assume they were courting and she'd brought him home to introduce him to the family. That was the most concerning scenario.

She could tell them he was there to help her hand out medicine. She pushed wisps of hair from her face as she peered at the unlit lamp. The kids would be thrilled to see a white man, the smiles on their faces—

"I take it your smile is a yes?"

"There's a slight problem though." She tugged at her skirt, needing a distraction. "My family might think you're my..." How could she say this without being too awkward? "Boyfriend?"

"Noted." His lopsided grin warmed her. "I'll be on my best behavior."

She'd make sure his wound was nicely wrapped, except…"There's also no beds. We sleep on the floor."

"I will sleep wherever."

"It's very far, like three hundred kilometers. About five hours from here."

"The adventure will give me something to talk about." He draped his strong arms over the love seat again, making himself at home. "I'd go crazy staying in a hotel room and thinking about all the opportunities I missed."

He wouldn't have time to think of anything but his discomfort in the village. "I'll be honored for you to come with me."

He gave a slow nod as he rubbed a hand against his freshly shaven chiseled jaw. He smelled so good, which reminded her she hadn't showered.

With nothing to entertain him while she showered, she pulled out her picture albums and handed them to him. "If it's okay, I'm going to take a quick shower. Feel free to browse through some pictures." She turned on the gospel music on her CD player and pressed the switch to the percolator. She didn't need a lot of hot water. Otherwise, she'd have to light the charcoal stove.

When the plastic jar whistled and steam rose within seconds, she unplugged the white jug and carried it outside to the back veranda. She poured the water into the basin and tilted the jerry can of cold water, sloshing in a generous amount and checking with her hand to keep a lukewarm temperature.

Women and kids eyed her door as she carried the basin to the bathroom. While most tenants shared their bathroom and toilets, Ruth and the other shop owners each had their private shower and toilet, making it easy to keep it clean.

She draped the bathrobe over her skirt before she returned to the house. With gospel music in the background, Brady was so attuned to the pictures that he didn't see her walk in. Perfect.

She slid behind the curtains of her bed, which now smelled like Brady, and she intended to keep it that way by not changing her bedsheets for another week. Then she unzipped her makeshift closet and pushed the hangers aside as she selected her attire. The burgundy cocktail dress she'd worn for her sister's wedding last year was perfect. She'd gotten compliments from her friends.

She rubbed some lotion on her feet and combed her bobbed hair. She then slid on her cross necklace, the only jewelry she had. Holding up her handheld mirror, she applied lip gloss, then moved the mirror up above her so she could see her dress. Her limbs felt light, and she smiled, pleased by her selection.

When she stepped out of the curtain, Brady's gaze swept over her, confirming her attire choice. "You look… stunning."

A little jolt charged through her heart. "Thank you."

He covered the album with his hand and stacked it atop the others, then stood and adjusted the collar on his short-sleeve button-down. "Ready?"

She nodded and grabbed her purse from the stand. Goosebumps shivered over her skin when his arm hit her lower back as they walked out through the clinic and exited the front door.

"I hired Dongo for the rest of the day." His breath brushed against her ear, making her knees slightly weak.

"That was nice of you to give him work."

As she took the final step down from her clinic, she overheard the onlookers talking.

"Who's that?"

"It's a mzungu. Don't you have eyes?"

Half a dozen heads swung in her direction, wide grins beaming at her, and Ruth smiled, waving at them. As the kids trailed them to

Dongo's awaiting Corona, he held the back door and said in Luganda, "Seems you finally got your mzungu, Musawo."

"For a week maybe?" she responded in kind before turning to Brady, who gestured for her to slide in first and took the seat next to her.

"I like your neighbors." He motioned back to their audience.

"It's... We never get white people here." Maybe she should explain they were not just being nosey, but rather, they were intrigued to see a new person, a tourist, in their midst. But he didn't look bothered by the prying citizens.

Having Brady next to her felt like a dream. Yet the people's smiles around them were real. She imagined herself a princess for a night.

"Where should I drive, boss?" Excitement trilled in Dongo's voice, raising it several notches as his voice reminded her that her dream was a reality. He must be glad not to compete with twenty other taxi drivers today, searching for customers. Brady probably paid him way more than the bargaining clients he usually got.

"Just call me Brady," he corrected. Apparently, he didn't want any extra titles or respect that came with the culture. He was different, diffident, delightful. His voice interrupted her thoughts when he called her name. He was real, too. "I didn't think ahead on where to take you to dinner."

"Oh." She only knew of the local African restaurants in her community. While she'd walked past the big hotels in Kampala, she'd never eaten in their restaurants.

"We can always eat at the resort where I'm staying. They have a restaurant."

"Is that the same resort you almost got the—"

"Yes." Light blood seeped through the tape on his forehead. She should've dressed his wound, but she'd not bothered to look at his bandages earlier. "After losing the deal, I thought I might as well stay there. It's close to the airport and to your place."

Had he thought of her when he booked the hotel? Of course, he had. Hadn't he said he—how had he put it? Wanted to hang out with her for the next ten days?

"Resort, then." Dongo fired the engine and drove to the smooth highway. Major traffic rarely reached this side of town.

Brady asked about her trip to the village and her shopping trip to the city.

"After I shop for medicine, I shop for toiletries and other items for my family... things they don't have in the village." Like oil, sugar, tea, and anything that didn't grow on a farm.

"Is it okay if I come shopping with you tomorrow?"

"I'd love for you to come." She'd need to do some coaching on how to hold his wallet while they shuffled through pedestrians, but she couldn't wait to be by his side. "I'll give you a tour of the city."

Brady confirmed with Dongo that he would be their driver tomorrow and to the village. "As long as we don't go by African time."

"Ruth will help me keep time."

But when Dongo smiled at her in the rearview mirror, a frown pinched her brows. She couldn't afford a taxi to the village. "That's a lot of money."

"It's on me." Brady scooted closer and took her hand in his. Even if she wanted to argue, how was she supposed to talk while her tongue was tied? "If I'm going that far, I'd like to drive in comfort."

Especially if he was going to sleep on the floor for five days.

"If you buy gas for the car and feed me lunch, I give you bargain," Dongo said.

"Just be on time, that's the bargain I need." Brady gave Ruth's hand a gentle squeeze. "If he picks me up at eight, I'll be at your house by eight thirty." His voice was light, radiating confidence. "I'm glad I missed my flight."

The car's temperature must have kicked up to another ten degrees as her heart warmed. Somehow, she managed to utter a response. "Me, too. I hope you enjoy your stay."

Their gazes held, his blue eyes so soft the air left her lungs.

"I know I will."

This was going to be one of the best weeks she'd ever had. Brady's week would be just as memorable, but would it be so in a good way?

CHAPTER 5

Brady wiped perspiration from his forehead with his palm as he held the Corona's back door for Ruth to slide into. After shopping for medicine and other medical supplies at the main pharmacy, she'd taken him to a low-end shopping center—different from the hotel boutique he'd shopped at yesterday.

"Remember, don't talk to the sellers," Ruth said as she clasped his hand while they entered another one of the many clothing shops.

Since she likely held his hand so they didn't separate from each other, he ignored the awareness flooding his veins—well, tried to—and yet remained grateful for her thoughtfulness. If he got lost in this crowded building, he'd have no clue how to find his way back to Dongo's car. Shop owners ushered them into their shops.

"They'll take advantage and overcharge you."

Apparently, nothing had a set price. Ruth did the bargaining while he picked out clothes and shoes. With the items so cheap, he got a bigger backpack for his trip to the village when they stopped at a luggage shop.

She bargained when they moved from one shop to another, speaking English with some shop owners, and Brady admired her confidence when she threatened to take her business elsewhere if they charged her more because she was with him. An extra pair of tennis shoes was necessary after Ruth told him it got muddy when it rained.

Surprisingly, most people spoke English. During their lunch at the African buffet, he asked why people understood English, yet spoke their native language fluently.

"Everyone who goes to elementary school learns English." She moved her fork through the steaming fish stew. "English is the national language so we can communicate with each other."

"There's very many culture with different language." Dongo spoke over his mouthful.

Brady frowned when he tested the creamy sauce. Peanut sauce, she'd said, and he didn't expect to like it. He scooped a bigger bite. Actually, it wasn't too bad. His fork clanked when he set it on his half-empty plate. "This doesn't taste like peanut butter at all."

"You like?" Dongo set down the chicken bone, his hands greasy from not using a fork.

"I think I like it."

"Try the tilapia." Ruth slid her plate in front of him.

He was stuffed, but her hopeful smile compelled him to reach for his fork and cut into her half-eaten fish.

It melted in his mouth. "Not bad." He doubted he'd tasted tilapia before to make any comparisons. He normally ate salmon.

After their lunch, Ruth needed to stop at the market—nakasero, she'd called it—to buy groceries for her family.

Dongo parked on the busy street close to the market entrance. Her soft fingers fit so perfectly as they clasped Brady's. With her other hand, she gripped her purse handles tight to her shoulder as they plunged into a sea of moving bodies.

He shuffled through a tangle of arms and legs. The scent of rotten onions mixing with body odor and fried food made him queasy.

"Keep your other hand in your pocket to guard your wallet."

He patted the pockets of his cargo shorts, thankful the wallet was still in place.

People shouted cheerful greetings, calling "mzungu," and others ushered them to their booths. But as they passed a butcher stand with slabs of meat and the seller swatted flies from the meat with his hand, Ruth kept a steady gaze on her destination. Soon, they entered open double doors to a spacious shop filled with sacks of grain and powdery items he couldn't identify.

Two gentlemen greeted Ruth by name, and they smiled in greeting to Brady.

"I'll take ten bars of soap, twenty kilograms of sugar...." Ruth skimmed a slip of paper as she read the items to the dark-skinned bald man. He bellowed for the young man in the back to scoop items onto the scale.

Brady squinted at the note. Was he seeing his name at the bottom of the list? Hard to tell through the paper, but it almost looked like she'd doodled it there.

People came in and out, making their transactions and taking their purchases. The shop owners obviously did this often, and the six cashiers had an easy-flow operation.

When they told Ruth the total, Brady pulled out his wallet. "I got it."

"You paid for all the medicine." She retrieved her wallet from the handbag and extracted some frail bills. "That was way more than I treated you for."

He still intended to pay so she could buy something for herself. He'd only used the excuse that he was paying for his stitches by buying the medical supplies since she was turning down his help. Even when he'd insisted on doubling the medical supplies on her list, it had cost less than his monthly Starbucks coffee.

The entire time they shopped, everything she bought was to benefit someone else, not herself.

At the end of their shopping, two of the shopkeepers helped push an overflowing wheelbarrow to Dongo's car. Brady shoved a gallon of oil in the back seat. "We might need to rent a truck for the village."

"There's no trucks for rental, anyway." Ruth set the box of biscuits on her lap.

Dongo pushed a sack of cornmeal—posho, as Ruth called it—in the back and slammed the door fast so the sack didn't fall out. "I shall tie some boxes on the top of the car."

Brady stifled a grin at the man's eager optimism. He didn't want to miss out on the business deal as their driver.

When Dongo started driving, Brady yawned, totally spent as they wove through afternoon traffic at the roundabout leading to Entebbe Road. He didn't mind waiting when they came to a complete halt. Ruth was a comforting presence. She pointed out the special buildings they passed.

"What's going to happen to you, since you missed the resort deal?"

She'd asked the same question during their dinner last night. But he hadn't wanted to talk about work, so he'd redirected the conversation toward her and her family.

"I'll be okay." Not really. It would push the company back to a different income bracket, but compared to Ruth, he couldn't complain. "I worry about the people who might lose their jobs if I have to shut down some branches."

"I'll pray everyone involved can be victorious in the end."

With the way her eyes gleamed, she meant it. His stomach fluttered. "Thanks."

As they approached Kisubi where she lived, Brady turned down her dinner invitation. He patted his stomach. "I feel like not eating for three days." The lunch buffet had been plenty. If he was sleeping on the floor for five nights, he needed a good rest before their trip. Still, he stretched out his legs as far as he could in the back seat and breathed in her floral scent, looking forward to this time with her. "I'm going to get ready for tomorrow."

"Good idea. Get to bed early." Ruth tucked a loose strand of hair behind her ear. "It's going to be a long day."

She and Dongo dropped him off at the resort parking lot. After a warm shower, Brady glanced at his phone. Only six p.m. Way too early to go to bed. His jet lag was wearing off, and after sleeping the day away yesterday, he doubted he'd be able to sleep again, so he wandered to the manicured lawn.

With the sky darkening, the orange clouds faded as couples sauntered around the property. A cool breeze stirred from the palm trees undulating throughout the gated resort.

He walked to one of the empty grass-thatched cabanas and perched on a wooden recliner.

The sound of water was relaxing. The Entebbe resort could've been his if he'd made it to that meeting. He'd asked the manager last night and discovered the owner had left for India, but he would be available the day Brady was set to leave the country.

He leaned back and closed his eyes, his heavy body relaxing.

Ruth. She looked like a Ruthie with that smile of hers. Gentle, yet feisty and hard working.

The way she'd navigated the chaotic city and haggled with shop owners made Brady admire her even more. She was a good businesswoman.

Why hadn't he invited her to stay for a while when Dongo dropped him off? The cabana would seem extra enjoyable with her seated nearby. She could probably use a day off—a day without treating patients or shuffling through a crowded market.

Good thing he'd withdrawn extra cash from the ATM. He hoped to spoil her when they stopped to tour Jinja on their way back from the village.

Exhilaration coursed through him, and his lips stretched into a smile. An entire week—maybe even the full ten days with her.

Business occupied ninety-eight percent of his time. Being responsible for people's pay, proving to his dad he could meet the standard, and staying ahead of the competition, made it hard to think of anything else but work.

But two percent of his time, he tried to remember that God had brought him so far. Ruth was an extraordinary woman. Yes, and he was a man who never did relationships because he had no time for romance. Even if being with Ruth felt so right, he'd better not entertain any ideas of her during this temporary exception from his chaotic routine.

SITTING ON RUTH'S LOVESEAT, Brady eyed the breakfast food on the table. It looked like lunch. A plate of steaming plantains with meat and collard greens. The spoon clinked when Ruth stirred tea with a hint of cream.

"Everything smells good." He lifted the cup to his lips, savoring the spicy scent. "What do you put in this tea again?"

"Milk and black tea." She balanced her plate on her lap. "I add ginger, cloves, and cinnamon sticks for spice."

Her phone chirped on the table, and she ignored it. He'd learned the village had no phone service. "What if your colleagues need to reach you for medical advice?"

"Eunice has the number to call the shop owner in the town center. There's just a tiny corner in the shop that has cell service. The shopkeeper can then send her message to my parents' house."

Since he'd emailed his assistant to reschedule his appointments, the lack of cell service was almost a relief.

Ruth's friend, Eunice, walked in from the clinic and knelt before Brady in greeting. Red lipstick contrasted her green blouse. "You're feeling better?"

"Yes." His shoulder still thrummed with a dull pain whenever he moved his arm, but he had a nurse to take care of him if the pain intensified. "Thank you."

Eunice handed Ruth a paper that she glanced over. "Just add it to his other bill from last month."

Since she purposefully seemed to respond in English, he assumed she didn't want to make him feel uncomfortable.

He helped her hand-wash the breakfast dishes while she hid his laptop in the safest place in the house. Brady had checked out of the hotel and reserved it for two nights after his return.

After she changed the bandage on his forehead, they loaded the car. Ruth carried cases of mineral water, insisting he'd need it. "I don't want you to get sick with the village water." She squeezed the fourth case onto one of the back seats.

Ruth snapped two pictures of the dispersing streaks of orange sunrise. She then asked Dongo to take a picture of her with Brady before they got in the car. "For the memories," she said, and Brady couldn't agree more.

Traffic wasn't an issue as they drove the long stretch to Kampala. Brady tried not to think about his injury at the sight of boda bodas swerving in and out of the flow as they arrived in the city. It would have to be a life-threatening emergency for him to sit on a motorcycle again.

Traffic thinned the further they drove toward Jinja Road, away from the city. He relaxed and shifted his leg. With the car jam-packed, his jeans brushed her knee, and warm awareness of her femininity jolted him. The soft scent of her shampoo offered a slight distraction—the kind of distraction he suddenly liked.

"That's the tea plantation." She nodded toward the left, then to the right. The road split apart green vegetation on both sides.

"That's where the delicious tea comes from?"

She lifted her purse from her lap and set it on the floor. She then told him about the work that went into growing tea.

"What's America like?" Her innocent eyes met his. "Do they have farms or just the flower gardens in their homes?"

"Yes, there's farmers in certain parts of the country."

He got the impression she had the wrong image of America when she assumed everyone had a smart-operated home with elevators and swimming pools. Either way, his mind started considering all the places he'd take her if she ever visited. With the nature of her job, she might enjoy an opera or anything relaxing.

When he told her about the ranches, she just shook her head and said she'd never seen any farms in the few movies she'd watched. Soon she asked Dongo to stop for a snack.

Dongo pulled over near the Mabira Forest nestled along the Kampala-Jinja highway. Underneath a flimsy tent across the street, smoke billowed where men manned the grills.

A few cars whizzed along the highway as men and women in blue and purple coats rushed to cross. Leaping in front of fast cars? "What a risk."

"I usually come in a minibus, and I've never paid attention to how they cross the road." Ruth reached for her purse when vendors thumped on his window since boxes stacked her side.

Brady opened his window, imitating Dongo. By the time Ruth dug out the money to order, the hawkers had shoved fifteen to twenty wooden skewers in front of him, and he had to lean back in his seat to avoid being poked.

"Guys, you need to step back so I can see what I need." Ruth shushed them with her hand, but they didn't seem to hear her over their shouts.

As the delicious scent of grilled meat permeated the car, Ruth's voice rose over the noise. She addressed the food vendors in Luganda. Soon she yanked four sticks of peeled-roasted bananas and then fumbled with cash, handing the money to whoever sold her the bananas. The man offered her newspapers to wrap her bananas.

She then passed money to Dongo, since he already had a meat skewer in his hand—two skewers actually. A drumstick and a beef skewer.

"What soda would you like?" she asked Dongo who wanted a Sprite.

Not wanting to compete with the bidding war over the window when she asked him, Brady said he'd have whatever she was having. Then he took the sodas one at a time as the man opened the lid. After Ruth paid for the drinks, she closed the window and drew in a sharp intake of breath.

It seemed like a lot of work. "Tired already?" He handed Dongo his Sprite, then Ruth her Fanta, and he took one for himself.

"I didn't realize the sellers would flood the car." She gave Brady one of the plantains wrapped in a newspaper. "This is gonja. A light snack, because Mom will have a big meal for us."

He wasn't hungry but was curious to try it. So he bit into the fluffy powdery banana and paused midchew as he tried to figure out the taste. Semisweet. "It's decent." Like most new foods he'd tried, he needed more time to get used to it.

She arched a brow, unconvinced by his response. "I understand if you don't like it. All the foreign food must be hard for you to get into."

"Not hard at all." He missed Starbucks and, well, New York pizza, but learning new foods was an adventure.

Dongo chucked the bones through the window and wiped his hands on the crumpled newspaper he retrieved from the console. Brady cringed when the man also chucked the wrapped newspaper through the window before he fired the engine.

Brady kept peering through the window, expecting blue and red police lights to chase after them for littering until Ruth asked if he was okay.

"Are we going to have a ticket for the trash?"

She chuckled. "They don't give tickets. People do it all the time."

She said they didn't have public trash cans. Brady sipped his Fanta to drop the subject. As they passed cars, he noticed trash being tossed out from random minibuses.

He took another bite of the plantain and guzzled the refreshing orange soda to wash the banana down. Stuffed, he folded the remaining plantain into the newspaper. Ruth said she'd add it to the ones she was taking to her family.

The deep-green forest surrounded them as they drove on for about twenty minutes. Looking at an expansive jungle somehow relaxed him, and he settled deeper against the backrest. "This is fascinating."

"Can you believe there's a hotel in that forest?" She dusted off the plantain remnants on her hand. "There's monkeys and other animals in there, too."

"Monkeys?" Brady set the bottle by his feet. "They're not in a zoo, right?"

Ruth shook her head, laughter twinkling in her eyes. "If you want to see monkeys, don't worry, you'll see plenty in the village."

"Let's add that hotel to our stops on the way back." Besides the source of the Nile where they'd originally planned to stop and stay the night in one of the hotels, Brady intended to utilize the last four days after the village to explore the rest of the tourist places.

"Maybe you'll end up buying the forest hotel instead of the resort." She shrugged, and her expressive mouth curved into a joyful smile that somehow energized him. "I've never visited the hotel before, but I've seen the pictures."

She was onto something. He liked her business mind. "That might be a good idea."

"Oh!" She drank the rest of the soda and set the bottle by her feet. She then pulled out a camera from her handbag. "I forgot to take pictures of the forest." Her face scrunched as she peered ahead. "But I can't miss the Nile."

"We're approaching Bujagali Falls," Dongo announced.

As they drove past a bridge, Ruth leaned into Brady and snapped pictures of the white rapids on his side.

It was hard to see through her window, but beyond the driver's side, the opposite side of the bridge had still water.

Having the height advantage and long arms, he offered to take the pictures on the opposite side.

When he sat back, he leaned into her, their heads almost touching while he scrolled through her Canon PowerShot camera to see the blurry pictures he'd taken. "Not my best shots." She'd have another opportunity to snap more pictures. "Good thing we'll be back."

"This one's not so bad." She tipped the camera his way so he could view the bridge with the Nile in the background. "It doesn't hurt to take more if you're going to show your friends pictures of your trip." She talked about the many beautiful places on the east side part of the country—places she thought he might like. "If you had time, I'd take you further to Mt. Elgon."

He'd heard of Elgon. "How far is it from your village?"

"One hundred and thirty kilometers, but it will be out of the way to get back to Kampala."

Hmm, eighty miles wasn't too bad, but they had enough plans. Perhaps he'd come back and visit her someday. "Maybe next time."

Her dark eyes glowed. "Yeah, I hope you can come back."

Even if he didn't have a business in Uganda, he could see himself coming back just to see her. "Definitely." It might be a while, but it would happen. "Maybe you can come and visit me in the States too."

Me that was a personal invitation, and his jaw tightened because he meant it.

She pressed her hand on her chest. "I'd love that."

A twinge cut through him when the realization of his invitation hit. Of course, she would visit as a friend who saved his life. If anything were to come out of their friendship, would she ever be willing to move to America? He wasn't relocating to Uganda.

What was wrong with him? Ruth pointed out sugarcane plantations. Nothing would be coming out of anything. His jaw twitched. He was only going to the village, returning for a tour in Jinja, and then heading back to his business in America.

"Would you like to take pictures of the sugarcanes?"

"Sure." He accepted the camera and snapped three pictures before handing it back.

"You'll have to give me your address, so I can send you some of these pictures."

"I will." His throat was hoarse. He closed his eyes, suddenly bothered by a possible friendship with Ruth. This could be the start of something different. Whether he left Ruth alone, he was pretty sure he'd be thinking of her long after this trip ended—he'd think of her more than the business deal he'd missed.

CHAPTER 6

Ruth's entire body shook as the tires vibrated along the familiar potholed road. If it wasn't for the dust stirring, she would've rolled down the windows so she could breathe in the fresh air and the familiar scent of home. She tried to ignore the warmth that radiated from Brady's shirt whenever his arm brushed against her shoulder. Only twenty kilometers, and they would be home.

Silence settled in the car as Dongo fixated on the narrow road while Brady massaged his temples as he took in the hills of pastures and farms.

Was the bouncy road the reason for his oncoming headache? Was it too much after his head injury? She doubted America had any dirt roads with potholes. Not the America she'd seen in those movies. "Are you feeling all right?"

He winced. "I have a dull headache."

Not the best way to start a vacation. She reached for her purse from beneath her feet and retrieved medicine. He held out his palm when she opened the container and shook out two pills. "The bumpy roads don't help either." She then twisted off the cap from a bottle of mineral water and handed it to him.

"Thank you, Ruthie."

Her breath caught at the way this name he called her rolled off his tongue... *Ruthie*. She liked that.

How could she make him feel comfortable? She always hated getting carsick during long trips, so she asked if he felt nauseous.

"I never get carsick." He lifted the bottle to his mouth and guzzled more water as she told him about her first time in a car.

Her stomach tightened, and warmth tingled in her ears. How could something so long ago feel so familiar? "It was a tight-packed bus when I first left the village to go to boarding school," she whispered, rubbing the sudden cold sweat from her arms, feeling the strangeness of the motion. "So I was glad to be with my dad when I vomited."

"Eww!" Dongo said over his shoulder.

"There was no room to sit, and it was so hot." She could almost smell the mix of diesel and body odors. "My next trip was a little better, and the next one better still. Now, I never get motion sickness."

A frown furrowed Brady's forehead. "That's not fun. I'm glad you don't get sick anymore when you travel."

"Me, too." Because she traveled to the village more often than she used to.

When they approached a bend in the road, she directed Dongo to take a right.

"This is where you grew up?" Dongo asked.

"Yes."

Brady sat up straighter, craning his neck around. "What brought you to Kampala from a remote village?"

While most of the girls in her village were raised with one purpose—to get married—her dad believed in education and wanted them to pursue a career. "We don't have good schools here. Kampala has many boarding schools." If you were getting a quality education, boarding schools were the way to go.

Brady's brows rose when she told him about the three months she used to be away from her family while at school.

"I missed my family, but I got used to it after several years."

The shrubs slapped at the windows as the road narrowed. Pink and white wildflowers were crushed in between the thick green vegetation, the way it stayed all year long.

Bicycles and motorcycles were the villagers' main means of transportation. On rare occasions like today, someone from the city hired a private driver.

Kibale Village unfolded around them as they drove past maize fields and banana plantations. Grass-thatched houses poked through the trees. The mud and wattle walls would be a challenge next month when the rainy season began. The inhabitants would have a hard time staying dry if they didn't keep adding more grass to their roofs.

The familiar surroundings always resurrected special memories of her childhood. Though she couldn't see most of the spread-out homes from the road, she knew the pathways and shortcuts leading to the well, and from one house to another. She knew the adults and their children by name.

"Mama Kato," she whispered when she spotted her almost falling off her bicycle as she halted to look at their car. "Sorry." She leaned over Brady and lowered the window before sticking her head out and waving. Mama Kato waved back, grinning, then adjusted the jerry cans on her bicycle's back seat.

"What are those kids carrying on their heads?" Brady asked when they passed three kids twelve and thirteen years old. They carried ten-gallon jerry cans on their heads as they smiled and waved at them.

"It's water." Mangoes dangled from the branches on the tree overshadowing them. "They're coming from the well." She told him of the well not far from there. Just below the hill, Ruth and her siblings used to walk fifteen kilometers to get to it. "These days we have a borehole."

Thankfully, the water pump was closer to her house.

A sense of exhilaration coursed through her when the familiar brick house nestled between mango trees and papayas came into view. Her childhood home. "We're here," she said, and Dongo turned into the expansive dirt compound, parking meters away from the corn sprawled on the ground.

Grandmom hunched over, peeling husks from the corn and spreading it to dry. She stood, frowning. Perhaps she'd heard the tires approaching.

Her gaze flitted to Dongo. She then looked at the back and blinked, rubbing at her eyes, then doing a double take at Brady. Ruth never came home in a private car, and certainly never brought a white man.

Ready to rescue Grandmom from her confusion, Ruth leaned over Brady and waved. "That's my grandmom, Imelda."

"Huh." Dongo cocked his head and waved too. "I've never heard of that name."

"Lovely name." Brady lifted the handle and pushed open the door, and Ruth followed him out.

Imelda patted her short salt-and-pepper hair, then fumbled with her raggedy floor-length dress. Given the time of the day, they'd likely come from cultivating the fields not more than an hour ago.

"You didn't tell them you're bringing company?" Dongo stepped out of the car as Ruth led them toward her grandmom.

Imelda cupped her mouth when she turned to the half-open door and called for Mom. "Ruth's here." She spoke in Lusoga, her native language. "She's brought us guests—not just any guests. One of them is a mzungu."

Ruth could only imagine the panic going on in the house as Mom, Dad, and Granddad yanked out their Sunday-best outfits in preparation for the guests.

Imelda turned to Dongo, then faced Brady as she smoothed a shaky hand over her tattered dress. "Sorry, I didn't dress nice." Her English was halting as she seemed to think before each word, but Ruth's heart warmed as Grandmom acknowledged Brady didn't speak Lusoga.

"I'm not complaining." He outstretched his hand. "I'm Brady."

"Uh..." Her jaw dropped as if she were thinking of her next words as she shook his hand and knelt before him. "Welcome. Call me Daada or Jajja."

"That means grandmom." Ruth could only hope Brady was comfortable with all these random rules.

"Jajja is easy enough." Wow, that smile of his was captivating. "You have such a beautiful home." Brady peered at the chickens pecking on the corn at the far end of the yard.

Ruth introduced Dongo as her neighbor and driver, and Imelda greeted him in Lusoga, which wasn't much different from Dongo's language.

When Grandmom turned to Ruth, she threw her arms around her. The sweet smell of Grandmom, passion fruit, and home filled Ruth's senses. "Those blue eyes! Is that what angels look like?" Grandmom whispered in Ruth's ear and stepped out of the embrace. Her callused fingers touched Ruth's cheek. "I've been praying for a husband for you. Finally, you got one. You went for the best."

Even if Ruth had different reasons to be drawn to Brady, Grandmom, like many Ugandans, assumed white people to be rich—assumptions furthered by the TV show. A white person was like financial security, but again, money was far from driving her choice for a future husband. Before Ruth could correct her, Grandmom broke out into a song, and danced as she clapped her hands.

"Your grandmother is... interesting?" Dongo crossed his arms over his chest. Perhaps he meant interesting in a good way.

"Sorry, I forgot to warn you." Her neck and ears burned, and she ducked her head, afraid to look at Brady. Being happy or excited triggered Imelda's love for singing.

Ruth twisted her neck when she heard Brady clapping. His broad grin crinkled up the skin around his eyes again as he watched Imelda spin around, and Ruth's embarrassment whirled away.

"I love your grandma!" When Brady smiled at her, their gazes caught, and a delicious sense of promise hung in the air between them.

"I'm glad." What a relief! She only needed his approval because he was staying with her family for an entire week. Well, that, and maybe not to scare him off.

The rest of the family emerged as Jajja's song ended.

Brady stepped forward and shook Mom's hand, and Ruth introduced her. "Florence."

Her dark face was shiny. She must have smeared it with the lavender facial cream Ruth bought her two months ago.

Ruth then introduced her father, Fred. The gray in his dark hair had increased, no doubt from long hours of hard work.

"And this is Granddad Joseph."

After they shook Brady's hand, they greeted Dongo.

Granddad led them underneath the four mango trees to the side of the yard, his radio in hand. He never left the house without it.

The men sat on worn wooden stools Dad had built with Granddad years ago.

"Where did you snag a mzungu?" Her mom exchanged looks with Dad who was across from them. "Sending your kids to boarding school is paying off. One of your daughters is marrying a mzungu."

"No... I'm not. He's a friend." She sat on the mat next to Mom. "He wants to help me hand out medicine." She'd leave out the part of Brady being on vacation.

Ruth glanced in Brady's direction. Dongo was asking Granddad something, but Brady's eyes found hers, no doubt curious upon hearing "mzungu" and knowing they were talking about him. If she were in his position, she'd want to know what every word spoken in front of her meant. She'd better make sure her guest was comfortable.

When she had her family's attention, she said, "For the next five days, can we all speak English?" Everyone knew the language. They were not fluent because they rarely spoke it, but even Grandmom had gone to school up until primary seven.

"You want to rip my tongue out?" Granddad huffed and crossed his hands over his chest, then fiddled with his radio.

Mom fumbled with her braid. "I'm going to make a fool of myself in front of my future son-in-law."

Had she already forgotten Ruth's explanation about her relationship with Brady?

Ruth eyed her mother and grandfather. "It's good practice." She spoke in English, keeping her tone firm as she would with a stubborn patient. "Brady will not grade your English."

His face colored, and he gripped the back of his neck. "You don't need to speak English on my account."

"It's no problem." Granddad adjusted his tunic. "You're already in a foreign country. No need to keep you feeling like an outsider."

Brady's appreciative smile warmed Ruth's heart. "When you put it that way, I like it."

When Dad started talking to Brady, Ruth joined Mom and Jajja on the opposite side of the yard, by the grass-thatched kitchen. A blackened pot waited on the fire pit outside. She lifted the lid, and her stomach growled at the simmering scent. "What're you cooking?"

"Chicken." Imelda spread out another mat and set the plates on it—the ceramic plates they reserved for special guests. "Flo, can you squeeze the passion fruit?"

Ruth remembered the water. She touched her mother's arm. "Brady can't use our water. I'll make his passion juice separate."

"When did you start courting a mzungu?" Jajja scooped mashed plantains and ladled them to one of the plates. No use in correcting her family anymore. How could she blame them? She'd expected this to happen because, culturally, you didn't bring a man to your parents' house unless he was going to be your husband.

"Imagine the respect your father will get when you marry a mzungu." Mom spooned sugar to the seeds in the sieve. "Is he married?"

"I didn't see a ring on his finger." Jajja waved away the question. "If he's staying with us for one week, you must mean something to him."

"Did you notice the color of his eyes?" Mom pointed the spoon to Jajja.

Jajja set a plate on the mat, then placed her hand on her cheeks. "Blue." Her brown eyes lit up. "He looks like an angel."

This would be a perfect drama. "I think angels have wings." Ruth sliced a passion fruit in half, grateful she hadn't called ahead to warn them. Otherwise, they'd have the pastor handy and ready to marry them by the end of the week. "For the last time, we're not courting." She told them about his accident and his missed flight, hoping they'd drop the subject. "He wanted to see what a village looks like."

It was safer not to tell them he'd taken her to dinner and she was attracted to him.

She ignored Jajja's excitement as she insited that Brady's missed flight must be a part of God's plan for him to meet Ruth. The man was leaving, but Ruth didn't want to get into this conversation.

"Who do I need to see after lunch?" She usually visited a few ill patients on her first day, and then met with the patients who showed up at their house late in the afternoon.

"Musa." Jajja carried food trays toward the gentlemen. Mom added two other names of emergency patients Ruth would be visiting within three hours.

Dad prayed for the food, and they ate. Dongo didn't need a fork or spoon. He was happy using his fingers.

When they'd finished, Brady joined everyone in unloading the boxes from the car. Ruth made sure all the boxes were stacked in the main room, fighting the urge to assess the one bedroom and figure out how they were going to sleep that night.

When they'd emptied everything, they said goodbye to Dongo. "You're sure you don't want me to come back for you?"

"Ruthie is my guide." Brady gave her that sunny smile, and for a second, she had to think of her words to Dongo.

She finally remembered. "I... I'll go into town and call you if we change our minds." Since they intended to stay in Jinja for two nights, it would be easier not to be tied to Dongo's schedule.

Brady patted Dongo's shoulder. "Drive careful."

What a sweet man. He was her kind of dream. When he faced her, his kind blue eyes danced over her face. Her knees felt unsteady, and she glanced away, turning toward the tree. "I better get ready."

Had he even heard her with her words coming out so weakly?

CHAPTER 7

Ruth changed into a knee-length flared skirt with shorts underneath. Wearing pants while riding a bike would be more practical. But the villagers were not used to women wearing pants, and her priority was to make everyone comfortable.

She slung the medical bag over her shoulder and said a prayer for the patients she was going to visit. Several times, she didn't know what to do for the patient, besides giving them pain medicine, but it was either her treatment or no treatment.

She closed the window to keep any mosquitoes from entering the house. Even though they'd tie a mosquito net above Brady's bed, she'd do her best to make sure not a single mosquito entered the house. Malaria could ruin his entire trip.

She grabbed a cap she'd bought for Brady to protect him from the sun. Then she stepped out of the house and reached for the bike propped against the front veranda wall. Dad and Granddad stood talking to Brady. With their heads bent into him, they must be in a serious discussion. Brady gripped the back of his neck and winced. The two chickens eating corn darted off with a squawk when she rolled the bike past them.

"Ready to go?" Brady rose when he saw her. Yes, the poor man was in a hurry to escape Dad and Granddad.

"Have you ever sat on the back of a bicycle before?" Walking would take way too long, and they wouldn't make it to three homes in one afternoon.

"I'm having a few firsts here." He accepted the cap she gave him. "Thank you."

"It will be easy." Dad walked over and pointed at the feet stands where Brady could rest his feet. "If you get scared, just wrap your hands around her waist."

Ugh. Ruth fumbled with the handle on her bag at the thought of Brady's steady arms wrapped around her. They'd fall off the bike from her loss of concentration.

"I'll carry the bag." Brady's face colored. Perhaps he was thinking the same thing. Not wanting to linger on the matter, she handed him the bag.

"Well, then." She tilted the bicycle to climb on, and Brady sat on the seat behind her.

He didn't have his arms wrapped around her, but she could feel his nearby body temperature. She pedaled the bicycle to the back of the house. A shortcut would get them to their destination twenty minutes faster.

She needed to say something, and she did as she started through the cornfield. "What were Granddad and Dad talking about?"

"A little this and that." His tone was light before he burst into a rich laugh that echoed through the fields as she weaved on an uneven path. His breath tickled her neck. "Guess your grandparents moved in when your grandpa was sick?"

"He used to work too hard on the farm, and they lived too far from my parents to check on them often."

Sunlight filtered through the mango tree leaves, dappling the path as monkeys chattered at them. Brady asked her to stop so he could watch the nimble creatures. She didn't argue. Pedaling the bike with him aboard was harder than usual, and the path was about to get steeper through here. Minutes later, she started again, straining her muscles with each push uphill.

A great blue turaco swept up the path. Though not a good flier, the silly-looking bird mocked her chugging efforts now with its ability to glide from tall branches. She tried not to laugh as it missed the branch it was aiming for and tumbled into another.

"Your dad is so funny."

"Just like his mom, Imelda." As long as he wasn't too direct.

"How did you make it to college when your siblings didn't?"

"Ambition. I thought if I took nursing, I'd make a lot of money and take care of my family."

"But?"

"God happened. My spiritual life changed during the first year at the main hospital." She gasped for air as she pedaled around the jutted rock. "I started thinking how I could make a difference by using my career."

Her decent salary at the hospital began to seem less rewarding as she thought about the scarcity of hospitals in the area and the many people who didn't have money to make it to the hospital. "I assumed that's why God enabled me to get a college scholarship, so I could take care of others."

He was silent for a while. When he responded, he somehow seemed to wrap the soft words around her like a hug. "Your family must be proud of you."

"Kind of." At times, Dad was disappointed she wasn't earning as much as she used to. "I don't bring them as many things as I did when I worked at the hospital." He'd sold several cows and worked endless hours on the farm so she could get a good education. She intended to take care of them someday.

As she biked past torch-ginger flowers, the conversation moved to her siblings when Brady asked their whereabouts. Dad must have told him about their family. "Seven kids is a lot."

"Could have been ten of us, but three died before I was born."

"Oh no!" A sudden intensity lowered his voice. "I'm so sorry."

She always wondered what life would have been like with nine siblings. "I'm the fifth born—second, I guess, after my siblings died."

But God had different plans. "Many people have eighteen, or even more kids. With malaria, meningitis, and other complicated illnesses, most kids don't live past six years old. People will have many kids, just in case they all don't grow up."

A brief silence followed as short-tailed warblers cried out from the undergrowth, the ground rustling with their movement.

"Maybe they wouldn't die so rapidly if they had a hospital."

"Probably." It was high time she learned a thing or two about him. "Any siblings?"

"It's just me… and my brother."

He hesitated before mentioning his brother. Then he jumped to ask another question, so he mustn't want to linger much on his family.

Based on what Brady asked about the family, he'd gotten ample information from Dad and Granddad. Dare she ask? She'd better leave that alone. As long as they didn't make him uncomfortable by assuming he was her fiancé.

Panting from the exertion of climbing a slight hill, she almost swerved when a giant rat darted through the pathway.

More warblers chirped, filling the brief silence before Brady spoke. "This is a lot of corn."

"Yes, it's our main staple." The cornhusks were turning from green to gold, and ears of corn stuck out as harvest time neared. "They use it to make *posho*, porridge, and also boil it or fry the corn for snacks."

He spread his arms out on either side as if reaching for the ears they rode past. His shadow cast before her wiggled its fingers. "What does posho mean?"

"It's a type of maize flour. We use it for food and porridge." Hmm, how could she explain it better? "I'll make sure to cook some before we leave."

The cornfield led her to another path through the sweet potato plantation. Her parents had bought acres of land when they settled in the village. The land paid off when harvest time came and they never ran out of food.

"The woman we're going to see is old and takes care of her great-grandkids." A brief background for where they were headed might help save them from introductions. "Their dad dropped them off after his wife died and he married a woman who didn't want someone else's kids."

"Whoa." Brady's arms flopped to his side, his shadow seeming to sink. "That's so sad."

She heard such stories often, but it crushed her every time.

They crossed two people cultivating their crops and waved. A grass-thatched house came into view, her family's closest neighbor who lived thirty kilometers away.

When she parked, Brady eased off the bike, and Ruth stepped down as well. She propped the bicycle against the tree in the compound. The midafternoon sun beat down, bringing perspiration to her brow.

"I have to say, I'm impressed by your skills on that bike." He took off his hat, his brown hair feathery in its rumpled state. "I almost thought we were going to fall when we rode past the rat."

For some reason, his compliment made her feel mushy inside. They would've fallen, not because of the rat, but because his nearness caused her mind to wander. She pointed to the bag slung around his shoulder. "There's some water in there for you."

He patted the bag and retrieved the bottle from the side pocket. "Thank you!" He saluted her with it, then capped off the lid. "Is there another one for you?"

"I'll be fine." She wouldn't waste his fancy water. "I'll get some from the neighbor." Speaking of which... where was the older woman or her three grandkids?

She pointed to the closed door. "They must still be in the garden." Which was an odd place to take a sick child.

The woods rustled from behind the hut, and the woman appeared with the seven-year-old hoisted to her back. "Musawo, welcome..." She froze midsentence when she saw Brady. "You brought a mzungu?"

Ruth ushered Brady forward, and he fell in step with her. "She's just surprised to see a white person."

"Just like all the others, I guess."

"I hope it's not offensive to you." She raised a brow when his face seemed neutral. "They think I'm the coolest person to be walking with you."

"You've got it wrong." He gave her a sideways glance. "It's the other way around."

Her heart quickened at the compliment, and her mind went blank on how to respond.

Underneath another tree, the woman set her granddaughter down on the dirty silk clothing. When Ruth introduced Brady to the seventy-three-year-old, she fumbled with her working gown and knelt before them. "Webale kwida."

"She says thank you for coming," Ruth interpreted.

Brady put a hand to his chest. "It's my pleasure."

Ruth interpreted the words for the woman.

While Ruth again interpreted, Brady's eyes shifted to the little girl lying on the ground, and he knelt beside her.

"Her throat hurts the most," the woman said after explaining Annie's symptoms.

It was either mumps or strep throat. Since Jajja had told her about the pain, Ruth had packed antibiotics. She couldn't run a strep culture, not in the village.

"We have a snake in the house." The woman rubbed her arms. A shiver shuddered over her slight form. "One of the children forgot to close the door this morning. It must have crept inside."

Ruth gasped, her hand to her heart. "Did you get it out?"

"No..." The woman's eyebrows creased together. "I can't mess with a cobra."

Brady was talking to Annie as he let her touch his hand, the child fascinated by his hair. Even if the girl was smiling now, her cleft lip made it look as if she always smiled. Ruth's heart constricted. She'd never heal the child of her cleft lip. She could only treat symptoms of random illnesses whenever she came. She'd deal with the snake after she checked the girl's temperature.

When she knelt beside Brady, his eyes glistened. She took the bag, and he gave her a sheepish grin. Then she rested the stethoscope over Annie's heart. "How are you feeling, sweetheart?"

The child smiled. "Not so good."

"Where are your sisters?"

"At school."

Ruth touched Annie's cheeks and probed the swelling. Then, with a flashlight, she checked her mouth, and her tight shoulders loosened. Her throat wasn't red. But when she took her temperature, it was way too high. In the past, the girl preferred taking pills over getting her medicine through an injection.

Ruth asked Annie's grandmom for water. For now, she would treat her for malaria and mumps. She'd have to make another trip before she left the village so she could immunize Annie and her family against mumps.

Breathless, the old woman shook her head and pointed to the house.

Brady offered his water, and Annie gagged as she took the bitter pills. "Good job." Ruth rested a gentle hand on Annie's shoulder as she gulped more water to force the medicine down. Ruth dreaded swallowing Chloroquine. When she'd had malaria, she preferred taking her medicine with a soda.

She handed Annie vitamins and a clear bag with two packages of biscuits. "Be sure to share with your sisters."

The girl's smile warmed Ruth's heart as she pushed herself to her feet. "I need to help your grandma get rid of the snake in your house."

Brady gawked when she explained her plans. "No way. You're gonna get killed."

Someone would, but she'd need God's help. She shrugged. "They need a place to stay tonight."

"I can't let you do it alone." He put the bag on the cloth next to Annie. "What's your plan?"

Ruth didn't have any. "Let's first open the door and see if we can spot the snake without going inside."

"Can we build them another house?" His question came out shaky as he took her moist hand in his.

She stifled a chuckle, despite her rising fear. "That might take the rest of this week, and they need a place to stay tonight."

"What do you usually do with snakes?"

"Kill them before they kill you." She'd rather not take any living thing's life, but she would have to save the human being first. She ducked and reached for the flimsy wooden door and pried it open, then shivered at the reality.

Brady pulled her behind him. "Wait!"

She was shaking before they even looked in the house. Brady's face was pale when he stepped in front of her and walked back to the hut.

"Ruth," he whispered, motioning in the house. "Look."

The giant cobra was curled, stalking a lizard meters away. It struck its prey in one swallow. Ruth gasped, and Brady's strong arm curled around her waist, pulling her closer. "Have you ever killed a snake?"

She shook her head. They'd encountered dangerous snakes. Her older brother had killed two. Unfortunately, he wasn't around. "I'm going to see if I can find a long stick." Perhaps poking the snake could prod it out.

He dropped her hand and followed her to the wooded area as they picked up different sticks, then returned with four of them.

The old woman sat by her granddaughter with a protective arm around her. Thankfully, they were meters away from the house, in case the snake cooperated and rolled out of the house. It could then return to the woods.

"I'll go first." With a shaky hand, Ruth tossed her stick through the door and assumed it landed on the snake. She jumped and turned, screaming. "Run!"

Brady didn't run. He winced. "Unfortunately, your stick never made it past the door." He sounded less unnerved than she was. At least one of them was brave.

Sure enough, her stick had fallen. "After all that mental work?" Her efforts had been in vain?

"You did great." Brady ducked below the prickly grass roof. He jabbed with the stick, probably poking at the snake. Then he jumped and moved his stick before letting go and sprinting toward her. "It moved!" He grabbed her hand. "Let's get out of here."

As they ran toward the woman, her wide smile revealed straight pearly teeth as she pointed behind them. "There it is!"

The snake slithered through the dirt into the nearby forest.

Brady gave her a gentle squeeze and exhaled. "We did it."

His blue eyes warmed her like the sunny sky had earlier.

"You're..." What was the word? How could she think when he was looking at her like that? "Brave." For someone who'd never wrestled a snake.

He pressed a hand against his chest, his face pale. "That was as thrilling as it was scary... life-threatening."

Annie's grandmother thanked them and extended an invitation for them to stay until she fixed them something to eat.

Ruth glanced up at the darkening sky. The damp air promised a coming rain. Turning down a meal was always rude, but she couldn't get Brady caught in a downpour. It wouldn't be good for his wound. "We still have to go to Zubaili's house, then Musa's." The two other patients. "And then we have some people coming to get their medicine tonight."

As the woman patted Ruth's arm in understanding, Ruth remembered the gospel tract she'd brought them. After unearthing it from her bag, she handed it over. Then they said goodbye.

"Tunakubona ku Sabiti."

Ruth agreed in response before she translated for Brady. "She says they will see us on Sunday."

"Do you have an appointment?"

"She knows I go to church whenever I'm in the village."

Brady squatted by Annie as Ruth crossed the yard to ready the bike. He patted the little girl's hair, then strode toward Ruth. His blue shirt stretched taut across his shoulders. He sure had a lean, hard waist. She came to her senses a little too late. *Caught in the act when he smiled.* She jerked and gripped the bike handles as if pretending to test the grip. How embarrassing.

"I'd offer to drive, but I've never ridden a bike through a dirt road before."

Without looking at him, she handed him the bag and climbed on the bike. "I don't mind driving."

Brady sat on the back seat.

As they rode, he kept asking about the little girl, and compassion flowed through his voice. "What's going to happen to her if she doesn't get surgery?"

"She will live like that for the rest of her life." Her heart squeezed at the thought. "She might have a hard time making friends." No doubt kids would make fun of her. Could be the reason why her step-mom didn't want her and her sisters.

He asked more questions about the village and her childhood.

"I spent most of the time in boarding school." She panted as she pedaled over a hill, gasping for air. "When I was at home, we spent most of our time working in the field."

The ride didn't feel long while talking with Brady. He was great company, and she was looking forward to getting to know him better during this week. That's if he stayed after wrestling a cobra and sleeping on a flat mattress.

CHAPTER 8

To say Brady expected a camping experience was an understatement. When he'd volunteered to come, even after Ruth explained the sleeping arrangements, he'd thought it would be sunshine and daisies—okay, it *was* daisies and sunshine with Ruth. Whenever he caught her staring at him with her doe eyes... the moments they shared an intimate smile... the times her laugh warmed him...

After they returned from their snake herding and home visits, a line of patients waited at her parents' house. She'd busied herself taking blood pressure and body temperatures, administering vaccines, handing out medicine, and applying antibiotic ointment and bandages to infected wounds.

Brady, she'd put in charge of handing out the pictures she'd taken the last time she'd visited. He also handed out the biscuits and treats she'd brought for the kids.

When the crowd died down, he leaned against the mango tree. As the weather stirred, he felt something stirring in him as well while he watched Ruth. The way the corners of her lips curled before she smiled sent a rush of warmth through him. He only had to look at her, and his mouth went dry.

Not that she'd catch him staring, since she was tending to her last patient of the day. She held a stethoscope to the frail woman's chest. The sharp collarbone that stuck out announced illness. Whatever Ruth was saying to her had the woman's sunken eyes light up.

From what Ruth had told him, most patients who suffered from human immunodeficiency infection (HIV) and other deadly diseases never recovered. Although she seemed like their only hope for medicine, she felt helpless when she didn't have a cure. Yet she made her patients smile. Ruth had that priceless effect that made everyone feel at home, cared for, cared about. That calm gentleness was so rare and precious. The longer he was in her company, the more her quiet, attractive traits drew him in.

The humid heat had been building since they'd left the cobra hut, but it hadn't rained yet. Ruth's family was stashing corn into sacks and storing the full sacks in a hut designated for food storage.

A warm droplet of rain struck his arm, and he moved back to the table to gather whatever was left of the pictures. As he slid them in the manila envelope, raindrops plopped on the ground.

"Let's get inside," Ruth invited those still lingering.

He sprinted with a box of supplies and the pictures. People stood on the porch as they waited for the rain to pass.

When it ceased and people left, Ruth boiled water on the charcoal stove for his shower. "If you don't shower now, before it gets dark, you'll not be able to shower until tomorrow."

Sticky and grimy from the earlier sweat, he definitely wasn't waiting until tomorrow. "How does this work?" He switched the towel for the basin of water from her as she led him through a narrow path in the woods to the bathhouse.

"Just rub the bar soap on the wet sponge, then scrub your skin." She left him to it.

At first, standing in the shrub-built shower, with no roof or door, felt odd. Then he felt how silent it was—sensed the stillness with his whole being, with parts of him that hadn't been still since his scouting trips to the mountains. Unless a wild animal interrupted, he was alone.

The rocks poked through his sandals as he attempted to use his hands to pour water onto his body.

Though brief, the cool stillness refreshed him, and when he finished, Ruth went to shower while her mom and grandma cooked dinner.

It rained again while they ate. Ruth hadn't been kidding when she'd said that the one-bedroom house was cozy. His arm brushed against hers whenever he lifted a spoonful of rice. They shared one of the two wooden chairs in the house, while her dad and grandpa sat in the other chair and the other two ladies perched on the mat.

Then Ruth's grandpa tuned the crackling radio to find a clear channel, and her mom and grandma talked about their life on the farm and their urgency to plant more corn and peanuts before the rainy season next month. Her dad asked about Brady's business and wanted to know how different it was from agriculture. He was interested in growing coffee in the near future so he could start a business.

"Don't you think sixty-six is too late to pursue a farming business?" The spoon clanked when Ruth set it on her plate. "Maybe think of something less taxing for your body."

"I'll do that when you and your siblings can take care of me and your grandparents."

Ruth drew in a deep breath before she moved the spoon through her half-eaten food. "I will—soon." Her voice was barely above a whisper.

"Our Ruth is the smartest in the family." Her grandma set the metal mug down on the mat. "She takes care of us even with the little money she has."

"Thank you, son, for the groceries."

Brady had no idea what her dad was talking about. Ruth was tugging at her ear. He'd tried to talk her into letting him pay, but she'd refused. "Ruth bought everything."

"You bought medicine," her grandpa added. "That left her money to buy extra paraffin, soap, and oil to last us for a long time."

Fred, her father, cleared his throat. "It's great she finally found a man—"

"Dad!" Ruth snapped, but Imelda continued where her son left off.

"She's always been our picky one when it came to men."

Ruth touched Brady's arm and looked at his full glass on the table. "Can I get you some more passion juice?"

So this is what she meant when she warned him about her family misinterpreting their relationship. He'd chosen to come, so he'd do his best to make her comfortable too. Time to redirect the conversation. His spoon touched the porcelain when he set it down. "I feel stuffed."

"Uh... What does this 'stuffed' mean?" Ruth's grandpa asked as he dipped the mashed plantains in the chicken sauce.

"It means he's satisfied and not hungry anymore." Ruth gave Brady a half-smile. Gorgeous brown eyes poured into him, seeming to pass through to his very soul. Something was brewing between them. His heart racing, he moved his gaze to the open door.

The rain pelted the roof, and he stared at the buckets overflowing with water that dripped from the roof.

Jajja and Ruth's mom carried the empty jerry cans out and filled them with the water from the bucket.

Intrigued, he asked why they were filling every empty container.

"If they get rainwater, they won't have to go to the well." Ruth stood and stacked dirty dishes into a bucket. "Plus, the rainwater is clean, and they don't have to cook it before they drink it."

Man, he appreciated America. Everything seemed harder here.

While her mom and grandma filled every container with rainwater, Ruth carried the bucket and headed for the door. "I'm going to go wash these dishes, and I'll be back."

"I'll help." He stood and smoothed the crinkles from his soft shorts.

"Men don't do housework," her dad called after him. "Only farm work."

"At home, the ladies do everything," Grandpa added.

How interesting. "I'm not good at farming." Brady also believed in taking his share of work for the food he just ate. Plus, she'd worked all day. He gave the men a curt nod and followed her to the front porch where she set the bucket.

She walked to the far side, reached for the whistling kettle on the charcoal stove, and poured the steamy water over the dishes. Then she swirled the rest of the water into another bucket. "You should rest. You're on vacation."

"You wash and I'll rinse." He left her no room to discuss the issue, though a sudden self-consciousness over his dish-rinsing skills prickled him under the scrutiny of Imelda and Ruth's mom.

Jajja clapped her hands and sang something he couldn't understand. Her smile indicated it was a positive song. He may have thought something was wrong with her if Ruth hadn't mentioned how much she loved to sing.

"It's very unique for man to clean dishes." Her mom smiled at Brady after Jajja's song. She then explained the song's meaning. "You're Ruth's gift from God."

"Seriously, Mom?" Ruth lifted the bucket to dump the soapy water into the muddy compound. She then whispered to him, "You don't have to do dishes."

"Just like you didn't have to make your family speak English on my account."

After the dishes, he was ready for a bathroom break. He'd trekked to the bathroom during the day, but now that it was getting darker, he asked if they had another toilet close by.

"Long call or short call?"

"Uh…" He scratched his jaw as her words registered. Perhaps short call meant number 1, or was that number 2? He went with a short call.

"I brought an umbrella." She gestured toward the woods not far from the house. "For a short call, you can just go to the bushes."

Good thing he didn't need a long call, since the latrine was far away and his tennis shoes were already sinking into the soft earth.

Could he survive day one? He could only hope he didn't need to go potty at night. At least he'd not drunk the entire glass of passion juice.

At bedtime, Grandma led them in a song that had both English and another language. They all seemed familiar with the lyrics. With Ruth's melodic voice echoing right in his ear, the repetitive words made it easy for him to join them by the fourth time they sang it.

The lantern gave her face a soft glow, and her smile—man, he fought the urge to take her hand in his. Perhaps he was dreaming, but he had no idea how he turned his thoughts into action and clasped her warm hand. Stiff at first, her tension vanished by the time the song ended, and those delicate fingers curled around his.

After they prayed, Ruth dimmed the paraffin lamp and hung it by the bedroom door.

They all took their spots on the thin mattress pads lining the floor. Brady's was against the wall with the mosquito net hanging above. He'd gotten malaria shots, but Ruth insisted he sleep under a net—more afraid for him to get malaria. She shouldn't be. *He* was in good hands even if he got sick. What about her?

When Ruth spoke, he could almost feel the warm air from her lips caress his face. His heart leaped. "I hope you don't wake up with back pain."

He hated making her apologetic about their sleeping arrangements. She already had enough to worry about.

"You warned me, and I knew what to expect." Although he'd expected a mattress, not a pad, he was not complaining. At least the surface was flat and not bumpy.

"Ruth bought us the pillows last time she was here," her grandpa bragged.

"And the mattresses too," her grandma added. "Otherwise, we would be sleeping on mats."

Ruth groaned, seeming uncomfortable. It was sweet how she took care of her family. She took care of everyone in her life. Who took care of her?

Ruth's mom whispered questions about what America was like. Brady talked about the four seasons of the year. Ruth asked about snow, then laughed. "I can't believe water turns into ice."

"Do you wear a sweater the entire winter?" Imelda asked.

How could they imagine the temperature change since they never got snow? "Sometimes we have to wear something warmer than a sweater. We need scarves and gloves too."

They continued to ask questions about each season, which he happily answered.

Then the conversation shifted to family, and they discussed her siblings. No one made him talk about his family. It wasn't as close-knit as theirs.

The room fell silent after they said good night to each other. Thunder pierced the quiet night as the breathing deepened around him.

Brady looked up on the roof, the dim light comforting in unfamiliar surroundings.

How had someone who'd come for a twenty-four-hour business trip ended up camping in a remote village? Well, not necessarily camping, since he had shelter.

Images of the evening taunted his mind. The kid with a cleft lip. He'd seen another kid similar to Annie that evening. His chest pressed tight. What could he do to make a difference?

Huh? A shadowy creature flew from one corner to another. He blinked when another flappy thing whizzed above. Panicked, he crawled his hand under the net to reach for Ruth's. With no legroom between their mattresses, he found her hand instantly.

"Brady?" She lifted her head, whispering.

"Are you awake?" A silly question since he'd woken her.

"Yes," she imitated his whisper.

"I saw something flying in the house."

She gave a soft chuckle. "Those are bats."

Her response came as relaxed as if it were the norm.

"In the house?"

"They have a nest in the beams."

A cobra, now bats. What else was in store for him? Brady shuddered and gripped her hand tight. He was not letting go of her and definitely not sleeping. "Is it okay if I...?"

"You can hold onto my hand if it's of any comfort."

It was a good excuse anyway, and he savored the warmth and comfort radiating from her. Images of his accident stirred. Those brown eyes and how he hadn't wanted to let go of her hand.

His body warmed. He almost didn't pay attention to the roof when he closed his eyes. Best not to watch the night creatures. Just as his body relaxed to give in to the pull of sleep, a thick wet drop struck his hair, and another. Rain was making its way through the roof.

He eased his hand out of Ruth's and sat up, not wanting to wake her or anybody, but unsure of what to do. He would have to sit and wait until morning. It wasn't like they'd wake up and command the rain to stop.

Perhaps Ruth had been used to his fingers wrapped around hers. She rose onto an elbow. "Can't sleep?"

He told her the fate of his bed.

"Oh no!" She tossed her blanket to the side and stood. "I'll trade spots with you."

No way. He'd sit all night rather than have her sleep under the rain. "You have a long day tomorrow."

"You're on holiday."

Not the ideal vacation. Maybe he could consider it some sort of mission trip.

"If the rain gets on your wound..."

"What's happening?" Another head popped up, Ruth's grandpa.

Brady started shifting the mattress while Ruth relayed the situation.

"Guys, wake up!" Her grandpa tapped all the bodies next to him. "Brady's bed is wet."

Great. Now he was the reason for everybody's lack of sleep. Ruth carried his wet mattress to the main room and returned with another blanket and an empty bucket to catch the drip. They shoved the three remaining mattresses next to each other, to the dry side of the house.

If he'd thought it was cozy earlier, then he hadn't experienced a thing. He tilted his head back and stared up at the metal roof. Ruth shifted, and his body stiffened when her shoulder brushed against his, awakening each nerve in his body.

He could almost hear her racing heart, but he kept his arms straight on his legs so he didn't shift. Otherwise, he'd end up in her face.

The bats would be a great distraction about now, but they'd vanished.

The arrangement didn't seem to hinder her family's rest since steady breathing settled. When her dad moved, his long arm fell in Brady's face. He winced as the callused fingertips scraped his bandaged forehead.

"Sorry," Ruth whispered, sitting up and moving the heavy hand out of his face and away from the gauze.

How had her parents managed to conceive ten kids in this house? *When I go back to Manhattan, I'll send Ruth some money.* It couldn't cost much to build an additional room.

With the hand taken out of the way, Ruth lay back, and Brady tried to relax. He yawned, exhausted, yet doubted he'd get any sleep. With no watch to keep track of time, he had to remind himself he was on vacation.

Yet a part of him wished he'd taken the five-day flight.

Okay, but who lived like this? He had a five-bedroom, four-bathroom penthouse awaiting him. What was he thinking, extending his trip and coming here, of all places?

This was a mistake. He'd have Ruth call for Dongo tomorrow or the day after. He and Ruth could hang out after she returned. He turned on the thin mattress pad. His emotions conflicted, and he had no idea when he drifted off to sleep. But distantly, he heard a rooster crowing just as his eyes closed.

CHAPTER 9

Brady woke to a quiet house and winced at the bright light streaming through the curtains. He was the only occupant on one of the three mattresses. In last night's commotion, they hadn't moved the net above him, but he hadn't seen or heard a mosquito.

Voices resounded outside. Ruth was no doubt already at work, and her parents already tending their farming activities.

He massaged his temples to rid himself of the dull headache. He was crazy if he stayed another night in this house.

Where else would you sleep? Go to the grass-thatched house of the woman who had cobras and lizards?

If his mind served him right, Dongo had driven a dirt road through nothing but farmland for a good thirty miles. Brady hadn't seen a single hotel, unless it was another hut somewhere.

Ruth would figure out a way to call Dongo so he could get back to the resort with its warm showers and touristy comforts.

A sinking feeling settled in his heart at the thought of leaving. He'd regret it, wouldn't he?

He closed his eyes. Perhaps he could still remember how to pray. *Lord, what do You want me to do?*

Ruth's sweet face hung in his memory. Ruth kneeling beside Annie. Ruth laughing and encouraging her parents. Ruth smiling at him from her bike.

He prayed for her and the kids with cleft lips, the women and children with no hope for a brighter future. His heart grew heavier as he prayed, burdened for God's people—the ones in the village who were less fortunate.

The burden lifted as he prayed. He yawned and stood up. His back hurt when he bent to retrieve his luggage from the corner. He needed to brush his teeth and get his day started if he was going to help bandage Ruth's patients' wounds. She'd given him a rundown of his job last night when he'd demanded she shouldn't be shy about putting him to work.

Using last night's brushing regiment, he stepped out with a glass of water and brushed on the back porch, spitting on the dirt. It seemed odd, but he'd better get used to things if he was going to pull through the next four days.

He was in no rush to take a shower. After the downpour last night, he might be standing in a pool of water in the bathroom.

Having the house to himself, he changed into athletic shorts and a blue T-shirt.

The air hung so humid around him after the torrential downpour he could almost feel its texture, but a clear blue sky beckoned through the trees. Melodies of unusual songbirds welcomed the morning to the remote village. A soothing way to start the day.

His earlier whining vanished when he saw Ruth's barefoot clients in colorful, but worn, apparel. They'd lined up before her, and some walked down the muddy roadside to join the line.

His breath caught as Ruth lowered herself to a boy of nine or ten and wiped his runny nose. Compassion radiated from her when she wrapped her arm around the boy and brushed a hand over the teary face. Brady had no idea why the lad was crying, but his feet led him to them.

"What's up, buddy?" He patted the boy's hairless head. The boy's eyes lit up.

"John's scared of injections." Ruth glanced at him before looking at the boy. "He has a fever, and he dislikes taking medicine."

Last night, Brady had learned it was much easier to treat kids with shots than make them swallow tablets to cure malaria and the flu. Too bad they didn't have liquid medicine. "That's a tough one."

"Good morning, by the way." Ruth eyed him, her voice soft. "I didn't want to wake you after the rough night you had."

Compared to what the villagers were facing, how could he complain when he had a penthouse to return to in less than two weeks? "Could've been worse." Sudden guilt over the fancy house he slept in assailed him. He gestured to the long line waiting for Ruth before taking the boy's small hand in his large one. "I got John."

He led the boy to the far side, hoping to persuade him to get the shot. He succeeded when he showed John the medic tape on his forehead and told him about his accident.

"I had to get injections to prepare for my trip." He'd heard Ruth use injections rather than shots. Perhaps the boy understood, because he was not interested in discussing shots anymore. He was now fascinated with Brady's hair as he tugged at strands of it. He would've grown his hair before the trip if he'd known it would bring the kids smiles.

"Is your blood red like mine?"

Brady chuckled, surprised by John's innocent question. "God made everyone the same. Even if we have different skin colors, we still have the same color of blood."

A Sunday school song echoed in the back of his mind. "Jesus loves all the children of the world. Red, yellow, black, and white."

"I'm ready for the injection." The little voice pulled Brady back to the present. He walked him back to Ruth, and after she took the stethoscope from the man's chest, she mouthed a thank you to Brady.

He held John's hand as Ruth lifted the boy's waistband, barely revealing his skin. She poked a needle on John's upper bottom. "Great job!"

The triumphant smile she gave Brady melted his heart.

He then took his station at her left side. Putting bandages on people's wounds. With so much to do, he ended up taking over wound care so Ruth could focus on other patients. He disinfected wounds, deep cuts that frazzled him. But he'd been a Boy Scout, prepared for the task. Although he'd never had to apply the skill.

Ruth looked his way, wincing after he finished the last person in his line. "Sorry," she mouthed.

He didn't have a sanitary mask to prevent him from smelling the extreme foot odor, but at least he had gloves.

He gave her what he assumed was a reassuring smile and then mouthed back, "It's okay."

Upon Ruth's request, he snapped photographs of the people. The kids' serious faces when pausing for a photo fascinated him. Then, when he encouraged them to smile for the camera, their toothless grins tugged at his heart.

The kids' happy screams at the yard's far end invited him for his break. He joined the boys and girls in kicking the flimsy, handwoven fiber ball, and the kids' excited squeals left him feeling lightweight. Until they got a kick out of him calling the game soccer.

"It's *football*." A seven-year-old girl jammed her hands on her waist and stared him down.

She looked so cute and so serious, he struggled not to laugh.

Instead, he gave a solemn nod. "Football it is."

Then he kicked the ball, and the kids darted for it in the banana plantation. How many soccer balls could he get in the States for little to nothing?

His shirt was damp, and he was thirsty as he ran to keep up with the kids. He welcomed the break when Ruth called him for breakfast.

"It's time for a break." She ushered him toward the house. "Let's go eat something."

He could finally have a few minutes alone with her. But the kids pleaded for him to play with them after his breakfast, and he assured them he would.

"Looks like you have some new fans." Her dark eyes softened as she looked back at the kids already kicking the flimsy ball. He needed to add those to his list of things for the money he'd send Ruth. Soccer balls.

"I love my fans." He walked toward Ruth, her eyes wearier than they'd been yesterday. With a silk cloth wrapped around her hair, an apron over her skirt and blouse, and a face free of makeup, she was the most beautiful woman he'd felt drawn to.

His pulse kicked up, and heat flooded the back of his neck when she gave him a questioning look. He had to say something even if it didn't make sense. "Breakfast this late?"

He held a hand over his eyes and tipped his head toward the sky, trying to judge the time. The sun shone bright as if it hadn't stormed last night.

"We usually don't have breakfast, but Mom came back from the garden early to fix something for you."

He took her hand and entwined her fingers in his. He loved the way her fingers fit so perfectly in his, how they felt soft despite hours of hard work. "I guess we could call it lunch." Man, he was sweaty and grimy. "Any chance I can take a shower and change first?"

She kicked dirt with her flip-flop. "I was thinking the same thing. I'll also get our laundry washed after lunch."

He'd seen her mom and grandma hand-wash clothes. He'd never had to hand-wash clothes, but he intended to learn whenever Ruth did their laundry.

They took turns using the shower, and after they'd changed, Ruth's mom sent them to a clearing in the woods where she'd set up a mat and promised to bring their food.

She suggested it to keep villagers from interfering with their break. Which worked out for Brady as they lay side by side with elbows resting on the mat underneath the shade of an overhanging tree.

Vibrant red, blinding white, and delicate pink flowers of different shapes and sizes splashed the green shrubbery.

Brady stretched his hand to pluck a red hibiscus flower and tucked it behind Ruth's ear. "This one complements your outfit."

Her smile was shy. "Thank you." She fumbled with her ear, and her lips parted. "I know this is not your ideal holiday, but if you want to leave, I can call Dongo this afternoon."

"Honestly, I entertained the idea." He hoped she didn't think he was a whiner. "But after being a part of what you do, there's no other place I'd rather be."

"If you change your mind—"

He touched her arm. "You promised me two days in Jinja." Three, if he could talk her into it. "I'm counting on that."

Two kingfisher birds flew to a nearby branch. She asked about his family, not that there was that much to tell. "Do you miss them?"

He missed seeing his mom weekly. "I rarely see them because my business is far from home." He doubted she would understand New York and Virginia if she'd never been to America.

"Do you take after your dad or your mom?"

"More like my mom in some ways." Partially flexible and a risk-taker. "The business mind comes from my dad." Type A personality.

Her eyes lit up. "Is your dad in the hotel business too?"

"He has a law firm." His jaw tensed just at his mentioning Dad's work... the high expectations and demands for Brady to be proper and perfect. "He and my older brother work there. He was hoping I'd follow in their footsteps, but I let him down."

He talked about his distant relationship with his half brother. His mom had married a single dad, but the boy obviously hadn't wanted a brother. "I don't have a single memory of us ever playing together." That could have been due to the ten-year age difference. "But I guess he's more like our dad than I am."

She tipped her head sideways, her silk scarf falling back and springy curls slipping across her forehead as her eyes dimmed with something—concern? "He must be proud of you for running a successful business."

He doubted it. Dad kept reminding him he was in the wrong career. Especially whenever one of his locations was shut down or bought out. "Attorneys make more money without sweating for it." How many times had Dad rubbed that one in? "I guess a part of me lives every day working hard to prove my dad wrong... to prove I can be successful without being a part of the family business."

As she rested her hand over his, her compassion touched him. "You don't have to prove anything to anybody but God. At the end of the day, someone's going to be disappointed. It's the nature of humanity."

A bushy caterpillar crawled on the mat. She reached for one of the many twigs on the ground, putting it in the caterpillar's path. Once it crawled into it, she tossed the stick back into the woods. "I'm trying to learn that not everybody will be happy with what I do or offer. If I do my best as if doing it for God, then I don't have to worry about what my family or anybody else says."

Her words made sense. "I need to remember that."

Enough about his family, while there were people with real problems. "Annie... and the kids like her." His heart ached. "We have to do something."

A clear pain tugged her brows together. "Do you ever feel helpless... no matter what you do?"

In business, he did. "Sometimes, but not like you."

Her eyes glossy, she talked about women she'd grown up with, and patients who suffered from AIDS with no hope for recovery.

"I'm trying my best, and people still die." A chipmunk skidded a few inches from them. "I don't know if I'll ever do enough."

If she didn't think she was doing enough, then Brady was making no difference in this world. "You do a lot more than... many of us." She seemed to carry people's burdens as her own. It wasn't good for her health. "You're doing your best and letting God heal these people."

The gloss in those vibrant brown eyes turned to a shine as a firm nod dipped her dainty chin and sent her curly hair bouncing. "You're right. It's up to God."

But he could do something with the money God had entrusted to him. "Where do people go when they get ill?"

"Most of them just wait and die." She blew out a breath, plucked a blade of grass, and rubbed it between her fingers. "The one hospital is like fifty kilometers away, and they don't have medical equipment. Sometimes I think when I bring simple malaria medicine and teach people how to keep the fever under control, it might save some kids from dying."

"You said you know lots of doctors in Kampala who could use a job?"

She tossed the crushed blade away and peered at the stain it left on her fingertips. But her gaze was distant, making him wonder what she was seeing. "There's few hospitals, and they can only hire so many doctors."

If he paid to build a hospital and brought in doctors to run it, that would be a minor solution. "You need funding."

"Sometimes, God brings wealthy patients to my clinic, and they end up paying more just so they can support the clinic." She explained how she treated her landlord's family in exchange for free rent.

"Not that kind of funding." He eyed the stack of logs to the side, each one bracing on the ones below it, dependent on the layers built first.

That's what he needed. A well-constructed plan. So how could he start a charity and find immediate support to put such a plan in motion? His friend, Eric, ran several charities. He'd have to ask him as soon as he returned.

"What's going on in your mind?" Her voice interfered with his thoughts.

Unsure how his plans would work out, he kept them to himself and motioned to the logs. "What's all that wood for out here?"

"For cooking. My dad keeps meaning to cut it, but he rarely finds the time."

Whenever Ruth ran out of supplies, Brady would have nothing but time. "If he shows me what to do, I'll be glad to help." He doubted they had a chainsaw.

She touched his shoulder. "You're so wonderful." Twigs crunched when her mom approached through the woods, a tray of food in her hand. "I was feeling melancholy, but you brightened my spirit."

She was a breath of fresh air. "The feeling is mutual."

CHAPTER 10

Utilizing the quiet house, Ruth pulled on a loose sleeveless dress with shorts underneath. Besides catching up with laundry and cooking, she doubted she'd work in the fields today. She'd had twice the amount of medicine she usually brought, but rumor of a mzungu had a flood of people showing up on the first and second day. So they'd run out of medicine yesterday, too soon, but her family wouldn't like it if she left. Plus, it was safer to stay the planned period, in case villagers who expected her to stay for another three days needed her.

After opening the windows for natural light, she grabbed her toothbrush and tin cup to go outside.

She'd look for Brady afterward. She'd woken up to empty mattresses with blankets tossed to the side. Her family rose before dawn to work in the fields.

Just as she was putting away her toothbrush, she realized he might have gone with her parents. He'd entertained the idea last night. Problem was—she had no idea what part of the fields they were cultivating today.

She'd done devotions with Brady yesterday before people showed up, and she'd assumed they would read the Bible together again today. He seemed familiar with the Bible verses, which was surprising if he wasn't a Christian. Or was he? His actions represented a godly man. She'd almost asked him yesterday before early arrivals interrupted them.

She reached for her Bible and ambled back to bed, then settled in, lying on her stomach. She closed her eyes to thank God for the good rest. She'd needed it after the last two days. She prayed for

Brady's business to succeed and then prayed for the health of the families in the village, and her family, too.

Just as she flipped open the Bible, the front door jerked open. With no door to the bedroom, her gaze shot straight to Brady's tall frame in the doorway.

Her heartbeat thudded, and before she could steer her gaze back to her book, his eyes found hers.

"Ruthie!" he said breathlessly and ran a hand through his rumpled brown hair. He then bent and slid his feet out of Dad's boots. "Did you do devotions without me?" He walked to the bedroom and braced a shoulder against the doorjamb.

"Yes... I... no." She looked at the Bible, hoping to clear her blank mind.

"You're shaking."

Glad you noticed. By his amused grin, he knew how he affected her.

"I just... It's cold." Actually, it was warm. "Did you plant corn?"

She glanced up at him, not long enough to see if he was sweaty from corn planting, before redirecting her gaze to the Bible.

"It was so fun. I decided to leave early. We have a roof to fix and a well to dig this afternoon." He pushed away from the doorjamb and stretched out on his bed next to her. "Your dad said all the village men will be there."

He was working too hard. "You need to take a break. You're on holiday, remember?"

"Taking a break is not in my nature." The small gap between them wasn't far enough to keep his hair from brushing against hers as he bent over the Bible. "Are we reading in John today?"

"I was going to... read John." Not exactly what she'd planned, but rather the random page she'd opened.

"John 10. Would you like me to read?"

She nodded, afraid her voice would sound funny if she spoke.

" 'Truly, truly...' "

Brady's deep voice sounded like a recording. The scent of healthy male sweat increased her nerves, hence her fluttering stomach. His voice, so smooth and cool, somehow made the Bible verses more refreshing, brought out the Living Water on a hot day. If he read the Bible to her often, she'd listen to it every second of the day.

"Huh." He paused to reread John 10:27–29. " 'My sheep listen to my voice; I know them and they follow me. I give them eternal life, and they shall never perish; no one will snatch them out of my hand. My Father, who has given them to me, is greater than all; no one can snatch them out of my Father's hand.' "

He peered at her before looking back at the Bible. "These words never made much sense to me, until now." He nodded, staring at the suitcases in the corner. "Even when I drifted far from God, a lost sheep that wandered away, He's always surrounded me with people who love Him—people who lived their lives for Him."

Drifted away from God? A lost sheep? If she wasn't sure, she would assume they shared the same faith and he'd backslidden for a while. She sat up to create distance when it became hard for her to form words with him so close. "What do you mean by drifting?"

"I was about fifteen when I met Eric in Scouts, and he invited me to a youth church camp." He let out a slow breath and sat up. "I asked God to forgive my sins, to make me new. Since then, I have made God a part of my everyday life, and not just when I had an emergency. I spoke to Him as a friend...." He talked about his business and how he relied on God daily for his life and business in the first years. "I started working long hours. Six days became seven, and soon I didn't have time to do or think of anything besides work."

He rested his back against the wall and peered at the ceiling where it had leaked his first night here. "Eric's been a mentor since then, not only in exhibiting what the Christian walk should be, but also as a business mentor. A selfless, godly man who lives his life for

Christ." His sad chuckle hurt her heart as he stretched his legs out and rocked his head against the wall. "And this? How can I say God isn't trying to get my attention? Missing my flight and ending up here... no electricity or distractions." He drummed his hands on his thighs. "It's hard not to think about God."

She wanted to reach out her hand to let him know he was a wonderful man, but they shared a smile instead. God was at work in his life. *Lord, could he be the man I've prayed for?*

"You're on the right trail, Brady."

He ducked his head, his smile turning sheepish as he rubbed the back of his neck. "You think so?"

How could anybody go wrong when they were trying to pursue God? "I know so."

Voices in the yard drifted through the door. Her parents wouldn't be back for another two hours. "I think we have company."

"I forgot to tell you, I ran across three families." He pushed to his feet and reached a hand down to help her up. "They said they were stopping by to say hello as soon as they finished cultivating."

Saying hello most times lasted hours. "We better go make some breakfast for our guests then."

"You don't have to cook for them."

"It's custom to feed anyone who stops by in your home." She could only hope there weren't many people. Otherwise, they'd be having porridge instead of fried eggs.

"Interesting." Keeping her hand in his, he walked to the door, and the warmth of his strong grip somehow radiated clear to her heart, taking hold of it as well.

"Hello!" Brady waved at the men and women in the yard.

"Welcome!" Ruth ushered them to the chairs under the tree. What would the villagers think about their relationship after seeing him holding her hand? The men in her culture never held their wives' hands. Again, with Brady, everything was different. Adults here didn't play with kids or interact with them, but Brady threw himself into their world, playing and laughing with them.

Ruth slid her hand out of his to kneel before their guests in greeting. He shook the men's hands, and the ladies knelt before him. He'd given up on reminding people not to kneel for him.

While she listened to the women's corn harvest plans, she also half-listened to him making plans to dig the well.

He wasn't the typical money-hungry businessman. He made everyone feel comfortable and welcome. He had this... genuine tenderness about him that made him more attractive, eroding her resistance to falling deeply in love with him. He was everything she needed in a man.

If only he wasn't leaving.

CHAPTER 11

"Mzungu!... Mzungu!"

When Ruth awakened the next morning, some girls and boys hunched around a sleeping Brady. After these days in the sun, his face was tan, his breathing steady, as he lay on his back.

"What are you doing here?" She rubbed her groggy eyes as Brady shifted onto his elbow, now frowning as if confused over where he was.

"We wanted to greet Mzungu."

They should be scolded for invading the house this early—well, maybe it wasn't too early, since her parents weren't around to have stopped the kids.

Their hopeful grins softened her reaction.

"You need to wait until he wakes up."

"We must have slept in." Brady covered a hand over his face. Then he spread his fingers open and glanced at the bright light streaming through the curtains, then the eager faces of the kids kneeling between him and Ruth. He smiled. "Good morning."

A boy touched Brady's hand, rubbing the little hairs there. "Are you going to stay in the village?"

"No."

A girl cocked her head sideways, tucked her knees up to her chest, and hugged her arms around her blue skirt. "When will you come back?"

"I don't know."

The boy scowled at her and tugged on Brady's hand for attention again. "Does America have streets of gold?"

"No." Brady's lips spread in a grin, but he managed to keep his answer serious. He sat up and stretched. His strong muscles moved beneath the white T-shirt.

One of the boys handed him a mango. Another one gave him leftover yucca root from last night's supper.

Brady patted his flat stomach. "This will make a great breakfast. Thank you." Then he pinched an edge of the nearest boy's crisp-blue sleeve, nothing like the playclothes they'd worn last time. "Why are you all dressed in uniforms?"

"They're on their way to school, but they wanted to see you." They had another ten kilometers to walk, given that the village had the one primary school—the only school in the area. If you graduated from primary seven, you either settled in the village or ventured out to a boarding school far from home. She gave the kids a look. "They'll be late, too."

The last few days had been exhausting. Ruth's and Brady's bodies must have needed the extra rest. After he'd fixed the leaky roof yesterday, he'd gone with Dad and worked with the villagers to dig a well. From there, they'd helped two elderly people add straw to their huts. That hadn't stopped him from joining Ruth and her mom and grandmom to plant corn in the afternoon.

Brady had been a trooper. He dove right in when he saw a need, surprising her family when he didn't mind getting dirty, and they were falling in love with him.

The chickens better have laid enough eggs for her to make him a hearty breakfast.

After she sent the kids off to school, she and Brady stepped on the back porch to brush their teeth side by side as the birds chirped their morning lullabies. Then she told him she'd head to the chicken coop and get some eggs. "You can have the house to yourself for a few minutes."

He laughed, a deep laugh that left her stomach all aswirl with loose-tied knots. "Privacy doesn't seem to be the norm around here."

She was used to the way people just came and went anytime. Most of them ate lunch or dinner with them, but she had no idea how Brady's culture operated with guests. She patted his arm. "I'll guard the house so no one comes in."

"I'll change and be right out."

Unlike him, she knew how to change her clothes under the covers. A trick she'd learned in boarding school when she shared a room with strangers, some of whom became friends.

In the coop, she crouched and picked up the first three eggs from the hay, then set them in the basket.

"Any luck?"

Ruth almost dropped the basket at the sound of Brady's voice as he ducked into the chicken coop. He looked good in all his T-shirts. Today, he wore a gray V-neck over dark sports shorts.

"I... found some eggs." Ugh. She sounded breathless. Her body tingled when his hand brushed hers while taking the basket.

"I wanted to find some, too." His voice was low.

Why was she having a hard time breathing? "Yes... there's, uh, two more." She gestured her chin to a corner where one hen always nested, then started walking to create space between them. The coop stank from chicken poop, but it felt too tight and intimate.

With the eggs easy to spot, she didn't need to talk. A good thing because she didn't trust herself anyway.

He nestled the brown egg in his palm and extended it toward Ruth, his wide grin overtaking his face. "Feel how warm this is."

She shook her head. His presence already warmed her. No need to ignite a fire in the grass-covered hut.

"Come on, Ruthie." He tilted his head to the side, his face playful. "You're sure?"

Completely sure about that, she nodded, then rubbed her arms—completely *un*sure about everything else. How did any of this work? Most men in her culture didn't flirt. Some married any woman who could cook and bear children. Attraction wasn't an issue.

"I'm going to, uh..." She walked backward toward the door. "Get the fire started."

Right, getting a fire started was the last thing she wanted to do.

He raised a brow. "What happened to watching my fire-starting skills?"

Seemed she was watching him do that right now. Which couldn't be what he was saying—at least, it better not be! She'd challenged him to start the fire when he talked about how he used to do it in Boy Scouts. "Yes. Okay."

She swept wayward spiral curls off her forehead. Her voice sounded funny. Brady must have sensed her awkwardness, because he picked the rest of the eggs before he gestured her toward the door.

Finally outside, she took a deep inhale, needing it.

While she whipped eggs in a bowl and mixed maize flour in water, he struck the match and tossed it on the newspaper beneath the twigs. He talked about his adventures as a Scout. "Besides trekking in the mountains and throwing popcorn sales' pitches, this part was my favorite part." He placed a piece of kindling over the flame. "In the outdoors with the smell of fire and roasting marshmallows..." His eyes twinkled, and his cheeks crinkled up as he added more logs. "S'mores—"

"Sm... what?"

"Oh." His grin widened, and then he smacked his lips together. "They're chocolate with marshmallows and graham crackers."

She had no clue what he was talking about. Except for chocolate. She'd heard about it but never tasted it. Such a luxury required her to go shopping at a fancy supermarket.

Perhaps he saw her confusion. His expression settled into something tender, and he reached over and grasped her hand, giving it the gentlest of squeezes. "When you come to America," he whispered, "I'll make s'mores with you."

He seemed genuine about his invitation. "I can't wait."

She'd panic venturing out of the country for the first time, but she'd do it if it meant Brady would be there.

He stacked logs over the fire as the smoke slowed. "Being a Scout was good for me. The skills I learned there factored into my love for entrepreneurship."

Ruth stirred the maize flour in the pan over the fire while he discussed his business goals for the next year. She nodded and tried to comprehend such massive undertakings, interrupting only to ask him to pass the milk so she could add it to the porridge to keep it from getting thick. When the porridge was ready, she took it off the fire. "We will need some sugar in this."

"Got it." Brady reached for the sugar bowl on the nearby table and scooped three spoonfuls into the pan while she fried the eggs.

As he ladled porridge into bowls, she peeled a papaya and diced it into a serving bowl. After he prayed over their food, she asked more about his resort businesses and hotels.

"Since I didn't get this resort, I might have to close four locations." His shoulders inched up as he scowled at his porridge. "That means all those people will be out of work."

He truly cared about his employees. No wonder God blessed his business.

"I'm glad you got your dream job."

He was silent as he chewed the eggs. "I thought I'd found my dream. Now, I'm not too sure."

She forked some egg into her mouth. Unsure about his uncertainty, she still felt guilty for bringing a rich man into a dingy place. "Sorry your vacation is uncomfortable."

He arched a brow. "Are you kidding? I needed this." He set down his plate and spread out his hands. "This has been wonderful for me. It's reminding me there's more to life than a business… reminding me my business belongs to Him."

She was on the same journey, no doubt. "We all need those reminders. I tend to forget I'm just a vessel being used by God." The times she felt responsible for someone's death because she couldn't do anything about it. The times she got frustrated because the need never seemed to end. The times she let pride invade her actions when she should be humble, giving God glory for her ability to help. "You reminded me healing comes from God." Not her effort in treating a patient.

"We could remind each other." He spooned his porridge and lifted it to his mouth, his Adam's apple bobbing when he swallowed. "We'd make a great team."

Warmth flooded her. "Yes… we would."

"This porridge reminds me of Cream of Wheat." His spoon clanked against the porcelain.

How maize could remind him of wheat she couldn't imagine, but she smiled anyway. "At least you have something that reminds you of home."

When her parents returned from the garden, they ate the eggs and porridge Ruth had saved them.

Mom was anxious to finish planting groundnuts before the rainy season started. When Ruth offered to help, Brady stayed to help Dad split the wood.

"I'm going to shower and mend some clothes." Grandmom unwrapped the cloth from her head.

Minutes later, Ruth's toes sunk in the moist ground of an open field. Mom dug the holes while Ruth fell in step, dropping the seeds and kicking dirt with her toes to cover them.

"He's so perfect for you." Mom seemed more interested in talking about Brady. "Why can't you be together?"

"He's leaving and I'm staying."

"Go with him."

Not possible. There wasn't anything besides her infatuation and misinterpretation of the way he looked at her. She couldn't mean more to him than being his nurse. Either way, obstacles blocked their path. "Who will take care of people, patients?"

"God will take care of them."

"By using me."

Mom tossed the hoe to the ground with a thud, then wiped her moist forehead. "There's a time for everything, and God used you for the time. If He sends you somewhere else, He can put someone in your place." She picked up the hoe and crouched to dig another hole. "You need to take care of yourself, too. Have you asked God lately what He wants you to do?"

Why would she? "Doesn't God want everyone to take care of the needy?"

"He does, but if you want to pursue other things—like a marriage—you should ask God and see how He wants you to find a good balance."

Her heart picked up speed. As the sudden rush of blood dizzied her, she sank to her knees and pressed a hand to the dirt, dropping seeds into the hole Mom made. Was Mom right? Ruth had been so afraid of pursuing someone who would prevent her from doing what God needed her to do. Brady didn't seem to be the type to hinder her from doing her job—unless he asked her to follow him. But...

"What if God wants me to stay single?" The whispered words slipped out in Lusoga, part of her almost afraid to say them.

"One way to find out is to pray and make yourself available if Brady wants to marry you."

With such thoughts, Mom was harvesting something that hadn't been planted yet. "I don't know if marriage is something he wants right now." He'd just laid out his future business plans with no mention of a wife.

"I've never seen a man look at his wife the way he looks at you." Mom dug another hole. "I've no doubt that he loves you."

Love was one thing, but marriage another. Ruth just shook her head and nudged Mom on to dig the next hole.

When they returned, Ruth carried a tray of Grandmom's passion juice through the woods to Brady and Dad. She followed a path of dappled light, tall grasses tickling her ankles and monkeys chittering in the trees. Then she stepped through to the clearing. The glasses almost tumbled off the tray when she saw Brady and Dad without their shirts on. She stood and swallowed. Her eyes swept over Brady's tanned back as his hard muscles moved while he swung the ax and split the log clean in half.

He stood and wiped his dampened forehead with the back of his hand. Dad gathered the split pieces and stacked them on the finished pile.

"Ruthie!"

She startled, and some juice splashed on the tray. Caught in the act of gawking.

"How was the peanut planting?" Brady reached for his T-shirt from the tree branch and wiped one side of his forehead, careful around the bandaged area.

"I got... ama..." What did he ask again? "I was..." She glanced at the tray to clarify what she was carrying.

"Passion juice couldn't have arrived at a more perfect time." Dad brushed his hands on his work pants.

Her shoulders loosened when Brady put on his shirt before walking toward her, his smile secretive as if pleased he'd caught her checking him out. "Thank you," he mouthed as he took his glass and raised it.

Because of the difference in the water they drank, Brady had been designated a unique glass so they didn't have him accidentally drink the well water.

Dad reached for his glass and sat on one of the round tree stumps.

"You guys are working so hard." She meant Brady because Dad was used to his hard labor, except on Sundays.

A green caterpillar crawled on her foot, and she shook her leg for it to fall back on the sawdusty ground.

"Have some." Brady held out his half glass of juice. Accepting it would only encourage Dad's assumptions of their relationship. Plus, Brady needed all the liquids he could get.

"Grandmom has some for me."

"It will give you the energy to walk back." He wasn't easily persuaded. Several days' worth of scruff covered his jaw. Dad had offered him a razor, but Brady didn't want to shave without a wall mirror, afraid he'd cut himself.

"The man shares a drink with you, just take it." Dad gulped the rest of his juice. "It would be rude of you not to."

This was getting to be a bigger deal than she'd intended, so she accepted the juice. "Thanks."

Brady winked.

Her knees buckled. She was going to need a seat after all. The stump next to Dad might be the perfect spot.

WITH THE EARLY EVENING sun warm on her shoulders, Ruth took Brady to one of their fields. The land sprawled before them as he snapped pictures with her camera, fascinated by monkeys leaping from one banana plant to another. They passed fruit trees, and he plucked a couple of oranges from one.

"Is this a guava tree?" He handed her an orange so he could pick one of the yellow round fruits. "I usually see it on the juice box in the store."

"I didn't know if it's guava in English. We call it mapera." Ruth didn't care for it too much. "It has a rough texture."

Brady bit into it, squinting as he chewed. "Maybe the juice is better." He chucked the rest of the half-eaten fruit into the unplowed field. The camera dangled down his chest as he peeled his orange and gave it to her, then took the one from her hand. "I'm going to test all the fruits we come across."

"You might get a stomachache." Jackfruit tended to cause runny stomachs. "Then we'll be making a night trip to the toilet."

"As long as it's not raining, I'm good." He popped an orange slice in his mouth. "I have to eat some mangoes." He motioned toward the five trees right next to each other. Green and yellow fruit crowded the overhanging branches.

Her lips curved up, and her chest warmed. She dangled one hand as they walked, letting tall grass tickle her fingertips. Memories of her time at the farm resurfaced whenever she saw those mango trees. "When I was younger, each time we worked in the field, we would be so hungry, but Mom and Dad wouldn't let us eat any mangoes until we finished working." It motivated them to work faster. "By climbing those trees, we'd eat as many mangoes as we could manage." It had felt so refreshing. "We would be so satisfied we didn't need lunch after."

"Can we go back to memory lane?" His blue eyes sparkled against tanned skin. "Climb and eat mangoes?"

Her laughter slipped loose. Sounding like a little girl—*feeling* like a little girl—she clasped his fingers, blistered from hours of manning the ax, and led him into a sprint through the moist ground to the shaded trees.

"It would be easier to climb if you take off your boots." She'd encouraged him to borrow Dad's boots since his tennis shoes had gotten muddy when he went to plant corn yesterday.

"I've climbed a tree before, missy." He slid off the boots and his socks, and his face went all squishy as soon as his toes sank on the rotten mangoes littering the ground. "Looks like we'll both need to take our showers again after all."

Low, sturdy branches grew out in every direction. Even a non–tree climber could easily hop from branch to branch. "I'll race you up." Ruth reached for a low branch on the middle tree and planted one foot on the trunk, finding the perfect foundation for her ascent.

"Are you climbing with your skirt?"

She had shorts underneath, but they were too short by themselves. She spoke over her back, ducking from a cluster of mangoes that almost whacked her face. "I've been biking with my skirt, so climbing a tree is no different."

Brady was pulling himself on a branch across from her. The skillful way he moved from one branch to another made the monkeys seem less entertaining. "You're an expert," she said when he sat on one of the flat wide branches beneath a canopy of leaves.

"I've rarely climbed trees, even when I was a kid, but this one's fun."

Ruth climbed one more branch and swung up to where he sat. The branch was strong enough for the two of them to sit side by side. With the leaves so thick, no one casually observing the tree could see them there.

He rested his back against the trunk. A cool breeze stirred the leaves, the air refreshing.

"Ruthie Kirabo..." Brady shook his head, the admiration in his blue eyes sending her heart in a frenzy. "What a beautiful name. Is there a meaning to your last name?"

In her culture, they didn't have one family name for every family member. "Jajja named me both names. Kirabo means gift."

A brief silence embraced them as they looked at each other. Her throat went dry, and she had no water.

"It's a perfect name for you." He plucked a mango from the cluster dangling above them.

"That's not ripe." She slid it out of his hand. The green ones had a bitter taste. "Find a yellow one."

He plucked another and held it in his broad hand, studying it. "I think this is yellow enough."

"Perfect."

He passed it to her. "I'll let you eat first so I can learn how to eat one."

Even in the city, people didn't know how to eat a mango without slicing it with a knife first.

Although nervous under his scrutiny, she bit the top and dragged off the peel with her teeth before savoring the juicy fruit.

He plucked another mango and imitated her instructions.

They ate mangoes as they tossed the peels and seeds through the leaves to the ground. The seeds always grew more trees, but her parents cut them down since they didn't want mango trees to take over their land.

"So this is your hiding spot?" He licked the juice off his fingers.

"Yes and no." They rarely had time for hiding. "Sometimes, I came down here to think, but whenever I felt tempted to escape chores, I'd have to know no one was going to get my work done for me."

He tossed the seed to the ground. "In other words, you'd have double work."

"Exactly." She licked her fingers, tempted to wipe them on her skirt.

Brady licked his fingers again. Perhaps he was as full as she was. "If fruit back home tasted this good, I'd never need dessert."

Was there anything sweeter than mangoes or jackfruit? "This is dessert." At least, that was what they served in the local restaurants if you requested dessert.

His Adam's apple bobbled when he laughed and wiped his mouth. "We have other sweets like chocolate, and so many baked things they add sugar to."

"Oh!" What did this chocolate he kept mentioning taste like?

"You're better off with the fruit." He tossed a seed to the ground.

Their feet dangled below the branch as they talked about their faith. She talked about her family being new to Christianity, except for Jajja, who had always been passionate about God.

Brady nodded. "That's like my mom. She was always the only one interested in church for as long as I could remember. I went with her a few times..." He rubbed his hands together and rocked his head against the tree trunk behind him. "Thank you for reminding me what I'd lost. I tend to make money a priority."

His lopsided grin warming her, she kicked her feet a bit, feeling a little like the girl who'd climbed this tree with such carefree delight. What had happened to that girl, anyway? "We need money. Nothing's wrong with that. As long as we don't lose ourselves in the process."

"I was on the journey to losing myself."

She didn't intend to make him self-conscious while she had faults of her own. "I tend to falter and need friends for accountability." Eunice being one of them.

"Tell me about your life, Ruthie. I want to know everything about you."

She pushed back the wispy hair tickling her forehead, unsure where to start. It seemed he'd already experienced her life—her world here with her parents, her time with the village patients, her work at the clinic. What more was there to speak of? "My life's not exciting."

"Any past boyfriends?"

Boyfriends. Ah. That. "What if I say I'm not the perfect girl for any man looking for a wife?"

He touched her shoulder, and a wave of electricity shocked through her.

"That's not true."

It *was* true, but having him say otherwise warmed her. She broke off a spear-shaped leaf and spun its stem between her fingers, the leaf changing color as it danced through sunlight and a shadow. She told him about her first boyfriend, a doctor who broke up with her after one year. "Even though he didn't say why, I assumed he wanted a housewife. Six months later, he married a career-free woman."

She'd then dated a pastor. She peered down through the branches. Wild turkeys roamed an open space to the far side of the cornfield while she peeled open her past for Brady. "He thought he liked me, but his family didn't approve because I was so into my work."

That had hurt, because since he was a devout Christian, she'd trusted him to only marry one wife, but he'd taken his family's advice to marry someone else.

"I love your career." Brady draped a hand over her shoulder. "I love how you're passionate to help people... I love everything about you, Ruthie."

He did? Mom had said so, but hearing it...

The breeze didn't stop her from heating up, too overwhelmed by his words. She liked him for his flexibility and attractiveness. "I like your teeth."

His teeth? Had she just said that? He'd said he *loved* everything about her, and she said she *liked* his teeth?

A grin pulled his lips away from his teeth, and his warm chuckle rushed past them. "Is that so?"

Not what she'd meant to utter, but yes, it was the truth. He had the most white and perfectly aligned teeth she'd ever seen. Needing to change the subject, she asked about his past relationships.

"The only serious relationship I had, my girlfriend ended things when I went to college in another state. She couldn't do long-distance dating."

Long-distance dating. Ruth played the words in her head. Trying to make sense of them. They sounded like her only hope if Brady were to court her.

"I thought I could do it, but she didn't think so." His lips twisted up, pressing together so tightly she could find the outlines of those perfect teeth beneath his skin. "Later on, I realized, it was for the best. I never could've managed to date long distance."

Her stomach dropped. She needed to stop entertaining any ideas of them together.

He surveyed both sides of the land. "Can we take a walk in the cornfield?"

"As long as we don't get lost." She jumped off the branch and made her way around the tree, climbing over and ducking under branches. Brady followed her down and slid on his boots.

His boots fell in step with her bare feet as they approached the cornfield.

"It's amazing how your family has miles of land for different crops." He touched the golden stalks taller than both of them as they strolled through straight rows.

"Ruthie!" He tugged her into his broad chest. "A snake."

By the time she craned her neck around, she only saw its tail slither through the weeds.

"I hope it's harmless gardener snakes in here."

It was hard to know what snake was harmless or poisonous. "It's safe to assume all snakes we encounter are poisonous."

Her heart drummed against his, not necessarily because of the snake but from being in his arms. She moved back enough to look at him, his arms still wrapped around her. He was even more handsome up close. His eyes were a soft blue. Her body shook when his fingers trailed on her forehead as he brushed a strand of hair from her face and tucked it behind her ear.

The sound of their heartbeats mingled with chirruping frogs and crickets. Her mind wandered when the tips of his fingers trailed over her jaw.

Was he going to kiss her? Oh no! The thought exhilarated and scared her. Kissing and falling for him was a start of heartbreak, but wow, he was so worth a broken heart.

"Should we get going?" His voice was raspy, his eyes too soft, yet filled with uncertainty.

Ruth could only nod before she turned to lead the way. They laughed when they walked in circles and couldn't find their way out. Yet they were relieved when they exited.

The evening had almost lost its light when they started on the trail home. Brady scratched his strong arms. "The stalks are so itchy."

They'd been scraped as they wove through from one dead zone to another. "It will be worse when you shower." They'd need another wash after their adventure.

He stepped over a rock and held out his hand, then grasped her fingers and helped her over. "It's getting hard to see."

With her hand in his, her wobbly knees might not be in great condition to walk home. "Thank you."

When they were safely down, he kept her fingers clasped in his. Despite his thoughts on that long-distance dating thing, despite his clear plans for the future that didn't involve her, maybe one week of feeling loved, admired, and respected by a man—one week with Brady—was worth dreaming about.

CHAPTER 12

Joyful screams and shouts rang in the mud-built shelter as drumming and clapping accompanied the songs. Brady sneezed when more dust stirred from the feet clambering the dirt floor, and people's wide smiles as they sang about the joy of the Lord being their strength—an English song, surprisingly—enthralled him. Everyone had dressed in their Sunday best, different from the worn clothes he'd seen them wear all week.

It almost felt like he'd never stepped in a church before. Unlike the gatherings in the churches he'd attended, these people went all-in, and burst out serious dance moves without caring that anybody was looking at them. In such an engaging service, he felt awkward *not* dancing, so he clapped his hands and shifted his feet the best he could as they switched the songs to Lusoga. Learning the songs was easy since the words were repetitive.

When they finished singing, people shared testimonies on what God had done for them that week.

Ruth interpreted whenever the local language was spoken, which was eighty five percent of the time.

Someone was grateful his cow delivered a calf so he could have milk for some time. Another man was grateful for the new well, another appreciated a new roof, and Annie's grandma thanked God for protecting her and her grandkids from the cobra in her house. She also credited Ruth and Brady for risking their lives.

His chest puffed, satisfaction coursing through him. God had used him to help some of the people and bring smiles to their faces. He hoped he could do more. That was his new prayer.

When the pastor preached, people shouted 'amens' at every other sentence, so Ruth's interpretation didn't distract those seated next to them.

The stocky pastor taught about true worship, and where God is on our priority list. It had taken being stuck in Uganda for Brady to realize he'd had his priorities backward. Business first, then if he wasn't too tired, God might be remembered.

After the sermon, Brady rasped the repetitive tunes as he clapped his hands and wiggled his body to imitate everyone else. When the service ended, he took Ruth's hand in his out of habit as they followed everyone outside.

Across the dirt yard, three large pots nestled on wide firepits. The community was putting on a farewell feast for him and Ruth to thank them for coming and giving them medical attention.

He bent slightly to whisper in her ear. "I didn't even do anything."

"You did a lot more than you're giving yourself credit for."

After they ate underneath a bamboo tree, they shook people's hands to bid them goodbye.

People presented sacks of food, woven baskets, and all sorts of handmade gifts. Brady felt guilty for taking the little they had, not that he needed any of it, but Ruth said it would be rude if he rejected their gifts. And the last thing he wanted was to spurn their heartfelt attempts to thank him.

Then a woman plunked a chicken in his arms. He ducked and dropped the flapping bird when it scratched his arm. What was he supposed to do with a chicken? His eyebrow lifted to the woman kneeling before him, then to Ruth.

Ruth seemed to understand his concern when she spoke to the woman in Lusoga, and the woman's shoulders sagged.

His heart ached over hurting her unwittingly. "Did I do something wrong?"

"She wants you to take the chicken back to America, but I told her you can't take it on the airplane."

A chicken? To America? Even if he took it, where would he pen it in the penthouse?

Yet, if it would make the woman smile, not look so desolate, he had to come up with a solution—fast. So he rested a hand on Ruth's bare shoulder, feeling the warmth radiating from it. "Ruth will take care of it for me."

"I'll send him pictures of his chicken." Ruth smiled at the woman.

One corner of the woman's lips lifted, and somehow, his heart felt light. "Mukama akuwe omukisa. Webale okwida."

"God bless you," Ruth interpreted the woman's words. "Thank you for coming."

Brady crouched to shake the woman's hand again. "Mukama"—he could only remember God, and not the rest—"bless you too."

They had nothing, yet they sacrificed all they had for him. His chest squeezed tight at such generosity. The thought of leaving the smiles behind, not seeing Ruth again, was all too real. Tears threatened to blur his vision. Time was running out.

He still had three more days with Ruth—days of them relaxing in Jinja—and he intended to make sure they were their best days together.

EVEN WITH THE TWO MILES they'd walked to church, the gifts were so many for them and Ruth's family to carry back home. So people helped.

"I usually take some food back to the city so I can share with the neighbors."

There were fewer farms in Kampala. "How do you take all these things?"

"They don't give me chickens and cows." She nestled the woven basket against her chest. "I get food and baskets sometimes, but I take whatever I can carry with me in the minibus."

Even though she'd thought they could take the public transportation back to Kampala, it seemed impossible if they were taking even half the items. "You said there's a place you can call Dongo to come and pick us up?"

She nodded.

When they got home, after a sweat-filled walk, a shower was necessary.

Ruth changed into a white sleeveless shirt and orange skirt. Brady changed into shorts.

The sun had dipped low on the horizon by the time Ruth brought out her dad's bicycle. Her bone-melting smile had Brady's heart racing so fast he could scarcely breathe.

"It's about ten kilometers away." She mounted the bike and gestured to the back seat. "Hop on."

"Ruthie..." He sauntered closer, stepped in front of the bike, and leaned his face down to hers as he placed his hands over hers on the handlebars. "You don't seriously think I'm going to let you carry me for *seven* miles."

Granted, that was a long way to chance on unfamiliar roads. All the places they'd walked and the wells he'd seen people bicycling to, he hadn't encountered a steady enough path for him to be confident he could pull this off. But the idea of her working while he sat...

Her hands were warm under his, and his blood quickened as her doe eyes blinked up at him. Could he do this? Be responsible for her on unbalanced roads, with her closeness distracting him? He'd most likely lose balance.

Her fingers twitched beneath his, but her gaze didn't waver. "You don't know the way."

"You can guide me." Seemed she'd been guiding him in everything lately.

But she was shaking her head. "I can tell you which direction to go. I can't tell you what problems to avoid—that's more instinct after years of riding the paths."

He opened his mouth to argue, but he couldn't. How could he risk it if he was driving her? He slid his hands from hers. "Maybe next time, then."

"Today is your last day here." Ruth blinked up at him.

Those words pierced his heart, As much as he wanted to convince himself nothing was simmering between them, and once he left Uganda, he'd go back to his normal life, he and Ruth were far from over. Without even trying, she was challenging him. Something about her quiet faith in the Lord and her lifestyle so different from his served to make a permanent impact on his heart.

She was waiting for his response, and those soft brown eyes on him rushed his blood. "You never know when I will be passing through again."

"Whatever you say." She gnawed at her lips and gripped the handlebars. Her orange skirt hit her knee as she settled on the seat, and he perched himself on the passenger seat. His heart raced as he breathed in her subtle scent. It had taken all his willpower not to kiss her when he'd had her in his arms in the cornfield. There'd been several opportunities that evening when they ran from one row to another, laughing as they tried to figure out their exit.

He tried to shove aside the thick shrubs sticking out in the dirt path as Ruth pedaled forward. He didn't need a stick scratching against his healing wound.

"And this is the shortcut?"

"If we don't want to spend an entire night there." She was panting. He should be the one pedaling.

As long as he was with her, he didn't mind if they spent the night in the woods.

The path narrowed, growing more unstable as they rode past a plowed field. The bike swiveled, and his heart raced when she bounced from one rock to another. "Oh no!" Ruth was breathing hard as she pedaled toward a jutted rock in their path. The alternative was her hitting a mature tree.

Like the panicked patient he still was, he wrapped his arms around her waist and leapt off the bike, bringing her down with him as she screamed and they landed on the plowed earth. A dull ache gripped his shoulder, but at least, he had his arm curled protectively around Ruth. They lay down side by side, his heart thundering against hers, and when he met her gaze to see her reaction, her smile was wide.

"You could've been hurt," she whispered. Her soft fingers traced his bandage, awakening every bit of his skin.

How sweet that she still worried about him. "You could have been hurt, too."

"That... was scary." A nervous chuckle skittered up her chest and rushed out in a heated breath that fogged over him. "And thrilling, too."

Brady smiled, loving her laugh. When their laughter subsided, her gaze locked with his. They drank each other in as if quenching a thirst. Speaking of which, his mouth was dry, and his palms sweaty.

He shifted his hand and brushed her face with his knuckles. Smooth skin without makeup gave way to his touch. Those doe eyes softened even further, and warmth flooded him. He didn't know what to do with her, but he was growing more afraid of what he'd do without her.

"Ruthie." Somehow, he found his voice. He tucked loose curls from her face, letting them tickle his fingers. "What are we going to do about us?"

His longing reflected in her eyes. "Let's not think about tomorrow."

His thumb grazed along her full lips as he tried to understand her. Was she okay if they kissed only to end things when he left? He leaned in and pressed his face to the top of her head, breathing in the scent of her. "Is that so?"

She nodded and looked at his lips. "Brady?" she whispered and ducked her head so he couldn't read her soul through those eyes. "I–I want to kiss you, but... I don't know how."

Whoa. His mind went blank at her honest confession. What was a man supposed to do? "Oh, Ruthie..." He drew in a deep breath, everything in him screaming *no*. He was leaving. But it was her first kiss, and he wouldn't want any other man robbing him of it. He had to make this kiss memorable for both of them. He lifted his hand to the side of her face, his fingers finding her hair.

His good judgment evaporated in a flood of want when her breath teased his lips before he touched them. Hers were soft, yielding, and responsive. And suddenly, it was just him and Ruth. Forget the reasons they couldn't be together. He was having lots of firsts with her, and falling hard. Overwhelming was the desire to tell her that.

She made sounds of pleasure, which only enticed him to deepen the kiss. She kissed him back. Her hands were shaking as she curled them around his neck, her chest pressing into his, heat rising up from their shirts to meld in the humid afternoon.

Ruth's kisses were as sweet and innocent and new as her village. He'd never kissed a girl who'd never been kissed before. Each tender touch declared all that she was to him, and what would become of them when he went home.

He didn't want to stop, but he pulled back. Something had changed in him. Her eyes were still closed, both of them breathing heavily. When she opened her eyes and peered at him, her expression was one of wonder. She was so beautiful and pure, she filled his heart to overflowing.

The crickets' chirps and frogs' croaks played in the background to the percussion of their pounding hearts.

Head propped up on his hand, he brushed his thumb along her jaw as they studied each other. His thumb skidded in the sweet moisture of her tears. Was it joy or regret? Her lips trembled when she let out a little sob, and with every bit of tenderness, he felt it. He pressed her face to his shoulder, holding her there. "Oh, Ruthie!" What had he just done, causing her to cry? *Way to go, Brady!* He couldn't keep his lips intact. "You're okay?"

"I'm just happy," she whispered, pulling from his shoulder. "I'll never forget... this day."

The feeling was mutual. "Me too."

She was precious. She couldn't be much older than twenty-five. Would her thoughts of him change once she found out the wide age gap between them? Even if they may not be together, she'd better know his age. "How old are you, Ruthie?"

She shrugged. "You're only ten years older. I turned thirty-one yesterday."

She looked a lot younger than thirty-one. How did she even know his age?

As if reading his thoughts, she smiled sheepishly. "Your passport."

Ah, yes. The morning he'd stayed at her house when he let her look through his passport to see what a visa stamp looked like. She was aware of his age, yet she wanted him?

"Why didn't anybody say it's your birthday? We should have celebrated."

"We don't celebrate birthdays."

"Not even recognize them?"

"We're lucky if our parents remember what day we were born."

He brushed her face with the back of his knuckles. "Why wouldn't they remember?"

"My brother was born from home, and one of my sisters, so they don't have a birth certificate. We just guess their age."

How fascinating. He turned his fingers to skim across her cheek. "So they could be a year younger or older."

"Yes." She pressed her face into the curve of his hand. "Almost seventy percent of the villagers didn't know what year they or their children were born. With so many kids, most parents never take the time to record their birthdays."

Before he could figure out a response, she slid away from him. "We better get going to call Dongo if we're going to make it before dark."

He doubted they'd be back before dark, but he didn't care. He stood, drawing her up with him. Then he plucked a flimsy twig from her hair, and she brushed dirt from his shirt, then hers. Lifting her hand to his lips, he kissed it and lingered there.

As Ruth navigated the narrow path, the evening sun cast pink over the hilly pastures and farms they rode past. The red soil and landscape almost glowed in the magical lighting. He saw Uganda in a whole new way than when he'd first set foot on it.

All the years he'd chased one prosperous deal after another and lived in a bubble. Only one week with Ruth had opened his eyes to brand-new possibilities and unleashed a passion he'd thought was dead.

Thank You, Lord, for bringing Ruth into my life.

Now that she'd crept into his heart, he had a lot of work to do to figure out their next steps.

CHAPTER 13

Ruth stepped out of the house and squinted at the bright morning sun as she clutched her handbag on her shoulder. Brady had wanted them to have an early start so they could enjoy several activities in Jinja.

Meters from her, Dongo was rearranging the baskets and gifts in his trunk. She struggled to control her pulse when she spotted Brady in affectionate goodbyes with her family. Jajja danced while singing her old-time favorite. When the song said something about how she wouldn't be showing him this dance if he wasn't a good friend, Brady's shoulders shook, and his head tipped back as he laughed. Then he slapped Dad's shoulder so casually. Dad and Mom walked toward Ruth, and she met them halfway.

"Come back and visit us, son," Granddad shouted as he stepped away from the car.

"You can count on it," Brady called out before he slid into the back seat.

Ruth was smiling, her lips still tingling from last night's kiss. She touched her warmed cheeks.

"My goodness, Ruth. You're going to sit next to him on the long drive." Mom's voice drew her from her daze.

"Oh, hi." She'd already said goodbye to her parents, but they always had farewell words. So she closed the gap between them and hugged Mom. "I love you so much."

"I love you, too."

"When should we expect the courtship ceremony?" Not one for affection, Dad crossed his arms over his chest. "Neither you nor Brady talked about the courtship."

"Because there is not going to be one." She understood why Dad was concerned for her. And that he dreamed of having bridewealth—a share he deserved from educating his daughter. "Did I forget to tell you he's going back to America in four days?" No need to tell them she was spending the next three days with him in Jinja.

Mom's face fell, and she rubbed a comforting hand on Ruth's shoulder. "You like taking care of people, Musawo"—Mom used her title as a nickname the way the people often did—"but don't lose yourself in the process. By the time you start having kids, you will be too old."

Ruth lowered her head, burdened that God might have a different path for her than most girls in her country. "I know." Some girls her age were grandparents. "Someday, I will adopt some of the village kids who don't have parents, but not with Brady."

With her heart heavy, she didn't need reminders that he was going to be out of her life for good.

Her mom snagged her in another tight hug, and Ruth held back threatening tears. Leaving after she came to visit was never easy, but more fearsome departures were brewing in her heart today. Mom, smelling like lavender from her body lotion, patted her shoulder. "Eight weeks will go fast."

Ruth promised Mom she'd go shopping before she returned. "I'll get you designer shoes for church." She'd left her an extra pair of her sandals.

When she slid and settled in the back seat next to Brady, she let out a shuddering gasp as Dongo drove out of the compound.

Unlike last time when they sat shoulder to shoulder, a few centimeters separated them. It was for the best. She'd better get used to everything.

She fastened her seat belt and waved to her family. Brady waved before closing the window and closing the gap between them. A shimmer of awareness flooded her when his shorts brushed against her knee.

"You're okay?" He buckled his seat belt.

Her time with him was ending. After that kiss, she should be content and act like nothing had happened. Instead, she wanted more. The kiss had only lit something inside of her, a passion she'd never had. She was still surprised she'd initiated it. She didn't know she could be so bold. Still, she had no regrets whatsoever.

If they were to be together, they had boulders to climb. With a lump of tears clogging her throat, she swallowed hard to find a way to talk. "It's hard to say goodbye." She was not going to cry. That would be embarrassing. She clenched her hands and tightened her jaw. She. Would. Not. Cry.

She tried to grasp the lyrics from the song on the radio to keep her mind from what next week would be like—the weeks after Brady left. A shiver coursed through her when his strong and sturdy arm wrapped around her shoulder.

"I understand... I hate goodbyes." He dropped his hand from her shoulder and reached for her hand, clasping it in his.

Then he asked about Dongo's week from time to time. Dongo laughed when Brady told him how they got lost in the cornfield. Ruth laughed when Dongo said he'd never return to his home village because they had so many cockroaches.

"Eww!" Brady shuddered, his fear evident.

The strength of his fingers clasped around hers comforted her, just as it had all week whenever he clasped her hand in his. She felt loved. They stayed that way, holding each other. Ruth was afraid to move for fear he'd pull away.

Minutes, then kilometers, passed, and the silence stretched. He eased her against his shoulder, and she relaxed, breathing in his clean scent. They absorbed comfort from each other, as if this exchange prepared them for what lay ahead.

In Jinja, Dongo dropped them off at the Rafting Company at the Nile River Explorers. With a promise to see them in a few days and store her goods at the clinic, he drove off.

Brady hooted and rubbed his hands together when an employee suggested whitewater rafting and bungee jumping. "Let's do both." He clapped, his eyes sparkling.

Ruth studied the photos on the wall. Neither activity seemed safe. She wanted him to have a fun time, but... "I'll stay here, but I would like you to go."

"No way!" He clasped her hand. "I can't leave you here. I want to spend every minute with you." His face was so earnest, and she wanted to spend every remaining minute with him, too. But...

She glanced back at the wall, at posters of people riding over rippling rapids. She'd never set foot in the water, let alone take up the life-threatening sport. "That's mad!" She gasped. "Would you do that?" Why would anybody want to do that?

Brady gave a slow nod. "I can do worse."

Whatever worse he meant, she didn't dare ask.

A lanky man, obviously figuring Ruth needed some convincing, walked close and spoke to her. "We offer classes. You will be fine."

He had to say that if he needed to make money.

"You'll be safe." Brady squeezed her hand. "I'll sink before I let you."

Well, he didn't have to say *that*. How could she say no with his assuring smile and contagious confidence?

Nothing had prepared her for taking any adventures on whitewater rapids. Even though Brady wanted to be in Class 5, for the thrill-seekers testing their limits, navigating the river's violent sections, he opted for the Class 2 tours for beginners and families.

She tightened her grip on his hand. "Let's do Class 5." She was mad for saying that, but how else would he have a great experience?

He clamped both hands on her shoulders, his eyes so soft and warm. How she loved the mushy feeling he caused whenever his hand hit her skin. "You don't have to do this for me."

"I'm not doing it for you." No way would she ever entertain such a maddening idea. "There's a reason they offer safety training."

Or so she could only hope.

Almost thirty minutes later, a bus picked them up and took them to their drop-off point. Ruth was the minority out of the seven in their group. Not only was she a first-timer, but also she was the only Ugandan among tourists.

Even Keith, their rafting guide, was a foreigner, a Canadian with long blond hair to match the jungle atmosphere.

"Remember, paddle hard, harder, and get down and hang onto the rope!" Keith got them into rafts and taught them the different paces from Level 1 with flat water like a swimming pool, levels 2 and 3 a bit bouncy, and levels 4 and 5 tough. Level 6 was deadly, but none in the group wanted to go for it.

They learned how to paddle in sync, how to hold on, and how to get back in the raft if they got tossed out. The whole activity took more strength than Ruth expected.

When it was time to put their training to the test, exhilaration tingled along her veins. The raft floated on calm waters where canyons covered in a thick carpet of trees towered above them.

"This is a picture worth taking." Sitting across from her, Brady smiled at her.

She should've brought her camera, but they'd been warned to leave behind anything they didn't want to lose in the river. Keith assured them their company was taking their pictures and copies would be available after their tour.

Ruth gripped the oar when approaching rapids roared ahead. Her heart raced, but she stayed alert while the raft bounced them. She paddled like her life depended on it. Relief whooshed from her lungs as their raft plunged through the curl of a wave that bounced their boat. Thankfully the water was warm and clean, perfect for getting dunked into—fun even.

"We did it!" Adrenaline surged through her. What an accomplishment!

A couple of young adults from Australia squealed and leaped off the boat and into the water, then back on the boat. The middle-aged couple jumped in the water, but when Ruth asked Brady to do the same, he shrugged. "I'm fine just watching from the boat." His dampened hair clung to his face. "Isn't this fun?"

She dangled her fingers over the side of the raft as the couple climbed back in. Amazingly, she'd always driven by on a minibus and never stopped to tour the beautiful Nile River. Miles and miles of pristine woodlands with no homes or fences, but just cormorants and monkeys, and the occasional crocodile lounging in the sun. The skillful guides were careful about the crocs that did bite, and in the few known crocodile hangout spots, people weren't allowed in the water. Every once in a while, they passed fishermen paddling along in log canoes.

They explored waterfalls surrounded by the shimmering emerald leaves of alder trees, and Brady convinced her to join in when they jumped off cliffs near turquoise pools of creek water. She stuck with the lower boulders, and with him nearby, she didn't have to worry about drowning.

They stopped for a sack lunch along the shore and relaxed before climbing back in the boat. She'd grown confident in the water—so confident it caught her off-guard when their raft rushed into the Grade 5 Overtime Rapids. The whole experience was like riding a parachute, not that she'd ridden one before, but it felt like she was up in the air and being tossed by the wind. She tried so hard to remember their training, but her mind went blank when they plunged over a waterfall, and then smashed through massive rapids. Their raft flipped up and over. Then it tossed her upside down in an infuriated patch of the Nile. With a ceiling of white water above her, she lost her hold on the rope she'd been told to cling to. But it all happened so quickly and trapped her beneath the raft.

"Ruthie!" Brady's voice was faint over the roaring rapids. She kicked and thrashed to get out from underneath the raft. The second air kissed her face, she gasped, only to be overtaken by another wave, and another and another.

She fought to breathe after too much water intake. *This is it, God. Is my life over?* Just when she'd started something with Brady... Her family would never see her again... What a terrible decision she'd made.

"Hold on!" Perhaps it was Brady's voice. Maybe she wasn't left alone.

The current carried their raft—and all seven of them—into the calm pool where they gasped and sputtered for air.

Brady gathered her in his strong arms and kissed her, his heart pounding against hers. "I never should've let you come here."

She didn't feel pain from any part of her body—no broken nose or hurting feet. She pulled back and framed his dear face with her hands. A thrill as big as the Nile flooded her, and laughter burst from her lungs. She was alive! "That was the most maddening—the most *fun*—thing I've ever done."

He drew in a sharp breath and kissed her head. "I'm gl–glad." She'd probably scared him, but most of them seemed terrified, except the confident guide.

The woman was upset about the ring she lost. Her husband was squinting, struggling to see without his contacts.

When the bus dropped them off and they'd changed into dry clothes, Ruth's heart was still racing. She met Brady in the common area. He looked handsome with his damp hair. They still had time in their day. She sprinted to his side and grasped his hand, feeling bereft without it. Then she squeezed it. "You should go bungee jumping."

He strapped the backpack over his shoulders. "I've put you through enough for today."

"No... no." She suppressed a shudder. "I meant you."

"Not without you."

She could still hear the roaring waves rushing through her ears. As much as she'd loved the adventure of something new, dangling her head down would have to wait for another day—a year or two from now. But she didn't want him to miss out. So she clasped her hands together, hoping to convince him. "Please, you'll love it, and *I'd* love to watch you."

His chest rose and fell as he let out a breath. Then he closed the gap between them and wrapped her in his strong arms. "I'll do it, but I'll feel like I'm abandoning you on our vacation."

Our vacation. The words coursed through her, splashed and tumbled over her with the force of those rapids. She eased out of the embrace. "I'll take your picture." She held her hand out so he could hand her the backpack.

After kissing her forehead, he went back for the gear before he left with a man who told Ruth where spectators stood.

Minutes later, Ruth stood across the bridge and snapped pictures of Brady plunging 144 feet over the river.

She was shaking the entire time. No doubt, the pictures would turn out blurry.

When she met him back at the common area, he planted another kiss on her forehead, his smile priceless. "That was a perfect bird's-eye view of the Nile."

She shook her head. He was one adventurous man. But he had fun, and it made her happy.

When they left the rafting company, Brady wanted to use his new binoculars from the gift shop for sightseeing and bird watching at the falls.

They sat side by side on the grass, the Nile River rushing before them. How odd that, after almost dying in it, she still found the rippling water soothing. Perhaps having the right person with her made the experience more exhilarating.

"I can't believe the Bible talks about this very river."

Brady nodded as he looked at the water. "The river where baby Moses was placed."

"Thankfully, Moses was placed on the calm side." Even if it was rippling water, the God who controlled the storm would've calmed it that day.

"Seeing this up close sure brings the Bible to life." Brady laced his hands behind his head and stretched out his legs. They sat there as they talked about Moses and wondered what it might have been like for him to grow up in a castle, only to end up in the wilderness.

At some point, Brady pulled out pictures from his backpack.

"I'm so proud of you!" His head touched hers as they flipped through the photos the rafting company had taken.

"Look at this." He stifled a chuckle as he pointed at her gritted teeth and widened eyes in the picture of their first wave. "This is how I felt the first night I saw the bats in your house."

Ruth laughed. How goofy she looked! Hard to imagine him having looked like that his first night in the village. His rich laugh mingled with hers. Laughing at something silly felt good.

"Tell me it wasn't as thrilling!"

It was waterfall heaven for Brady, and honestly, for her too. "I thought I was going to die." She still had no idea how she'd done it. Her heart was still pounding from the thrills. "I wouldn't have done it without you."

Random people came and left as they sat there, talking about life in Uganda. He spoke of America and how different the culture was.

"Are you having a good time?" He wrapped his arm around her waist.

Just being with him was way too much fun. "You?"

"How hard would it be to get you an American visa?" His random question promised a glimpse into a future. "I mean if you ever came to visit me someday?"

"I've heard it's hard to get a visa." But with God, all things are possible. "Are you thinking of inviting me?"

The longing in his face reflected hers. "I'll even take time off from work." He squeezed her waist. "It would be nice for you to have a vacation."

"What do we call this?"

"This was your work trip." Smiling, he dipped his forehead to rest against hers. "Mom would be happy to meet you."

Wow. Something sweet and tender warmed her. He'd consider introducing her to his mom. "I'll start working on a passport as soon as I get back." She'd heard it took two weeks to get one. "I'll do some research at the embassy, too, on how visas work."

"I'll call the embassy as soon as I get back, too."

He tilted his head, his cheek resting against hers. "You were wonderful with the children in the village. Have you ever thought about it? About having kids and getting married someday?"

That may not be up to her, but... "If it's a part of God's plan in my life." Especially if she had a man like him, someone fun and easygoing. It was a serious topic, but it didn't hurt to know about each other. "How about you?"

"I wouldn't mind getting married someday, if I have the right woman."

A silence settled between them as they peered at the expansive rippling water, now sparkling with late afternoon sun.

He didn't say she was the right woman. But he trailed his fingers along her jaw and kissed her forehead, making her feel she might be the woman on his mind.

As they lingered, the sky lost its colorful clouds. Only one car remained in the parking lot. A breeze stirred, leaving his hair tousled and cute.

"You look cold." He reached for the backpack and retrieved one of his button-down shirts, then draped it over her shoulders. He'd carried the backpack, and she had tucked a bag of her clothes in it.

Surprisingly, though she'd grown up in the country, she'd never been to the falls. It wasn't one of those places you just woke up one morning and went to.

She rubbed at her forehead as Brady took pictures. "If we're walking to the hotel, shouldn't we get going?" Otherwise, it would be dark. She hugged his shirt around her. "We better get going. I don't have a flashlight." She'd left all of them at home with her family.

When Brady held out his hand, she took it, standing up. Then he hoisted the backpack onto his back and fastened the straps.

THE TEN-MINUTE WALK to the hotel was smooth. Like Ruth had hoped, enough rooms were available for them each to have their own.

She'd stayed here during a one-week nursing training she'd had. It wasn't fancy or bad, or the type known to be crowded, since it didn't attract too many tourists.

After checking into their rooms, Ruth showered and combed her hair with a wide-toothed comb. She needed to relax her hair, but going to the salon would have to wait until she returned to Kampala.

She straightened her wraparound floral dress. Although she'd kept minimal clothes, she'd selected her favorite outfits for the Jinja trip.

She met Brady on the restaurant balcony, easily spotting him amongst the black faces.

The late evening sun gave his brown hair a golden hue.

"You look gorgeous!" He pulled out the chair next to him for her. What a gentleman.

"Thank you." His jaw was squarer when shaved. How he'd managed to get to the restaurant before her, when he'd had to trim a beard, was hard to imagine. "So do you." His blue polo brought out the deep blue in his eyes.

When their server took their orders, she requested fish and chips, and Brady ordered beef kabobs and collard greens.

The vibrant flowers along the shore and the seagulls cackling above made Ruth feel like she was in one of those American movies.

When their food was brought, Brady's eyes widened. "Do they have to serve the fish with its head still on?"

"That's how they cook fried fish."

"Huh." His nose scrunched up. Then he prayed for God's blessing upon their food, eyed her plate askance, and shared his kabobs. As much as she suggested he tried the fish, he declined. "I'm afraid the thing might bite. If it makes you better at trading, I'll eat some of your fries."

Was that what Americans called them? Fries? Interesting.

Soft songs in different Ugandan languages played in the background as spoons and forks clanked against their plates. Ruth asked about the type of food they ate in America.

"We have way too many options." Brady dabbed a napkin to his mouth. "But my favorite is pizza."

What an odd name for food. "I look forward to trying it someday."

His eyes warmed and peered into hers in a way that made her feel as if no one else were in the world. "Very soon, I hope."

The palm trees below became mere shadows as daylight gave way to darkness.

After paying for their meal, they stayed and talked until the place went dark.

Brady groaned. "The first day we have electricity there's a power outage?"

Ruth glanced around the restaurant. It was just them and the two women hanging up the lanterns above the posts.

Perhaps they'd overstayed. "Are we in your way?" she asked the woman who was stepping down the ladder meters away.

"The restaurant closes at ten, but the balcony serves as a restaurant and lounge." She pointed to the sofas in the far corner overlooking the water. "You can stay as long as you want."

Her shoulders relaxed. If the power went out at her place, she could light up a lantern, but it was different in a strange place.

"We'll stay until the power comes back." Brady must have read her thoughts.

"We have power, but we turn it off in the common area and hallways at ten." It was already ten? "The light attracts so many bugs. This is the only way to keep them out."

That made sense. "Thanks for letting us know," Ruth said, and the woman moved to hang the next lantern.

"I'm not ready to go to bed yet." Brady squeezed her hand, joy lilting in his voice.

"Neither am I."

They walked to the far corner and sat on one of the sofas. His jeans brushed her dress.

Even if there was no future in it, she wanted to know more about him, and why he hesitated to talk about his family. Christmas seemed like an easier way to approach that topic. "Do you get together with your family on Christmas? Aunts, uncles, or grandparents?"

He was silent so long she contemplated changing the subject. "My parents divorced." His cheerful voice fell flat. "I was seven at the time."

Ruth reached for his hand, his pain reverberating through her. She couldn't imagine a seven-year-old being caught in the middle of his parents' separation.

"I'm so sorry." What else could she say?

"My dad has very high expectations. Which can be hard to cope with. He and my mom are so different." Great! Another obstacle to their relationship. "I believe in true love—marriage if you're with the right person."

As he talked about his friend's parents who had over fifty years in their marriage, Ruth's mind spiraled to all sorts of places. Was she the right person for him? Their conversation on the mango tree came to mind. *The only serious relationship I had, my girlfriend ended things when I left for college.* Was Ruth going to be one of his not-so-serious relationships?

She liked him. She could get used to being spoiled the way he'd already proven he'd spoil a woman. Most of all, he loved God. He'd backslidden, but deep down, he seemed to know his Creator.

He'd worked hard in the village, helping her family and playing with the kids. No way was he putting on a show. He enjoyed spending time with the people. Silence settled between them as the lanterns cast flowing reflections on the water lapping below the terrace.

As if recognizing her questions, he squeezed her hand. "I want you to know you're different—different from the women I'd normally encounter."

She clung to his statement, savoring the compliment when he pulled her toward him and pressed a kiss on her head. She inhaled his scent, engraving it in her mind.

They sat in contented silence, surrounded by the peaceful song of frogs and crickets from the water. She had no idea how long they lounged there, discussing spontaneous things, before they strolled back to their rooms through the dimly lit facility.

Not a sound came from the other two doors on their side of the hallway.

"Good night." She lifted her arms to hug him, but she put them down and licked her lips, contemplating a kiss. How was this done properly? She'd initiated their first kiss yesterday, and she was not about to give Brady the impression she was needy. Was she?

"'Night, Ruthie," he whispered, closing the gap between them and backing her against the wall. Her body hummed in anticipation when he moved his hands and traced his fingers on her cheek. His hand slipped to the back of her neck, his mouth warm and insistent against hers. She tasted the kabobs and mint. She breathed in his fresh and appealing smell and savored his warmth.

Her heart thundered as she kissed him back. Did the earth stop turning? That's how she felt when his hands wrapped around her waist, holding her like he didn't want to let go. She didn't want to let go either. Since when did she learn to kiss? With him leaning forward, she moved her hands to his shoulders and wove her fingers into the hair at his nape. They broke up in between to gulp for air, but by the time he came to his senses—since she had none—she could scarcely breathe.

"You're sure you've never kissed before?" His head touched hers, the dim light revealing his smile.

Her cheeks were on fire. "Yesterday, I did." She had no idea how other men kissed, but she didn't want to find out, because Brady was enough. It was either him, or she would die single.

"See you in the morning." He kissed her forehead and stepped back, waiting for her. Where was she? She slapped her forehead, needing to think.

"I'll wait to make sure you get in safe."

Oh yeah, the key. She patted her dress pocket, retrieved her key and stuck it in the door, and turned on the light.

Brady blew her a kiss before she closed the door and leaned against it. Her heart was pounding in her ears. Her knees were wobbly, her head light. Somehow, she forced herself to the bed and slid off her sandals.

She stared at the roof, tried to close her eyes to give herself privacy to replay both kiss experiences. The one in the field and the one that still had the rhythm of her heart beating. She could almost see and feel Brady's arms around her and taste his warm lips. If things didn't work out between them, she had some heart cleansing to do.

She needed to bring up the long-distance relationship conversation again. Would he reconsider? Otherwise, there was no reason for her dreaming.

CHAPTER 14

Using Ruth's camera, Brady hit the zoom button to get a strong focal point on a monkey. If it would only stop leaping from one tree to another, he'd get a decent picture before Ruth met him for their midmorning tour. Since they'd both forgotten their chargers when they left for the village, Ruth suggested they use her camera for taking pictures so they didn't run out of phone battery.

The camera shutter snapped when he pressed the button. Finally, the critter stayed still for the two seconds he needed to steal three shots.

After encountering a four-inch roach in his bathroom that morning, he'd been anxious to check out of the hotel. He'd screamed like a baby when the cockroach flew above his head, and he'd fled and knocked on Ruth's door so he could use her bathroom instead.

Having already showered and dressed, she laughed when he told her his debacle. "Quite unmerciful to laugh at someone's near-death encounter," he'd mumbled as she let herself out to wait for him at the balcony.

As soon as he'd showered and dressed, he'd asked if they could have their breakfast at their next destination. It would've been hard to eat the hotel's food without thinking a cockroach might have played in the pancake batter or whatever they served.

The forest lodge had plenty of vacant huts, and he paid an extra fee to check in early. Ruth had taken out his stitches, which had been much faster and less painful than he'd expected. He'd been so used to having the bandage that at times, he felt something was missing.

All the years he'd chased his business dream—the times he'd gone on a date or two but chosen work over romance, seemed a blur.

He'd relaxed more the last few days with Ruth than he ever had. Seeing things from her perspective made him feel warm and real. Made the world around him vibrant and new.

A group of yellow birds flitted from one tree to another. He readied the camera to take a picture and snapped the end of their V-formation.

He'd try for the birds another time. He spun around, looking for the next shot to capture. The spacious wooden lodge nestled in the lush green forest would be a great memory. He readied the camera and took the picture.

What a perfect place to unwind after their busy time in the village. Surrounded by quiet—except for the monkeys and birds—the atmosphere calmed him, and the huts smelled of lemon disinfectant, not cockroaches. It was a decent facility, and surprisingly, the place wasn't overflowing with tourists.

The grass-thatched huts could use some improvements, but he hadn't spotted any roaches when he checked under the bed, through the corners, and in the bathroom.

While the huts in Ruth's village were constructed with mud and wattle walls, these were sturdy with polished wood floors, indoor bathrooms, and electricity.

The air suddenly shifted, and his breath caught when Ruth walked from one of the huts beneath the trees. The sight made him nearly dizzy with longing. Did she look better in leggings, or the skirts she'd worn in the village? Hard to tell. She was gorgeous in both, but he'd go for the leggings. They showcased her curves.

Her eyes met his, and his knees buckled. He had to remind himself to breathe. No woman ever made his heart race this way. Ruth was the whole package—the kind of woman to fulfill a man's dreams. Beautiful, selfless, and compassionate. He was grateful he'd been too entangled with his work to think of romance. Otherwise, he would've missed out on her.

Did he just entertain forever with her? Yes, he wanted it to be, but how were the logistics going to work out? Her job, his job. His world, her world.

When she almost tripped, he realized he was staring. The camera dangled around his neck as he strode to her and took her tender hand in his. The smell of her soft conditioner did something to him. "Did you check for roaches in your hut?" Not that she was scared of them, but he had to say something so she didn't notice his flushed face.

"Do I need to?" She stifled a chuckle, no doubt replaying his morning debacle.

"Hey." He toyed with the spirally curls she always combed to her forehead. The hair was more tightly coiled, since she'd gotten her hair done before they checked in. "It's not very nice of you to laugh when I almost got attacked."

She peered up at him, her eyes so warm and brown, he fought the urge to cup her face and press his lips against hers. He might have if they didn't have a midmorning activity planned.

Someone cleared their throat. "Ready?"

They both turned to their tour guide. With his dark face already shining in sweat, he'd probably come from an earlier hike.

"Yes." Ruth squared her shoulders as if she'd been caught in a wrong act. She slipped her arm through the crook of Brady's elbow. Her strapped sandals fell into a slow rhythm with his tennis shoes. They circled a tree draped in hanging moss to follow Byambi's lead to a narrow forest path and ducked and shoved aside branches sticking out from the lush shrubs.

"I haven't seen any mosquitoes so far," Ruth said. They'd been told the forest had plenty.

"There's a lot during the rainy season." Byambi wiped his moistening forehead. "That's why we have few customers now. Rainy season starts next week."

Hard to believe it was almost September. Brady breathed in the aroma from the flowery shrubs. Savoring the serenity, he tried not to think about next week. He'd be walking on American soil—alone.

When they walked through an array of butterflies, Ruth wanted to take pictures.

"Someone doesn't trust my photography skills, I see." He handed her the camera.

"That's not true." She approached the bright flowering shrubs, snapping pictures before zeroing the camera lens to him.

The flash went off once, twice, and he reached for her hand, then tugged her to his side, and wrapped his arm around her waist. "It's unacceptable for you to take a picture of me when you're not in it."

"I'll need lots of your photos to look at when you're gone."

Byambi offered to take their picture.

After posing for three pictures, Brady used their picture break to press a kiss on her head. The subtle scent of her conditioner refreshed him. He longed to stretch out that moment, but their tour guide started walking. The short man probably didn't want to waste any more of his time.

Brady clasped Ruth's hand. "We better get going so we don't get lost in this jungle."

"We've only used one pathway." She hugged his arm to her. "We can find our way back."

"That's what we thought in the cornfield." He'd enjoyed every minute of it, except for the snake that interfered—although actually, without that snake, he wouldn't have been able to pull Ruth into his arms.

"Keep an eye out for snakes." Did Byambi just read his mind? Even though he said they rarely showed up, they encountered some as they walked deeper into the forest.

Brady's fear of snakes vanished when the trees parted, unveiling cascading falls. "We have to get our picture here." This time, Brady suggested it, and their guide was patient, snapping a few photos from different angles to get the right lighting as Ruth pointed out.

Byambi described the different animals living in the forest, and explained the activities they could do with their tour package for their two-day stay.

When he pointed out the zip line visible in the distance, Brady turned to Ruth. "Would you like to try it?"

She blinked and put a hand to her chest, her jaw dropping. "Have you done that before?"

Not wanting to appear like the expert, he shrugged. "It's been a long time." That was the truth, but he'd zip lined during his Boy Scout and college days. "You might like it."

"No way!" Ruth clutched harder against her chest, as if trying to keep her pounding heart in place. "Rafting was as far an adventure as I'm ready for. I surprisingly survived."

He chuckled at her drama. Yet he didn't blame her. He'd been terrified for her when the raft flipped, which he'd expected would happen, but had also been confident she'd be safe. Except, being her first time, the experience must have been intense for her. She'd done it for him, but she had fun. "I'm glad you gave rafting a try."

"I'd love to see you zip line." She gave a slow nod. "I'll take pictures."

When Byambi asked if they could find their way back, Ruth was confident they could. So Brady pulled out his wallet and handed Byambi several shillings for a tip. Appreciation beamed in the man's smile before he left.

As much as Brady loved doing all the firsts with her, she'd already rafted for him. He'd better not try to persuade her any further.

Zip lining was always a thrilling sport, but doing it through the jungle made for a far more daring adventure. Brady felt like a teenager again as he spanned the 820 feet across the river through the canopy of trees.

By the time he repelled the 256 feet back down, his heart raced, and his veins buzzed with adrenaline. He was ready for more. But whatever he did from there on would have to be with her. He walked back to the waiting area where he'd left her.

She let out a shuddered breath. "You're mad. Did I already say that?" Relief loosening her taut features, she sprinted to his side. "I was so scared for you."

Seeing her concerned and fearful for his safety twisted in his heart. Not caring that he was damp and sweaty, he gathered her close and wrapped an arm around her. "I'll teach you how to zip line so we can go together next time."

"You're leaving in two days."

Right, he didn't need that reminder. "When you come to the States, then." As soon as he returned, he'd find a way to get a visa going for her to visit.

The afternoon sun heated their brows. He welcomed the gentle breeze rustling the leaves.

As Ruth had said, they didn't have a problem finding their way back to their huts. Both needing to shower, they agreed to meet at her hut in thirty minutes.

Brady finished showering and changed into cargo shorts and a T-shirt. He glanced at his phone. He'd only used fifteen minutes. With the next fifteen, he could walk to the gift shop and find her something special.

Five more minutes. He stuffed his phone back in his shorts pocket. His palms were sweating as he shifted the box in his hand, glancing at her green door, then back to his. Only a few trees separated their huts. He could walk back to his room and wait there, or he could knock on her door, assuming she was ready. In three strides, he was at the entrance.

His knuckles drummed on the door. Anticipation beat against his ribs. When the door swung open and his gaze slid over her green dress, his tongue felt stuck.

"You're hungry?" Ruth's whisper pulled him back into focus.

Yes, hungry to kiss her again. But, if he even entered her hut, there could be a serious fire, and he didn't want to cause collateral damage. It was different when her shoulders brushed against his in the village—they had four others in the room.

His hand shook when he extended the white box. "This is for you."

She pressed a hand to her chest, her face glowing before she took the box and lifted the silver necklace. "A butterfly."

The gift shop didn't have anything fancier. "Since we saw them today, I thought..."

"It's beautiful." She stepped on tiptoes and curled her hand around his neck. Her lips brushed against his, an invitation he didn't take for granted. He snugged his arms around her and drew her close, kissing her with all the feelings inside him. They kissed until they were both breathless. He forced himself to pull back. The box and necklace had fallen on the ground.

Ruth threw both hands over her face, hiding her smile. "I think your kisses are turning me into something else."

Pleased she loved being kissed as much as he enjoyed kissing her, he could hardly contain his smile when he crouched and picked up the box and necklace. "Let's say I'm going a bit crazy myself—that's what you would call mad." He ushered her toward the trees separating her hut from his. "I'll help you get this on."

She tipped her head to the side as he slid the necklace on her, and goose bumps broke out in all the visible areas of her shoulders, filling his heart with contentment. He affected her the way she affected him. It went both ways, at least. His heart was getting caught in a new level of danger, but he'd have to process it all after he returned home.

How nice to have privacy with the way the huts were laid out. Plus, they'd shown up at the end of the tourist season. "Are we still having dinner? Or is it lunch?" It was only two thirty when he'd brought her the necklace.

With her eyes soft, she clasped his hand. "It's lunch." They walked toward the stone pathway. "We'll eat dinner at eight."

From the upper restaurant, they overlooked the pristine rainforest. Various papyrus swamps, streams, and a peaceful waterfall surrounded the breathtaking valley. A cool breeze stirred from the trees as the kind waitress took their orders.

Besides him and Ruth, two other couples occupied the restaurant tables. How did the place survive its low tourist season?

The menu had minimal options, and he ordered the same food Ruth picked—chapati with beef stew and a side of collard greens.

Except for its delicious flavor, the chapati reminded him of a tortilla and naan bread.

With three more hours of daylight, he suggested they take advantage of the pool hidden beneath the trees. He hadn't seen a single soul when he'd walked by it twice that day.

"I don't know how to swim." She frowned. "Even if I did, I don't have a swimming costume."

If she was bold enough to try rafting over the rippling falls, she could swim. He'd been a lifeguard for two summers before he found it boring. "I'll teach you."

"I'll need more than one day to learn."

"I'm a good teacher." They could swim today and most of the day tomorrow before they left for Kampala. And whenever she came to America, she could swim in his penthouse pool.

"I don't have a costume."

"I saw swimsuits in the gift shop." He needed to get one for himself, too.

BRADY WAS ALREADY IN the water when Ruth met him by the pool. She'd wrapped a towel over her chest and thighs. She was cute when she glanced at his bare chest, then peered over his head to the tall trees. She spoke without looking at him. "I don't think I can learn today."

He would've bought a swim shirt if they'd had one in the shop. "I'm your instructor, remember?"

The monkeys leaped from one tree to another, and Ruth gripped the towel tight as if to make sure it didn't fall down. Seeming lost in thought, she stared at the animals.

"You'll need to drop the towel if you're getting in," he teased, hoping she didn't change her mind. Waiting, he swirled water warmed by the humid air.

She could be bold, yet shy in some ways. Which was fascinating. She'd turned down every two-piece swimsuit the clerk had presented, until she showed Ruth the one-piece suits. She'd settled for the more modest burgundy.

He'd keep his eyes on her face while he taught her to swim. Whoa, his heart was already racing at the thought of holding her in his arms while instructing her in the water.

Ruth fidgeted with her swimsuit strap.

"Ruthie, I'm turning around." He pivoted and walked toward the pool's deep end. "I'm closing my eyes, too. You can come in the water, okay?" Perhaps that would help her feel comfortable. It did. He spun back when she splashed water on his back. Smirking, she sat on the shallow end steps.

"Is this how it's going to be?" He splashed water at her, and they went back and forth as she giggled, shoving him back in the water. He emerged and wiped water from his face, then scooped her up. "Drowning your coach before your first lesson?"

She squealed before he dunked her under the water, keeping her secure in his arms. *Oops.* He'd forgotten she'd never swam before. She coughed nonstop. "Sorry, I forgot..."

Her hand on her chest, she choked on her words. "Now... who's... drowning who?"

Brady shrugged. "I guess payback is my defense."

Ripples of sunlight reflected off the pool's surface, casting golden light on her skin, and shimmering water drops sparkled in her hair and slipped along the contours of her face, beckoning more than his attention. Somehow, he fought the urge to cup her face and press his lips to each droplet. If he did that, there'd be no lesson. He had to remind himself to focus so he could teach her the breaststroke.

He swallowed. "We will focus on four things—pull, breathe, kick, and glide." He started the lesson by having her practice holding her breath under the water. He showed her how to submerge and resurface. He then taught her how to float with her face in the water.

"Close your eyes if it's scary."

"So I can drown without seeing?"

He laughed, looking at her skeptical brown eyes. "You trust me?"

She rolled her eyes, nodded, and tipped her head back.

"You're overthinking." He pulled her up when her body started sinking.

After a few more tries of the exercise, both with her body straight and horizontal, he showed her how to stroke her arms and keep her arms and legs long. Soon she was floating and gliding forward and back.

"This is fun." She wiped water from her face. "I didn't think I'd like it."

He was loving it from her perspective. "I always enjoy it." Today the most. The beautiful birdsong echoed inside the forest, offering a wonderful nature lullaby.

He didn't want Ruth to overdo it. But he only had today and tomorrow with her, and he didn't want his day to end just yet. "Are you up to practicing some kicks?"

"Totally." She reached her arms forward to glide with her face in the water.

After splashing and laughing, she climbed up to sit by the pool stairs. He sat next to her, and they dangled their feet in the water.

"I can't believe you've never been swimming before." She was a natural.

"The only places with pools are the fancy tourist hotels."

Duh, this wasn't the States where pools awaited at almost each recreation center and neighborhood. "I didn't think about that."

The conversation shifted to their time in the village, and Brady asked what she was going to do with the chicken he'd been given.

She splashed water with her feet. "My neighbor—the tailor—has chickens, I might ask his help raising it."

Talking about the village brought up those faces. They made such unique baskets and intricate woodwork. The gift shop came to mind. What if they sold their items in the shop to provide some income? The place was only twenty miles from Ruth's home village.

"Can you remind me to get the manager's business card when we go to dinner?" He'd most likely forget while he was with her.

"You want to buy this hotel too?"

Wouldn't be a bad idea, but he'd already failed with the Entebbe resort. "I might let my property lawyer keep an eye out for when it goes on sale." He shared his thoughts with her.

"That would be such a blessing."

If he didn't succeed, he'd try calling the Entebbe resort to ask what it took for people to sell crafts in their shop. "They could at least afford to travel to a hospital if they needed to."

She took her hand in his. "You're a good man, Mr. Sharp."

He was far from it, but her compliment was a sweet encouragement. "I could do better." He needed her to remind him of things he'd ignored.

"I'm gonna miss you." He brushed damp hair from her face, sending shimmering droplets gliding down her skin. He didn't let his gaze follow them far.

"Me the most." Her eyes dimmed. "Regardless, glad to have met you."

His beautiful Ruthie was trying to be brave. "We still have another day together, right?" Unless she was planning on taking off in the middle of the night. He intended to stretch out the evening as long as he could. "I hear their bonfire stays lit until one, up for that?"

"If you're not tired of me yet."

It felt as if he'd only spent two hours with her instead of eight days. He was more relaxed doing manual labor rather than the normal work he did. He hadn't stressed about missed meetings and engagements. No doubt, her presence had to do with all the calm inside his heart. He draped his arm over her shoulder and held his breath. Could this moment last forever? His heart raced. Could she hear it?

"I'll never have enough of you." He drew in a deep breath, surprised by the sudden confession. Was that too direct?

Her smile when she tipped her head against his shoulder reassured him he'd said the right thing.

CHAPTER 15

After luxuriating in the resort's shower, which almost reminded him of home, Brady thought he'd feel refreshed and relaxed. He felt anything but.

Staring at the ceiling, he tried to pay attention to the TV. He'd turned it on for some background noise, but it merely enhanced his frustration as he tried to concentrate on the events of his trip.

The drive back from Jinja had been quiet, mainly because he and Ruth had been nestled in the middle of sticky bodies. A man on his side and another man to Ruth's side.

He'd held onto Ruth's hand, despite the heat radiating from the un-airconditioned and packed minibus.

He made a brief stop at her place to get his laptop before she took another minibus with him back to Entebbe and walked him to the resort's gate.

They'd agreed to say goodbye that night, but he wasn't content with the way they parted. With no words exchanged, he wrapped his arms around her, and teary-eyed, she sniffled and rested her head on his chest. He'd wanted her to linger in his embrace, but she eased out and waved before walking away and leaving him standing. The gate-keeper had been the front-row audience to their farewell.

They'd parted only five hours ago, and his heart was already wrenched. Why had he agreed to say goodbye that night? What was he going to do all day tomorrow before his midnight flight? Drown in sorrow?

He turned to his side. The nightstand clock cast garish red numbers back at him—12:07 a.m.

Ruth was just a phone call or a text away. He tossed the bedsheets aside, swung his feet out of bed, and grabbed his phone from the nightstand. His thumb teased the screen. He could text and ask her for one more day.

Forget tracking down the resort owner tomorrow. After parting from Ruth, he'd asked the receptionist and learned the owner would be at the place all day tomorrow. That's what he should do since he'd come to Uganda on business. He was starting to assume God had other plans for his trip, far better than his company's prosperity.

Could it be God planned for Brady to help Ruth fulfill her dream instead of chasing his own? The billionaire legacy he had worked so hard to accomplish?

He closed his eyes. Perhaps God would direct him. "If Ruth is for me, Lord, how can I make things different? How can I make our relationship work? She's here. I'm there."

Opening his eyes, he set his phone back on the nightstand. He'd call Ruth in the morning instead. She was probably sleeping after their long days. If he could only have one more day with her. One more embrace and one more kiss before they parted to an uncertain future would make things okay.

Wrong. One day with her wouldn't be enough, but he'd take what he could get.

Would she be available tomorrow? She had loads of patients to tend, especially after she'd been gone so long. *Forget it.* He lay back down and threw a pillow over his head and changed his prayer. "I have a life in America, and she has one here. Please help me not to obsess about her."

Too much was at stake. His employees needed him. He couldn't endanger their jobs should he have to sell out some of his resorts.

He forced his eyes closed, craving sleep, but images of the cleft-lipped kids, of *Annie*, consumed his mind. He growled and sat upto call the front desk for coffee or whatever caffeine they had.

A billionaire in the making was his legacy. That's what he wanted, right? Why was his heart now aching and confused about his dream?

AFTER A LONG NIGHT of lying there thinking about her time with Brady, Ruth gave up on sleep and started her day earlier than she intended. It was time to return to reality. Break time was over. The only holiday she'd ever have.

Her knees hit the rough woven mat, and she closed her eyes. She needed guidance and clarification on several questions. But first, she had to be grateful to God for the joy she'd felt in Brady's presence.

"Even if it was for a short time, Lord, thank You for bringing him into my life, for making me feel loved and cared for." Having a man look at her with such longing, the way Brady did, had felt so good. The best ten days of her life.

When she finished praying, she stacked her journal and Bible on the table. She moved the vase to the center. Although the petals were looking frail, Brady's flowers were still intact, and she intended to keep them forever. She should probably dry them before the petals fell. She just wasn't up for the task. Not today, anyway.

She needed a strong cup of tea. She walked to her small stove on the kitchen table and lit it.

The smell of paraffin permeated the room. With no milk to make chai, she boiled water before tossing in the cinnamon sticks, ginger, and tea leaves. It was the perfect blend for any tea to taste magnificent.

She only had sips left when the clinic door rattled and Eunice stuck her head through. "Oh my!" Her face lit up as she jumped up and down, screeching before she scurried to Ruth. "Tell me! Tell me *everything*."

She squeezed herself on the love seat before Ruth could say hello. "Since you didn't respond to my texts, I figured you were busy."

"I responded." Ruth set her cup on the table. She'd texted Eunice when Brady did the zip line. She'd been responding to her text on what Brady thought of the village.

"With one paltry text?" Tsking, Eunice crossed one foot over the other and wiggled back on the cushions, getting ready for a good story.

"Can I get you some tea?" Ruth knew what her friend's response would be, but she wanted to test her anxious energy.

Eunice brushed off her question by kicking off her flip-flops and bringing her hands together as if pleading. "Have you even noticed I came an hour early?"

Ruth had stopped checking the time once she got out of bed.

"So... tell me everything!"

"We ran out of medicine." She told her about Brady's hard work in the field, helping with bandages. "He even..."

"Seriously!" Eunice arched an eyebrow. "Do I want to hear this? Ruuuth!"

"Okay." Laughter slipped from Ruth's chest, but it hurt. "We had fun in Jinja."

"Did he kiss you like we see in the movies?" Her eyes lighting up, Eunice moved her hands to speed up Ruth's response. "Please, tell me."

Ruth's lips tingled at the warm feeling rushing over her. The first kiss in the plowed field, and how she felt the moment their lips met... She twirled a strand of her hair with her finger. The kiss when he'd walked her to her door had her touching her cheeks. She'd better get out the fan. She fanned herself with her hand. "Yes..." The wonder lingered on her lips. "Even better than the movies," she whispered.

Eunice threw her head back and clasped her hands to her chest. "Oh my! I'm going to die. Please, keep talking."

Ruth laughed at Eunice's dreamy expression. Those soaps they'd watched in college hadn't helped either of them. "You're still married, right?"

"Just because I'm married, doesn't mean I don't enjoy romantic stories."

With Eunice's insisting she divulge more about the trip, Ruth told her about her swimming lessons and daring adventures in Jinja. "I'll show you the pictures when I get them developed."

"I can't wait that long." Eunice wanted to see the pictures on the camera, but the battery had died right before they left Jinja.

"Well, you'd better get the pictures printed *today*."

Ruth shook her head. "We have patients." They never knew when a woman would go into labor, a kidney stone would pass, or some unexpected patient would show up. "Today might be"—what was the word Brady used?—"crazy."

"I figured you would be tired today, so I asked Rashida to come in." Ruth was one year younger than Eunice, but her friend was no-nonsense—well, except for today. She'd been silly today. Still, God knew Ruth needed a friend like her in business. "Take the rest of the day off and go get those pictures printed."

Going to the city took a lot of energy. Marching through bodies along the street exhausted her every time. However, she could use some time to look up where and how to apply for a passport. Perhaps she could combine the trip? Get prints and apply for a passport in one day? "I have other things I can get done besides getting those prints." Brady had left her money to take Ivan to the hospital. The facility they'd stayed at in the forest accepted credit cards, and Brady used the Jinja fund toward Ivan's. "I need to call Ivan."

"He stopped by, said he was having pain again."

"When was that?"

"Yesterday." Eunice frowned, twisting her red-lipsticked mouth to one side. "I think the day before. I gave him some aspirin. He didn't want to stay the night alone here."

"I'll call him tonight." His brother had the phone, and he didn't get home until six.

"Good plan." Eunice bounced one foot. "Thanks for the produce you sent with Dongo. I requested he divide it amongst your neighbors after Rashida and I took some. And I took the chicken to my house, but what are you going to do with all the baskets and stuff?"

"Oh no!" Ruth pressed both hands on her head. She'd forgotten Brady's souvenirs when they stopped by for his bag. "Most of those are Brady's gifts." She stood, wobbling a little as her blood rushed. "Are they at your house?"

"I stored them in the extra room since we didn't have an overnight patient."

Not that he'd take any of the baskets on the airplane, but it gave her the excuse she needed to see him one more time. "Maybe I should call and see if he wants to take them."

"He's not gone yet?" Eunice jumped to her feet.

"His flight is tonight."

Her eyes widening, Eunice slapped Ruth's shoulder. "*He's* still here, and *you* are sitting here with *me*? Why are you not spending the day with him?"

Saying their goodbyes last night seemed like a good idea. She wasn't convinced of that theory anymore. She shrugged. "The sooner we move back to our regular lives the better."

Eunice's penciled eyebrows knitted. "You've prayed for Mzungu for almost three years, and now he's here—and you're acting like it's not a big deal?" She slapped her thigh. "Do you know how many girls would die to be in your position right now?"

Yes, it was a big deal. But Brady was too good—far better than the man she'd prayed for. "What if God used him as a stepping stone to prepare me for my mzungu?" Except she didn't want another. She wanted him. He was fun and adventurous and made her laugh.

Eunice was already draping Ruth's curtains and walking to her closet. "You're leaving."

"What are you doing?"

Eunice tossed three sundresses on her bed. "Helping you get your man."

Ruth's heart was already racing. Brady had mentioned talking to the resort's CEO today. She retrieved her phone from the table. "Let me just... uh, send Dongo to take his items—"

Eunice snatched the phone and scrolled through it, then handed it back. "I just called Brady's number."

Nobody bossed her around. Ruth slammed her hands on her hips. "Really?"

"Put the phone to your ear," Eunice ordered, and Ruth did as she was told. But really, no one bossed her around.

"You're fired," Ruth mouthed as the first ring sounded.

"Ruthie!" Brady's voice rang out. "I'm so glad you called! I was going to call you."

"Oh, Brady." She tightened her grip on the phone and sank into the nearest chair before her wobbly knees could give out. His voice washed over her like the water they'd been in, and she lowered her voice as if he were in the room. "Did you sleep well?" she whispered.

"I tried... I just..." He stammered over some words. Wow, he was as nervous as she was. "Any chance you have some time to hang out with me today?"

Her hands were shaking. She needed two of them to hold the phone to her ear. "I was thinking the same. I have your souvenirs."

Eunice set a pink sundress on her lap and mouthed, "You're welcome."

Ruth had forgotten she was in the room. With plans to meet in less than an hour, Ruth hung up.

Eunice started jumping and clapping like a little girl. Then she jammed her hands on her hips and singsonged, "*When* is my last day again?"

"Shut up!" Ruth rolled her eyes and got the basin. A cold shower would have to do today. She had no time to boil water. "Please call Dongo while I shower."

"On it." Eunice snapped her fingers. "I'll even have your souvenirs ready by the time you get out."

"You're the best." Ruth spoke over her back as she carried the towel and water basin out the door.

One more day. She wanted forever, but she was grateful for an unexpected day.

WHEN SHE SAT IN DONGO'S car and he started driving, Ruth looked through the window, the green vegetation and blue sky rising into a new and vibrant glow by the sunrise.

She bounced her foot, her stomach tied up in knots as the thirteen kilometers dwindled into one.

"We're almost there," Dongo said when the expansive gated property came into view. "I have no doubt, this man will marry you."

"You don't know that." Either way, she was trembling. "He's leaving."

"Don't forget I had the audience."

Yes, in his silence, he'd probably witnessed them through the rearview mirror when he drove from the village to Jinja as they held hands, and maybe shared a few pecks. Despite all that, when she'd asked him if they could date long distance, Brady's response was maybe. What kind of word was *maybe*? Perhaps one of the worst English words. Did they even have a word like it in her language?

She couldn't think of a direct translation right now, but then, she couldn't think of anything coherent right now.

She rubbed the shivers from her arms. He had plenty of reasons to be afraid of a long-distance relationship.

She was just as terrified never to hear from him once he got back to his busy life, but she had nothing to lose—nothing more than to hope something was simmering between them, that he was the one she wanted. Maybe she was a fool to feel giddy about a man who didn't offer any promise for a future together, but the ten days she'd spent with him were better than not having him at all.

When they drove up, Brady was pacing in front of the metal gate. He stilled, and his face lifted into a wide smile as if he recognized their car.

"Stop the car!" she shouted when Brady started sprinting toward them. She pushed the door open and ran to meet him, and before she could say a word, he swept her up in his arms and kissed her until she could scarcely breathe.

"I'm so glad you're here," he whispered when he stepped back and looked at her in the way that always made her knees tremble.

They turned when the car honked. "Dongo." Brady led her back to the car and shook Dongo's hand in greeting before asking if he would be available to come back later and drive him to the airport.

"I will be honored to."

The hotels offered a shuttle, but if Dongo drove him to the airport, they could take their time depending on the hotel's schedule.

The guard grinned and waved as they walked through the gate and to the hotel lobby.

"We get to have breakfast together." Grinning, Brady rubbed his hands together. "I reserved a table."

A shiver went through her when he pressed his palm against the small of her back and guided her. As she slid into the chair he pulled out for her, her knees shook so much she had to brace a hand to the table. The wildflower bouquet centered over the white tablecloth wobbled.

"What can we do after breakfast?" Brady asked.

She had no idea what couples did, but she loved being around him. "I don't care what we do." As long as they were together.

As he suggested the things the resort offered, she couldn't stop wondering if today wasn't the beginning of their future. Yet it seemed like a long goodbye to their brief past. So, would everything end today, or would it create a memorable future neither would forget?

CHAPTER 16

The sun rose higher, warming the air as morning turned into noon while they swam and lounged on beach chairs. "Ready to get some lunch?" Brady stood and reached for her hand. Swimming tended to leave him hungry.

"You're hungry already?" She tightened the cloth wrapper around her waist before taking his hand.

"I was so excited to see you, I lost my appetite for food." Watching her fascination about the different juices she'd never tried was more interesting.

"Don't we need to change first?"

"You don't have to. I reserved one of the huts for us, and they can bring our lunch there." The resort offered private reservable huts as well as huts where any guest could walk in and wander.

She looked over her swimsuit and wrap. "I better shower and change first."

He'd paid an extra night just so he could keep his luggage in the suite. "We can use the showers in my suite if you want to."

When her delicate brows pinched together, he realized what he'd asked her, and his cheeks burned. "The suite has two rooms and two bathrooms. You will have your own, and I won't even..." *Stop talking, man.* Each word sounded more foolish.

She ducked her head, a secretive smile curling her full lips. "Even in public, I don't trust myself around you—let alone in close quarters."

It wasn't close quarters, but neither was it necessary to argue. "I understand."

He pointed out their reserved hut for the afternoon, and they agreed to meet there once they'd showered and changed.

After they shared their lunch, the server took the dirty plates from the table, leaving two milk chocolate bars and a bag of unopened chips left over from Ruth's lunch.

The huts were built with strong acacia wood, with no walls around them.

"I'm so satisfied, and I have no room for crisps." She nudged the Lays chips to the side. Crisps, an interesting name for chips. "I might take that for Eunice. Crisps are her favorite treat."

"Hope you have room for something sweet." He closed the space between them as the expansive Victoria Lake shimmered before them. Two huts from theirs, another couple was lost in their world, just like Brady and Ruth. No swimmers braved the side of the lake with the private huts, mainly because the crocodiles snuck into the water in certain areas. The wrapper scrunched when he ripped open the chocolate, broke off a corner, and handed it to her. "I want to see your reaction as you taste your first bite."

She twisted her face, accepting the square in her hand. "It doesn't look like something I'll like." She eyed it, her nose scrunching before she dropped it in her mouth. Her brows unwrinkled as she chewed. "That's good."

"Better than a lollipop?" He handed her the rest of the chocolate, his mouth watering by watching her lips puckering as her tongue licked the chocolaty remains.

"Much better." She broke a piece and handed it to him, but he slid it in her mouth instead. "That's your piece." She objected over a mouthful before breaking off another and sliding it into his mouth.

Chocolate had never tasted better than it did now as they fed each other the rest of the candy bar and ate another.

She handed him a notebook. "This is for you."

Brady opened it. Her printed writing was so neat for a nurse. She'd added several Bible verses they'd read together in the village. He skimmed them, heat radiating through his chest. "I think you forgot to add one here for me."

Her warm breath tickled his neck. "Really?"

"Can I borrow your pen?" He held out his hand. She carried one whenever she had a bag with her.

He spoke the words as he wrote. From her note when she'd first said goodbye to him. "Psalm 20. 'May He make your plans succeed.'"

"You memorized that?" she whispered, her voice breaking, her eyes glowing, and their intensity on his face heated the back of his neck.

They spoke about random things, her clinic, his business, and how different their cultures were. Which was good. He needed to know what Ruth would miss in her country, should she entertain the idea of ever moving to America.

Visiting was one thing, but for them to have a lasting relationship, one of them had to make a sacrifice. He exhaled a heavy breath. That was a topic best left for another time.

He touched the strap of her navy dress. Hibiscus flowers, like the ones in her village, flowed over its print. "This color looks so nice on you."

Ducking her head, she fiddled with her butterfly pendant. "You have good taste."

When he'd talked her into swimming, he'd taken her to the gift shop to get another swimsuit. While there, he urged her to pick out as many outfits she wanted, but she'd only taken two skirts, claiming the money could better be spent elsewhere. So Brady picked out two sundresses for her, ones with flowers he'd seen in her home village.

The afternoon turned to evening. Dusk deepened and darkened and fled. By ten, Dongo arrived to take them to the airport. Every moment with Ruth was as precious as the previous ones.

The silence stretched as the distance to the airport narrowed. Just like earlier, they avoided talking about what lay ahead, even as it loomed over them. At least, they'd been talking then, and he didn't have to think. Even Dongo's ethnic songs would be a welcome distraction, but the man had no music playing.

As much as Brady wanted to shift his hand from Ruth's shoulder so he could look at her face, he wouldn't dare, not when he could feel her chest fall and rise as she rested her head on his chest. She wasn't sleeping, not with the way she let out shuddered breaths from time to time.

Several lights illuminated the distance, and Ruth drew in a dreadful breath. "We're almost there," she whispered and straightened. She clasped his fingers in hers as if to hold on as long as she could.

Brady's heart thudded when Dongo turned into the lit parking lot. People were unloading luggage and embracing loved ones.

Their time together was up. His throat tightened. "I... This is it."

He didn't think his words made sense, but he had no idea what else to say.

Dongo parked the car. "I'll let you say goodbye."

The front door clicked shut, leaving just the two of them again.

Brady released her hand and peered through the window. In mere minutes, he'd join those people at the gate, leaving Ruth behind. A pain rose so fiercely he couldn't remember how to speak. This was it. He swallowed hard. He couldn't sit here forever. He needed to form the goodbye he'd planned. "I'll let you..."

How was he going to do this?

Tears gleamed in her expressive eyes. "Brady." She shook her head, hands to her cheeks, chin trembling.

Unable to look at her, he reached to open the door, to put this to an end. But his fingers were trembling so much he couldn't unlatch it.

Ruth swung open her door and stepped out, and he managed to open his and walk to the trunk to retrieve his luggage. She'd given him her luggage so he could carry all those handcrafted souvenirs.

She stood there, her head lowered, a soft wind teasing her curls and tossing her dress around her knees. She looked so fragile, even though he'd never met a stronger woman. She had her hands clasped loosely before her, and all Brady needed to do was wave and start marching toward the gate. But then her wide eyes searched his face so intently, and the devastation in them rose within him, nearly choking him on its way out. He let go of the luggage and in two strides stopped before her.

Clearing his throat, he couldn't form a word, but he wanted to say one, just one nearly as perfect as she was.... "Ruthie," he whispered with such force that it broke the dam blocking his throat. It fell from his lips so naturally. How long would it be before he said her name again?

"I'm sorry I landed in your clinic." The words ripped up his chest. Did he mean them? Did he regret their time together? Regret meeting her? No, not for himself, but he couldn't be that selfish. "And now, I get to leave."

He touched her cheek, warm smooth skin yielding to his fingertips. He had no right to break her sweet heart, the first boyfriend she'd had, and now he was leaving.

Her lips trembled. Her chin lifted. "I'm not... sorry."

Tears spilled down on her cheek, and he wiped them with the back of his hand.

"I'm just sorry you missed your business deal."

As her voice—a half-gasp, half-sob—swirled around him, the ache burned deeper. "I found a far better deal." He pulled her close.

Why did he feel as if he was leaving everything behind? He'd tasted a simpler life, and the American dream waiting the moment he landed in New York. But he wanted Ruth to be a part of that dream. He lowered his head to kiss her curls, breathing in her soft-scented conditioner. "I want to give long-distance dating a chance."

"Are you sure?" Ruth coughed and choked on her tears. He tucked her face against his shoulder and closed his eyes. Their breaths melded into one as her chest rose and fell against his. His eyes burned. If only they could stay this way forever!

No, not this way. Not this poignant sadness crippling them. He slammed his eyes shut, sending two tears plunging. He wanted to change this moment to another time and place.

His chest rose with the weight of it, heart thrashing against his ribs. Afraid of what he was about to say, he kissed the top of her head and whispered, "I love you." Maybe it was too soon to confess, maybe saying those words wouldn't change anything, but she had to know that, during their time spent together, he'd fallen for her.

"I love you, too."

When Dongo returned, Ruth eased out of Brady's arms, and he opened the front passenger door for her. He placed his palm on the small of her back and guided her to her seat, then closed her door.

He'd rather have her in the car when he started walking. Otherwise, he'd look back and change his mind.

"Thank you so much for your hard work." He shook Dongo's hands. He'd left an extra tip with Ruth for him when they withdrew funds at the gift shop. "Take care of her for me, okay?"

"I will, sir. May I carry your luggage?"

"Just take Ruthie home. Thank you." She'd had a long day, a long week. He imagined she'd have a long night.

Brady reached for his luggage. His vision blurred as he zeroed in on the entrance. He forced his feet forward, fighting the urge to turn around and lift his hand to wave, but he didn't—*couldn't*.

Minutes later, he boarded and settled in his comfortable chair.

"Can I get you something to drink?" The stewardess dropped her hands from the cart. "And a snack if you've had a chance to look at the menu?"

"Water is fine, thanks." He wasn't hungry, nor would he be for the rest of the trip. An empty hole hollowed out his heart, a hole only Ruth could fill.

When the lady rolled to the seat in front of him, Brady reached for his sleep mask, slid it over his eyes, and leaned back, blanketing into the growing dark.

Think of work. He had so much to do. The missed deal meant figuring out a new investment somewhere. How could he save the four properties from shutting down? How could he convince the wishy-washy investor from backing out?

But he couldn't do anything on the plane, except sleep while he could. No, he couldn't sleep. He'd already done that while on vacation. Think. It's what he did best whenever he closed his eyes.

Images of the two cleft-lipped kids taunted him... their lively eyes and curious minds as they investigated the mzungu. Annie. The frail women and men suffering from long-term illnesses. The broad smiles of the kids he'd played with. He needed to start a fund to send medical assistance and build a hospital. He shifted in his seat, bothered by the comfort. If he'd flown economy, the difference could've gone toward medical needs.

Ruth's words when he'd wanted to buy clothes for her because she'd never shop for herself, teased his memory—*There's more ways to spend that money than on my clothes.*

He rubbed his temples, but the thoughts kept hammering them. He could work harder toward becoming the next billionaire, or he could take two steps back and start a new charity. That would take time, given he'd never run one before. All he'd done was donate to Eric's charities.

Eric. He had lunch with him once a month. He'd have to ask him how to proceed.

Having a plan to work with, he relaxed and let sleep claim him. Ruth's face smiled into his memory. Then their laughter as they'd run through the cornfield to find their way out echoed in his ears. The day they fell off the bike, and her awestruck reaction after he kissed her—her first kiss. His body hummed, and he moaned inwardly.

He had pictures of her from their rafting trip. They would get him through until he saw her again.

CHAPTER 17

After a long shower, Ruth sank onto her loveseat for the first time since she'd said goodbye to Brady. She tucked her nightdress around her, blew out a breath, and reached for her phone. It felt like a month since they'd parted, yet it was only three days ago. The rainy season had kicked off, and the rain pelting the roof made her mood somewhat gray.

The night he'd left, she'd been called to a home where a three-year-old had put her hand in scalding water. She'd taken a boda boda twenty kilometers to tend to the child, whose frazzled parents had no knowledge of what to do. If Ruth ever recruited extra help, she'd hold first-aid classes to teach parents.

On her way home, she'd come across a road collision and had given CPR to the taxi driver before arranging another taxi to get the driver and injured passengers to the hospital.

It had been like that since then—one patient after another, including a woman they'd admitted to the clinic for two nights. Suffering intense pain from a kidney stone, she hadn't felt confident leaving the clinic until it passed.

That, and two labor deliveries, one with a complication. The baby's breathing wasn't stable, and Ruth had to arrange for Dongo's help to get the mom and baby to the hospital.

Ruth lowered her phone to her lap and closed her eyes against the sting in her chest. No texts from Brady. She'd received his text for his arrival. Despite the chaos, she'd called him twice, and the phone went to voicemail. She'd also texted him while waiting in the hospital.

She scrolled her thumb to call him, then sat up straighter. She'd missed a call from him!

A bit of laughter slipped out. Good thing Brady had bought her two years' worth of phone airtime when they spent the day at the resort.

Her hands shook a bit as she hit the callback button and pushed the phone tight to her ear. With the rain pounding the roof, hearing him would be a challenge.

One ring.

Two.

Three.

She held her breath. The line answered, and she sat up straighter. "Hi!"

"You've reached Brady Sharp...."

His voice mail message played. The phone on the other end made a flatline sound just as it thundered and the room went dark. "Hello." Could she still leave a message? "It's Ruth... Ruthie."

The message probably hadn't gone through.

She checked New York time—one p.m. He had to be working, just like she'd been when he called her as he'd promised.

She lay back on the sofa, her feet dangling over the armrest. The blackout should make it easier for her to go to bed. Instead, she slid her hand to the loveseat cushion, all too aware of the time he'd sat on the seat during the blackout.

She could still smell him in her tiny house, picture him walking on the same floor, imagine his muscular body sprawled on this seat. Wow, she should be in bed so she could smell him on her pillow. She may seem mad, but it would be a while before she washed the pillowcase.

Enough of the dreaming. She rose and lit the lantern before calling Ivan's brother.

She imagined how happy Ivan would be to hear they had the money to get him to the doctor. He'd also be glad to know he got a phone. Brady had left his phone for Ruth since it was fancier than hers. So she was passing hers on to Ivan.

"The number you've called can't be reached at this time." The line cut off.

It wasn't the right day to make calls. She plodded to her bed to pray. She knelt, pouring out her heart to God, then climbed into bed and refused to savor the sweet scent on her pillowcase.

It didn't work. The smell encased her, smothered her, drowned her. And she lay there enjoying every second of it. Then came the thoughts—Brady, her future, and her plans to go to the city soon to get the photos developed and inquire about applying for a passport.

IT RAINED THE REST of the week, offering an hour or two-hour interval breaks. Because of the downpour, the clinic walk-in traffic slowed. Ruth used the free time to look up the passport office, the applications, and their requirements. She called Ivan's brother's number, and the phone wasn't on.

Almost the same thing with Brady's number she'd called twice. One time, he answered and spoke for less than one minute—he'd been in a meeting. When he called her back, she'd spoken for less than two minutes—she was tending to a patient. It hadn't even been a month, yet their long-distance relationship was already challenging. He was busy running a company, so his unreturned texts weren't a brush-off. Brady wasn't like that.

On one of the slow mornings the following week, Eunice insisted Ruth get the photos developed. "Now would be a good time to look at those memories while we're not busy."

They *could* both use something better to look at. She the most, now that she couldn't hear Brady's voice. He'd taken the picture from their rafting trip, saying she had their pictures on the camera and he had none. Oddly, they hadn't taken a single picture with their phones—first from conserving the battery power, then later from habit.

"Don't forget this." Eunice handed Ruth their red umbrella as she walked out of the clinic.

"Thanks."

With the gloomy sky hanging over her, she avoided the shortcut, too aware of the muddy trail during the rainy season. The midmorning made it easy for her to hitch a taxi.

She got her pictures developed. Just in case it rained and she was on the street, she needed to keep the pictures dry. She double bagged them and slid them in the utility bag she'd brought.

She took a boda boda to the passport office, where they also took passport photos.

On her way back to the taxi park, a yellow sign among the many shops flashed KK's Internet Café. Although Brady paid enough airtime for her to have data, Ruth hadn't figured out how to add an email to it. Maybe she could email Brady. Why not? She had an email account she rarely used, and although she didn't have his email address, if she looked up his company's name, she'd find his contact information on the website.

She smiled at the thought, breathing in deeply. Thanks to the constant rain, the air smelled fresh. Her feet sped forward as she shuffled through the crowded street, ignoring vendors who flashed jewelry in her face to get her attention.

Inside, she retrieved the shillings from the bag and paid for twenty minutes of computer time. That should be enough to peruse Brady's portfolio and type up an email.

"Use Number 5." The heavyset woman clicked the keyboard to activate the computer.

"Thanks." Ruth scanned the room with dividers for each computer—most of which were occupied. There. Number 5, in the corner on the first row.

She clicked on the search engine and typed in Sharp Resorts.

Her body warmed when the top result showed Brady's picture. She clicked on it and took a few seconds to stare at his handsome face, sharp jawline, and blue eyes that could drown her more easily than any river-rafting adventure. She touched her warm cheeks, wishing he were here, or even a phone call away. How she longed to hear his voice. Was there a possibility they could talk on the phone for an hour instead of a minute?

The clock kept counting down. She only had thirteen minutes left. Had she been staring at him *that* long? She clicked back to the next link and read an article about New York's richest.

Brady Sharp of Sharp Resorts. It gave a bio of his company. A former broker before he founded Sharp Resorts.

Blinking, she stiffened when she scrolled through images of his resorts. Expansive pools, lavishly landscaped grounds, extremely tall and overly lit buildings in one compound. Oh my! If he had like forty-five of those and fit with New York's richest, what would he want with someone like her?

It was hard to believe he had lots of money, yet he'd been sleeping on the floor and splitting wood. If she'd known, she never would've agreed to take him to the remote village. Yet he'd never mentioned anything about his wealth. Ruth had suspected him to have money whenever he offered to buy and support her cause. But not that kind of money, not the kind to make internet articles.

Focus... She needed to get that email, only five minutes left. She'd probably pay more money to add extra time, so she clicked the arrow on the left corner to go back, needing to find a page for his website, instead of articles. As she scrolled, a headline glared at her.

Brady Sharp and Violet Saben. Dating?

Ruth's fingers shook as she clicked on the link. Brady's picture, his smile striking as he walked beside a stunning woman with long blond hair. The glamorous party dress and fancy shoes fit Brady's class. Ruth tried to comfort herself—after all, he seemed to be staring at the camera more than his date. He wasn't looking at her with longing the way he'd looked at Ruth. She had to cling to that so she didn't lose her mind.

Her heart raced, guilt gnawed at her for snooping, but if he had another life he hadn't disclosed, she needed to know. Her gaze sped over the article below the picture.

Toys for Tots at Sharp International Hotel, New York.

While rumored sightings of the two during the one-week toy drive abound, the pair hasn't made things official, but we've caught them on two dates...

The computer screen turned gray, just the way she felt. She could get more time and read the rest, but she'd read enough to torture herself. Her entire body shook as she gathered her bags and walked out.

She thought mzungus were better, thought they only fell in love with one woman. *They're all human. Sinful.*

Just as she approached the spacious taxi park, the rain started pouring, and she tipped her face to it, letting the gentle touch of God's raindrops caress her, cry for her. If it wasn't for the kids' pictures among the many in her hand, she'd let the rain wash away the threatening tears. She wasn't going to cry. She'd give Brady a chance to come clean, not even bring the picture up at all.

Ruth snapped open her umbrella as she squinted through several vendors and heads to find the sign with Entebbe taxis.

A man was shouting the towns where his taxi was going. "Nansana, Kisubi, Kajjansi."

"Kisubi?" she asked the skinny man holding the black umbrella. The man she assumed to be the conductor ran ahead of her and slid open the door, and Ruth squeezed in the last seat by the door. Slightly damp from the rain, she wrapped her hands around her bags and held her breath. The conductor was standing with his smudged armpit right above her head, but her mind quivered in all sorts of dark corners.

She welcomed the rain and fresh air when she stepped out of the taxi. The wind blew her umbrella, and rain slapped on her face as she sprinted through the mud, and her flats got stuck.

Mud was the least of her worries. She needed to mask her feelings from Eunice. She'd eventually tell her, maybe after she confirmed with Brady.

"Oh my!" Eunice glanced at the shoe in her hand when she slogged up the clinic veranda.

"I don't want to bring mud in the house."

Eunice took the bags and handed her a one-gallon jerry can of water. Ruth poured the water over her feet before she walked to the back and grabbed a towel. She needed a shower, a cool shower to numb her tattered spirit.

By the time she'd showered and changed, Eunice was browsing through the photos. "Sorry, I was too anxious to wait." She glanced Ruth's way before she saw the picture of the village kids playing football. She started shuffling through the rest of the photos. "Did you guys take any pictures of just the two of you?"

Ruth didn't want to think about Jinja, and neither did she want to talk about her revelation. "Those will be at the bottom."

Enthralled, Eunice bounced in her chair and patted the stool across from her. "I'll need you to give me a replay of the moment of each picture."

Ruth's patience was the reason she was a nurse, and needing a distraction from Brady, she felt an urgent pull to call Ivan. She'd ignored that feeling when she woke up, but before she could put things off any further, she held up a hand. "I need to try calling Ivan's brother again."

"I'm starting to think his brother switched phones." Eunice flipped to another picture, grinning at whatever she saw.

Ruth had only called Ivan twice to follow up after he left her clinic. "I wish I knew where he lived." Going to his house must be easier than playing phone tag.

"Ooh…" Eunice gushed, her voice all swoony. "Hurry and come tell me about this one."

How was she to tell Eunice that she and Brady had been a dream? Just like the movies were fantasy, so were Ruth and Brady.

Ruth leaned against the wall as she dialed the number, doubting the phone would be on. "Hmm?"

The phone rang.

"Hello?" A man's raspy voice sounded after the third ring.

Ruth wanted to ask why his phone hadn't been on for the last week, but she'd ask Ivan, not a stranger she'd never met. "I'm Ivan's nurse. May I speak with him?"

The man was quiet for so long she thought he'd hung up on her. "Ruth?"

She smiled, sagging a little against the wall behind her. "Yes." What had Ivan said about her to his quiet brother? He'd said he and his brother rarely spoke.

"I appreciate all the things you did for him—for us. He talked about you all the time—"

"Wait!" Did he just speak about Ivan in past tense? "What do you mean 'talked'? Is he—?"

"Died yesterday, in his sleep."

Ruth gripped the phone to her ear so it didn't slip from her shaky hands. The gloominess she saw through her window seemed darker, closer, realer.

"Hello?"

Right. She was still on the phone. She cleared the thick lump forming in her throat. "Hi."

No need to ask if he'd had any signs of dying that night because they had no idea, but she did. While she should've been around to tend to him, she'd been busy chasing after her dreams. She sniffled, her throat too tight to talk. "It's all my fault…"

Saying the words hurt her throat. Hearing them hurt her heart.

"Why would you say that? You were the one person he looked forward to seeing… Don't you see? You're the reason Ivan lived an extra year. Seeing you brought him joy and hope."

Whatever Paul said didn't make her feel any better. "When's the funeral?"

"His body is still in the house. I have no idea what to do with it."

From what Ivan had told Ruth, he and his brother had agreed to sell their parents' land in the village to start a business in the city. While Paul wanted to run an appliance shop, Ivan wanted to sell clothing. In the end, his younger brother insisted he had the best idea.

"Maybe I can help." She'd have to call her parents and see if they could let her bury Ivan in the family cemetery. The money that was supposed to help Ivan recover was going toward his funeral.

After getting directions to Paul's house, Ruth promised to call him once she made arrangements. Her parents might not get the phone message for another day, but she needed to start somewhere.

"Ruth!" Eunice called, but Ruth stilled against the wall, both hands to her head and her knees shaking.

"Are you okay?" Eunice's warm hand closed over Ruth's. A gentle tug led her to the love seat. "What happened?"

"Ivan…" Her shoulders shook while she rubbed her forehead. "I should have seen him last week. It's my fault."

"Ruth." Eunice patted a hand on her shoulder. "Ivan was one of the few lucky men to live that long, not many people here live to be seventy."

Her grandparents were still alive and strong, seventy-eight and counting, but she wouldn't say that to Eunice, who'd lost her parents at such a young age, and her grandparents before she was born.

So much was at stake. How could she not blame herself? If she'd been around when Ivan came to the clinic, maybe he'd be alive. Why didn't God keep him alive until he made it to the doctor? She rubbed her temples. Each pulse through them came loaded with questions for God, questions about everything. Her chest hurt, and her head shook.

THE GRACIOUS VILLAGE people had brought food and wood. Each family had sent a representative to stay the night. The women brought and cooked food while the men fetched water and split wood to cook through the two days.

Smoke hung thick in the air, and wiping her smoky eyes, Ruth walked around the huddled groups. She touched the women's shoulders and shook the men's hands, thanking them for their kindness to a stranger. She knelt before the village chief and thanked him again for blowing the emergency horn that alarmed people to show up at such short notice.

His dark eyes glowing, he took her shaky hands in his strong, callused ones. "Anything for you, Musawo." He squeezed his grip, then lifted a hand to cup her face and turned her eyes to his. "You look tired, sad. This makes me sad. You always take good care of our community. Any friend of yours is our family."

She ducked her head, half-afraid he would ask where her mzungu was, but he merely patted her cheek and let her go. So she walked toward Paul to say goodbye as he sat on a boulder staring at the banana plantation. "Your boda boda should be here soon."

He jerked upon hearing her voice. "You have a nice village here." He rubbed his hands on his dress pants. "Nice community."

"The people are nice." Knowing the history of selling their land, she kept a light tone. "But it's hard to chase your dream if you're stuck in the village."

In the brief silence, his jaw clenched. Clearing his throat, he said, "Thanks again for giving Ivan a proper burial. The service was nice." He ran a hand over his bald head. "Ivan would've liked this village."

"I hope so."

Rubbing his forehead, he chuckled bitterly. "I was... I was a terrible brother." He blew out a breath. "I could've done better for him."

Ruth still struggled with how to be a better sister to her siblings. "We all make mistakes, but..."

"When my girlfriend moved in, things changed..." He trailed off about his irritation sharing space with Ivan in the one-room apartment while he had a girlfriend.

"The woman took all the money from the shop last month and ran off, and the shop is not stocked up." His shoulders sagged, his dark face almost turning purple where the brows knitted together. He stood and clenched his fist. "How can I go back and fix things with my brother?"

If only Ruth knew the right words! She touched his fisted hand. "You can't change the past, just start doing better. Today is a new day, a new chance." She shrugged. "You can't do anything without God's help."

"Ivan said things like that. These last three months, he spoke of how you told him about Jesus. He kept saying if he died he was going to live with Jesus forever."

Praise God! Maybe something good had happened with Ivan's spiritual journey.

"He was always happiest when he talked about your conversations with Him. About Jesus this, and God providing that." Paul nodded and leaned against the tree trunk. "That's why I'm not too worried about Ivan, just worried about the time I lost."

And then Ruth knew what to do with the money left over from Ivan's hospital fund. She reached for the envelope from her skirt pocket and handed it to him. "You'll need to pay rent." It was enough to pay for an entire year, but he'd figure something out by then. "I wish I had a job to offer you."

She also handed him the phone she retrieved from her other pocket. "I was going to give this to him."

He smiled. "Thank you." It was rude to unwrap a gift in front of the giver. So he thrust the envelope into his pants pocket. He then glanced at the phone in his hands.

"My phone was giving me a hard time." He shook Ruth's hand, his smile wide. "Another way I can honor my brother is to check out the church he'd been inviting me to go to with him."

You hear that, God? "That's a good place to start." Ruth looked up to the dark-gray clouds as a motorcycle engine revved into the yard. "Your boda boda is here—that's if you don't mind riding in the rain."

"It would be cleansing if it rained on." He fell in step with her. "If the city doesn't work out for me, I might come and retire in this village."

"You heard my dad."

"The harvest is plenty, and the workers are few."

"Exactly."

Paul said goodbye to Ruth's family and thanked them for their hospitality. Thankfully, it being a funeral, the men had built two temporary straw shelters. Men slept in one shelter and women in the other. So the people didn't crowd their small house.

With a final lift of her hand, she closed her eyes and thanked God for how the funeral turned out. Even the rain had stopped for three hours during the pastor's farewell words before they'd buried Ivan.

Meters away, her family bid the locals goodbye. People gathered their belongings, rushing before they could get caught in the rain.

Whenever she left the village, she intended to take the advice she'd given.

Not to stress over mistakes. She'd wasted time in a fairy tale about a mzungu. It had been good while it lasted. She needed to start over and stay focused. No more distractions. Now that Brady had gone back to his world, she needed to get back to hers.

CHAPTER 18

Brady leaned back in his leather chair and massaged his throbbing temples. His morning meeting had gone as he'd expected—unsuccessfully. He'd lost two investors after he took the board's advice to sell the four properties with low return on investment. Two years was too long not to see a profit. He'd done the right thing. He had to remind himself.

He ran a hand over his weary face as he voiced a silent prayer for his former employees. *Please help those people find work soon.*

The Wise Corporation intended to turn his four former resorts into luxury vacation homes. That meant his employees wouldn't be hired at the facilities set for demolition.

After Beth communicated his delayed trip in Uganda, the board passed on the information to the investors who'd been anxiously awaiting his return.

The muscle in his jaw twitched. He'd wasted time trying to meet a higher financial goal that wasn't going to happen. He pushed back his chair and crossed the plush carpet to the window. From the ninety-second floor, he could see clouds darkening the New York skyline. He'd been too busy lately to take in the serenity through the window.

Although he was too high to see them from here, people would be bundled as they walked on the streets. The few trees had started changing color, an indication that New York's fall was rolling in and bringing frigid air.

A loss. He hated losses. He drew in a breath, grateful for the forty-one properties he still had. That, and this office building he'd bought five years ago. It provided a steady income from commercial tenants. He could guarantee he'd never have to worry about selling it.

I'm sorry, Lord. It felt as if he'd already forgotten his two weeks in Uganda. Two weeks of peace that helped him get back on track to his faith—Ruth.

Now, almost two weeks of working day and night, writing proposals, meeting with current and potential investors was trying to rob him of that destination. Meetings with his management teams and board of directors further waylaid him.

He'd slept in his office twice last week, and honestly, he was ready to take things as they came. Except he hadn't heard from Ruth. One-minute chats to tell each other they'd call back didn't count. Since she wasn't on social media, they needed to figure out how to communicate. They had to stay in touch more often. Otherwise, their romance could dwindle.

His cell phone rang, and in two long strides, he was back to his mahogany desk to grab it. Maybe it was Ruth. His heart quickened, but one glance to the screen eliminated his brief elation.

Dad. He only called when he heard of Brady's business mishaps. No doubt Dad had read the *New York Times* about him selling to the Wise Corporation. On rare occasions, his name made it into the *Times*, or he had his penthouse mentioned in *Forbes* as one of the best homes in Manhattan.

He drew in deep breaths, preparing the facade he put on for his dad's unpredictable conversations, but today, he was in no mood to be reminded of his wrong career choice. So he set down the phone. It could go to voicemail.

The office phone lit up, and his assistant spoke through the speaker. "It's your dad."

Beth didn't know his edgy relationship with his dad—likely never would. "Put him through."

I can do this. He breathed in and out and lifted the receiver. "Hel-lo." He rubbed his forehead at the reddened scar from his accident.

"Everything okay?" Dad's gruff voice heralded the coming "I told you so."

"Of course." *Why wouldn't it be?* Asking that wouldn't help. "How's work?" That should be a safer topic.

"So you decided to sell?"

Yep, there it was.

"Just wanted to see if you're okay."

Whoa. Brady's mouth slid open, and he pressed the back of his neck. Did he hear right?

"You still have the other forty-one thriving. You should be proud of yourself."

Who was the man on the other end of the line?

"Uh..." What was he supposed to say to this... stranger?

"I'm proud of you." Those magic words massaged the tension from his shoulders.

"Even if I'm not an attorney?"

"I still think you should've taken the easy side of things." Dad chuckled. "You're just like your mom. Risk-takers."

"Thanks," Brady whispered, almost too overwhelmed to form the word.

Was his dad holding something else from him? What if this was the last conversation they'd have? "Still up for tennis on Thursday?"

"Counting on it."

They met once a month in San Diego at one of Sharps' country clubs. San Diego was far for both of them, but Dad enjoyed getting away from Virginia and hanging out at Brady's beachfront home.

Even though their conversations didn't go deep, Brady still loved spending time with him, still hoped to bond. Dad mostly asked about Mom and if she was seeing anyone. Either way, his dad's words had still caught him off-guard. "Is everything okay?"

Dad cleared his voice before speaking. "Listen, I've had lots of time to think about all I could've done to keep my marriage... and family intact. Long story short, I want to be a better dad. I blew things with your mom already..."

Whoa. Dad was taking the blame? He'd never done so. What made him so vulnerable now? Brady searched for anything to say how relieved he was to hear his genuine confession.

"By the way, have you heard from your mom lately?"

"I've been in Uganda for two weeks." Maybe he'd forgotten.

"I thought you talked every night?"

For the most part, they did. Brady sat up straighter in his chair. Did Dad feel about Mom the way Brady felt about Ruth? Did the lack of communication hurt Dad like it was hurting him? "Why don't you call her?" Brady let his voice go soft, encouraging so it wouldn't step on Dad's pride. "Otherwise, you'll have to wait until Thanksgiving to ask her yourself."

Mom still invited Dad, Brady, and his brother for the holidays. They obviously both cared for each other, if they could get past their issues and make sacrifices.

"I'll wait. See you Thursday."

"See you."

When Brady hung up, his thumb scrolled his cell for Ruth's number.

"Got a minute?" Beth peeked her head in. Her graying hair slid over her shoulder before she shook the tight ponytail back in place. When he nodded, she sat on the leather chair across from his desk. "You got a call from Uganda."

Ruth. He gripped the desk edge. Maybe she'd looked up the office number online. "Did she leave a message?"

"She?" Beth lifted a brow. "Is there someone you didn't tell me about?"

He shrugged, not ready to discuss her. "Who called?"

"It's about the resort. They want you to call back."

Had they reconsidered?

Beth handed him the blue sticky note of the property lawyer's phone number, and he was punching in the digits on the landline as she closed the door behind her.

"Mr. Sharp."

Brady grimaced at the enthusiastic voice. Its volume normally didn't bother him. He normally didn't have a headache. "If you're still interested, the resort's all yours."

He leaned back in his chair. "What do you mean?"

"The previous buyer had some failings with their loan."

Just like that? "Of course I am." With Ruth in Uganda, he had further reason to seek investments in her country. "Except I can't come for another meeting." Like last time.

"Your presence is not needed this time. I told them about your accident..."

The pain in his head was almost gone. Either that, or the lawyer's excitement had overtaken him.

"One more thing, since you're not a citizen—"

"I can't be a property owner until I lease for at least forty-nine years." He'd learned that before his first attempt to buy.

When he hung up the phone, Brady closed his eyes and lifted his hands. "Thank You, Lord!"

How could this be? This could push him to the ten-figure window by next year. If he had the right team in place. Leasing versus ownership. He tapped his fingers to his temples as he calculated the best possible ROI. What if he bought the resort for Ruth? Put it in her name.

That wouldn't close his gap to ten figures. But she could save that money to help the needy. It would be their money—God's money, and not Sharp Resorts'.

He had a lot to pray about tonight. Wisdom was all he needed.

He'd better have some answers when he met with the board. First things first, Ruth needed to hear. He rubbed his hands together, then loosened his tie and reached for the landline's headset.

She was the first person he wanted to tell. Not the board or his dad or anyone else.

He rocked back in his chair, crossing one leg over the other. Hard to believe he didn't have her number memorized after thinking of calling her so often. Slipping the headset over his ear, he reached for his cell phone to hunt up the number.

Whoa.

Both feet slammed to the floor as he sat up straight and his heart constricted. There'd been *four* missed calls from her. *What?*

How come he hadn't seen a missed call?

The eight-hour time difference didn't make their communication any easier.

He leaned over the landline phone and punched in the numbers two, five, and six—the Ugandan code—before the rest of the digits for Ruth's cell phone. Grinning, he rocked back in his chair again as he listened to the first ring. She hadn't responded to his text because she hadn't gotten it. That's all.

His heart raced as the second ring turned to the third. He bounced his knee at the fourth ring, then released a huff as a British accent spoke. "The telephone number you've called is not set up for voice messages. Please, call again later."

Ruth probably had a patient. He nestled the receiver back on its bed. *There goes that.* He let his fingers trace the scar on his forehead, deflated instead of rejoicing about the resort.

He then remembered the cabin in Mabira Forest. He'd meant to call them last week. He found the business card and dialed the number. The manager himself answered. It must be his cell phone.

Brady identified himself and mentioned staying there two weeks ago. Even if the place could use some improvements, he started with the positives and how he liked it. He then got to the reason for his call. "When I came to Uganda, I visited this village..." The people's faces marched through his mind as he raved about their amazing talents and beautiful crafts. "I was wondering if the villagers could have some of their handmade gifts in your gift shop? It could help support their—"

"Sir," the manager interrupted. "I'm not the one to speak to. The place will be under new management. It's going up for sale."

Whoa! Interesting. "Is it already sold?"

"Not yet. They have some interested parties. I don't know the details."

Brady knew someone who could find out.

That place had potential. If he renovated it and built more huts and added a spacious hotel, it could pull in more tourists—especially if he boosted its media attention. All the funds could go toward Ruth's village medical clinic. The villagers could still sell their crafts in the gift shop if they wanted.

"Thanks so much for your time." His heart was racing, and his head throbbed when he slammed down the phone and reached for the property lawyer's number again. *Breathe! Breathe, buddy. Don't get too excited!*

After he'd called the lawyer and forwarded Beth all the information she needed to pass onto the board and schedule meetings, his cell phone rang.

"Ruthie..." Her name whispered past his lips, all the weeks of yearning slipping out when he heard her soft voice. Longing quivered through him, the excitement he'd felt moments ago nothing compared to this. He'd trade it all to see her beautiful face and smile.

"We..."

"I..."

He laughed as they spoke at the same time. Relaxing into his seat, he waved a hand as if she could see him gesturing her ahead. "You first."

She gave a soft chuckle. Perhaps he wasn't used to hearing her voice through the phone, but the laugh seemed off. "We keep missing each other's calls."

"We've been playing phone tag."

She told him how rainy it'd been since he'd left, and as they talked about spontaneous things, he learned she didn't get his texts, except the first one he'd sent to let her know he'd arrived. She'd sent him texts too, but he didn't get any.

"Thanks for the flowers."

Her flat tone made him miss her more. She'd been so full of hope, so giving of herself, not just to everyone else, but also to him. She'd held nothing back with formalities. So why did she sound stiff now? Was it just the way she spoke on the phone? Was it because he couldn't see her mobile mouth or shining eyes?

He rubbed the scar again—seemed he did it when thinking of her. "They reminded me of you... of Uganda."

He'd ordered flowers three days ago, after researching what florist shop in Entebbe knew the Blessings Clinic and would deliver them. Unlike the US, most homes and businesses in Uganda didn't have physical addresses. You had to have a good sense of direction to find your way somewhere.

"I have so much to say..."

He gripped the front of his chair, resting one forearm on the table. "I've missed you so much, Ruthie!" He wanted to tell her so much, yet he had no idea where to start. He could ask her to pray about the resort or the Mabira Forest cabin. But knowing how important her patients were to her, and remembering the old man she'd been worried about, he held off. "Was Ivan able to see the doctor?"

She drew in a long breath. "Ivan... died."

He winced and gripped the back of his stiffened neck. She must've taken that hard. He made sure to keep his voice soft. "Did he not make it through the surgery?"

"One week after you left." She spoke of his sudden death in his sleep, then sniffled. "It rained so much, and I didn't call him when I should've. I should've been there when he came by and wanted to see me, but I was on vacation and then..."

He ached to take her in his arms and comfort her, assure her she'd done nothing wrong. Instead, he somehow had to do it with an ocean and a continent between them. "It's not your fault. It's gut-wrenching that he died before going to the hospital, but you did your best, Ruthie. You have to know there's nothing else you could have done to stop his death."

"I shouldn't have stayed on vacation so long."

In other words, it was his fault she'd stayed on vacation. His jaw clenched. If she felt like this over a few days off, how would she ever make a life with him? "Ruth, I don't want you—"

"I didn't do my best."

How could he convince her God was pleased with her work? "You shouldn't feel accountable for people's deaths."

"How can I not!"

As her sharp words slapped him across the face, he almost dropped the phone.

"What's the point of praying for someone—for *something*—when God's going to do what He already intended to do?"

Tingles lifted the hairs on his neck and arms. She couldn't be doubting God, not the woman who helped him rekindle his faith. "Ruthie, you can't prevent people from dying." She was an intelligent woman, one of the most intelligent he'd ever met. So she knew that—*in her head*—but she was thinking with her heart now. He ached for what she was going through, but she needed to know some things were out of her control. "God's got this."

"Does He?"

The words hung between them.

His heart twisted. How he hated not being there to comfort her while she was hurting! But he was not a counselor or pastor, so he had to choose his words carefully.

"When were you going to tell me about Violet?"

"Who?" Her sudden shift flickered a faint recollection. "What do you mean?"

"I saw a picture of you and her. A toy drive or something."

"Oh... that." He almost chuckled, but Ruth wouldn't find it funny. "The fact that I can barely remember her face says there's nothing to tell."

"You date a model, and you don't think it's necessary to tell me?"

"I worked with her for the Christmas event she ran at one of my hotels. She asked me out to dinner, maybe liked me, but I wasn't interested." Not in a model, anyway. How was the article still on the internet after four—or was it five—years? No reason to tell her Violet had asked him out to more than one date and he'd declined. "I was too busy enjoying my time with you to remember a woman who had no effect on me years ago." Violet was attractive, but he hadn't been drawn to her for more reasons than her celebrity status. "She and I, it's a rumor."

"Why did the article say you're dating?"

Okay, this conversation was draining the joy out of him. He'd been looking forward to catching up with her, *not* delving into his past. He ran a hand through his hair. "You can't believe everything you read on the internet. If we're going to do this long-distance thing, you have to trust me just like I trust you. Otherwise, there's no sense in trying."

She didn't answer right away, and he held his breath, waiting. Then the softest sound came through the speaker. He almost imagined feeling a puff of air kiss his face.

"You were right. You're set there, and I'm here. I don't think a long-distance relationship will work out."

Whoa! No way!

He slammed his feet to the floor and sprang from his chair—where was he going anyway? He had no idea.

"Ruthie!" She wasn't breaking up with him before he had a chance to invest in their relationship. He cradled the phone to his ear as if he were holding her hand. "I *want* this. I didn't think it would work out, but after spending time with you..." Witnessing her selflessness and compassion for others. "You made me see things differently. I fell in love with you..."

Every bit of him desperate, he moved to the east-facing window, trying not to imagine the miles between them. Somewhere beyond that ocean, she was sitting on a little blue loveseat. And he needed to be there with her. "I want—"

A crackling interrupted him, followed by a flatline. He slammed the phone against his thigh and clenched his jaw. He hadn't finished. He needed to tell her that, whenever he had a moment to breathe, she was all he thought about. He dialed her number again, but only got a static sound. Could rain in Uganda be interfering with their call?

The headache had intensified, throbbing worse than ever. He'd better go home, take an Advil, and go to bed.

Telling Ruth about the resort would have to wait until he set her at ease. Violet! How had something like that interfered with his relationship with Ruthie?

He grabbed his coat, checked the pocket for his wallet and keys, before he walked out. At least, he could share the good news with Eric Stone when he met with him in San Francisco tomorrow. His friend was the right person to talk to—about both the business and charity. Whether Ruth meant what she said or not, Brady would fund her cause.

"I THINK THE SPEED LIMIT is forty-five, not twenty," Brady teased his friend and business mentor as they drove one of the back-country roads outside San Francisco.

"Brady... Brady." Eric shook his head. He'd lost weight, ever since his wife and ten kids died. Although his friend tried to keep the spark in his hazel eyes, a pain lurked there, buried deep for dark nights—nights when he called Brady to talk about a missed birthday, an anniversary, or a fresh encounter with a memory. "I take it your trip to Uganda didn't teach you about slowing down?"

Brady had learned a lot during the two weeks in the foreign land. But it wasn't the trip that taught him—it was Ruth. God had used an amazing woman. "A missed flight can teach you a lot of things."

Eric kept his gaze on the narrow road they'd taken since they left the dealership with a 2018 Bentley. Brady had shown up at Eric's office, and his friend's driver dropped them off at the dealership. Despite the tragic events in his life, nothing had shaken Eric's faith in God. He was still taking care of the needy. Sponsoring several hospitals and orphanages throughout the world made him travel abroad weekly.

"Things like?" Eric approached things a lot differently from the billionaires Brady had met. Being humble and a great listener earned him many friends, except most assumed he had far too many close confidants and never got to know him better.

Brady had thought so when he'd reunited with him at an entrepreneur's conference. He'd sought out Eric because he was one of the most successful businessmen with financial advisor firms throughout the country. Their business meetings only served to strengthen their friendship, and then Brady learned he was one of the few close friends Eric had.

"Tell me more about this nurse." The car bounced when Eric drove over a bump. "Those baskets you gave me were something else. Did you say she lives in the village?"

"She runs a clinic in the city, earns minimal money, and then goes to her village to treat the locals." Brady loosened his tie. Just talking about Ruth warmed his blood. "With all the orphanages and NGOs you run, you'd better give me some advice on how to help start a hospital in Uganda."

"And you still don't think God had a reason for your missed flight?" Eric pulled over to let the car behind them pass.

"At first I didn't, but after I met Ruth, I just knew..."

Eric put the car in park. The green valley below awoke memories of Ruth's village. A knot tightened Brady's stomach. "I don't know how to deal with long-distance relationships."

"Why do I get the feeling she's more than a friend?"

Brady's head jerked up. Had he said that out loud?

Eric had the seat pulled back and his hands crossed as if they'd arrived at their destination.

"Why are we parked?"

"This conversation requires my full attention." He always took his driving seriously and rarely went past the speed limit. Even before losing his family. "Let's start with the long-distance part."

"Yeah?"

"If you're determining your dating based on the location of your business, you may need to come up with a better excuse. "

Brady scratched his jaw. "It's not an excuse."

"You can live anywhere and run your business. Put the rest of your properties in franchise, or sell some. Invest in another country."

Like Ruth said in one of their conversations, wealth was only important if you shared with others, in his case to invest in others. Perhaps this was why he was working and God was using him to make a difference. "I might make more money from franchising and management fees than ownership."

"Exactly."

He hadn't entertained the idea of franchising. Why hadn't it crossed his mind? "I'll look into that."

"About dating." Eric gave him a knowing look. "If you ever want to get married, you might want to join the club real soon. You're not getting any younger."

"Whoa. Thanks for the reminder, Dad."

Eric laughed. "Okay, talk to me. Tell me more about this Ruth."

If he was going to tell anyone about his love life—or anything else—Eric was the man. His mom too, but with the way Ruth had concluded on the phone, he had nothing exciting to share.

His hand strayed to the scar on his forehead. It probably wasn't even visible in the mirror, but he could still feel it. Still feel her tending it. "That motorcycle accident I told you about..."

Brady drew in a deep breath, needing it as he told Eric how Ruth rescued him from the roadside, nurtured him back to health, and joined him during his extended vacation after he missed a flight. As he spoke, his words convicted him with her love for God and how it had challenged his faith. Eric had always challenged Brady to draw near to God, but he'd been too busy to let the words sink in.

"She's so different. I feel like I've known her my whole life." He kept his gaze over the valley as he told Eric about her passion for her job, her ability or curse of taking her patients' burdens upon herself. "She lost a patient recently, and she blames herself."

He stared down at his hands. "She's having doubts about God—about our relationship."

Eric was silent, his eyes closed in meditation, the way he did when he gave thought to something. "Everyone mourns differently."

He opened his eyes and rubbed a hand over his shaven jaw. "Give her some time and call her again. Don't try to give her advice on how to mourn, what she should and shouldn't say. Try to understand her struggles with her shaken faith—and more importantly, *pray*."

Brady grimaced. He'd tried to tell her not to blame herself. Talking to God was his only hope with Ruth. "Guess it wouldn't hurt to pray."

"Why didn't you get that picture taken off the internet?"

Seriously? Some gossip half a decade ago? Brady shrugged. "Never thought it would come back to haunt me. I never even look at the gossip articles, and it shouldn't have been a problem for her. I don't think she realized how old it was or even noticed it was from Christmas, not now."

"Seems to me Ruth still loves you. She's also aware of God's sovereignty, but when you're hurting, it shakes your confidence and faith in God."

Except for Eric. At least in Brady's presence, he'd never heard his friend blame God for taking his family.

"The circumstances of how you met show God's hand at work—that's the kind of relationship meant to last forever." Eric pulled his seat forward and started the car. "About the hospital, I have some people I'd like you to meet. In the meantime, I'll direct half the winter fundraisers toward your charity."

Eric fastened his seat belt, and the ease with which Eric presented the news awed Brady.

He cleared his throat. "I don't want to impose on your donations."

Eric drove with his eyes fixated on the road. "We've already met next year's financial goal. Plus, there's no imposing when it comes to God's work. We have enough donors always passionate about a new hospital built in a third-world country."

He thought of the hospital fundraiser he attended in Colorado for the last three years. Eric founded the hospital where Brady's childhood friends, Ryan and Lucas, worked. Brady grinned, thinking of seeing them again.

"By the way, tell your mom I'll be having Christmas in Colorado this year," Eric said.

How could his friend be talking about the holidays already? Eric had spent the last two Thanksgivings and Christmases with Brady's family, or at least Brady had dragged Eric there, since he didn't want him spending the holidays alone. "That's a long time from now."

"The sooner I let her know, the less disappointed she will be."

"She'll be disappointed to not have anyone challenge Dad in chess."

Sadness etched across Eric's brows. "My parents are ready to see me."

Eric hated lingering on bitter memories, so Brady changed the subject as they neared a few abstract buildings.

"Why did you buy a Bentley for the old man, again?"

"The man almost died six months ago. I don't think his restaurant would earn him a Bentley any time soon."

He'd bought the expensive car to support a used-car dealership, as he blessed the dad of one of his employees with the gift.

Brady testified Eric's generosity, and it wouldn't surprise him if Eric insisted they have lunch at the local diner to support the man's business where he was parking the car.

CHAPTER 19

Brady signed the last paper and handed it to Beth. "As soon as you fax this, you can go home." She'd worked overtime the last two weeks. He'd put up some of his properties for franchise. The board had been busy negotiating what properties would be more profitable under franchise, and evaluating possible candidates.

"It's my job to make sure you go home before I do." She stuck the papers in a manila folder.

"Don't worry. I won't sleep in the office." Not since his property lawyer had told him he knew the owner of the forest lodge and Brady was the most serious buyer out of the three contenders.

Beth pushed back her chair and stood. "Do I get to meet Ruth before Christmas?"

Brady nearly groaned. Trust Beth not to let the matter rest. Too bad Ruth's name slipped out that day. That handmade salad bowl and spoon he'd given Beth from Uganda had further heightened her curiosity, and he'd eventually talked about Ruth and his time with her family.

There wasn't much to say now. He was still hopeful he could mend things, somehow assure her she was the only woman for him. He'd been tempted to shower her with presents to apologize, but Ruth would resent the money "wasted." Acting like that would only terrify her into believing she wasn't his type. So he'd sent flowers and chocolate instead.

He arched his eyebrow. "If my memory serves me right, isn't October when you start writing that four-page Christmas letter?"

Beth chuckled and walked toward the frosted glass door. "I'll make it five pages this year. I have to add my boss's trip to Africa."

Despite the many things he had to do, Brady always read Beth's Christmas essays about her new cats, and each grandchild's sweet antics, growth, and accomplishments. "I'll not read it, then."

She wagged a finger. "Don't stay late." Her words bounced off her back as she closed the door.

No way was he staying late. Not when they'd earned an hour off early after the news of properties from abroad. He intended to call Ruth when he got home.

It had been two weeks since his time with Eric. Surely, two weeks was long enough for the space Ruth needed to mourn her patient.

The flowers he'd sent had contained his only communication, but he needed to know if she was still interested in him. They needed to clear the fog from their relationship.

He opened the desk drawer and retrieved the picture of them. As he touched her face, memories of their rafting filled his mind. He could almost hear the rapids echo in his ears. It felt as if it were yesterday. How she'd been nervous but trusted him when he assured her she'd be safe. He touched her face again. She'd been so cute and shy when she'd first worn a swimsuit. Rafting, swimming, and all the firsts he'd shared with her created a deep connection between them—a connection he didn't want internet gossip to sever.

Brady set back the picture in the drawer. It should be in his house, but he spent more hours at the office than at home. He called his town car driver before closing his laptop and zipping it in the bag. He'd resume work tomorrow.

When he got home, the front desk buzzed him for his care package and mail. Familiar handwriting swirled over the white box.

Anticipation took over, his hands shaking when he traced the sender's name. Ruth Kirabo.

He needed to be comfortable when he opened this. He went through the hallway before making it to his living room and loosening and yanking off his tie.

This kind of mail might require pacing, so he walked to the kitchen and set the box on the counter, then sat on the barstool.

As he struggled to rip open the box, he shook his head. He'd thought he was saving time not reaching for a knife. He grabbed one now to speed things up. The box surrendered.

He started with an envelope on top of random items, then unfolded the pink paper from inside it, smiling at Ruth's familiar writing. For a nurse, she had good penmanship.

My dearest Brady,

I hope you're well. I wish I could apologize in person or on the phone instead of in a letter. Not only is it hard to get in touch with you, but also I tend to get tongue-tied on the phone, forgetting what I wanted to say.

I'm sorry I wasn't nice to you when we last spoke. I was scared and let my emotions get the best of me. I trust you. Pretend my last call never existed. I need you in my life, and I'm willing to date long distance since that's all we can do right now.

I got my passport and will wait until God enables me to come and be with you. That is—if you can forgive me. I've had so much time to research how to get a visa, to pray, and to think. I'll do whatever it takes for us to be together again.

I know one thing—I will never love anyone but you.

Remember when I told you I wrote down three things I prayed for?

His pulse raced. He remembered everything she'd told him and almost every conversation they shared. One night in the village, they'd sat up by the fire after everyone had gone to bed. She told him about praying to start her clinic, and another clinic in the village. "I will tell you the third thing someday, God willing," she'd said.

He glanced back to the paper in his hand.

> I wanted to tell you the third thing, face to face, but just in case I don't get the opportunity to see you....

> I prayed for God to drop a white man on my lap, a man who feared God. I prayed this mainly because I thought meeting one was impossible. I'll tell you someday why else I prayed for a white man. But I had given up praying until that morning before I found you on the roadside. I revisited my journal and saw my prayer request and decided to pray again. In other words, I prayed for you. I believe you're the man God dropped on my lap.

Brady smiled. His palms were suddenly moist, his heart racing. He was Ruth's first love,based on what she'd told him about her past dates. He touched the delicate print on the letter, trying to hear her voice as he read her sweet words, seeing her sitting at her table as she wrote.

> Whether we spend the rest of our lives together or not, I'm so glad you came into my life, because those ten days with you will always be the best moments in my life.

> I hope you enjoy the pictures. I made some scarves for you and your family since you told me you use them to accompany a winter coat. I hope they're warm enough.

With only two lines left on the page, she squeezed the remaining words onto them.

I love you.
Yours truly,
Ruthie

He raked a hand through his trimmed hair, missing her, wanting to get on a plane and tell her how much she meant to him.

But he wouldn't. He couldn't see her and leave her behind this time.

He spent the next hour looking through the pictures she had sent. Pictures of them in Jinja. Pictures of the village. Yes, he could hear the children's happy squeals behind their sweet smiles. Speaking of which, he needed to shop for soccer balls. Since Ruth didn't trust things to be safely delivered through the mail, she'd recommended FedEx or DHL, where she could go to their offices and pick up the items.

One of the pictures had a written note on the back—"The corn you helped plant."

Another was the cornfield with a note—"Dad hired people to harvest the corn, but it's been too rainy to plow the field." The once-tall stalks were flimsy, with no ears of corn sticking out. How clearly he remembered them running through the cornfield and getting lost. The rich red soil with all the sweet fruits. The mangoes he'd eaten while up in the tree.

A smile lifted the corners of his mouth, making him feel light and joyful all at once. He flipped through pictures of him zip lining through the thick forest and bungee jumping with a bird's-eye view of the Nile. Anyone would want to start a business in such a picturesque country. No wonder they called the place the pearl of Africa.

The pictures would boost the charity fundraisers next month and in December. But right now, he needed to call her. It was six p.m., so it was nighttime in Uganda. "What time is it in Uganda?" he asked his HomePod speaker on the long counter.

"Thanks for asking, Mr. Sharp. It is two a.m. in Uganda."

Even if she kept her phone on all night, he didn't need to disrupt her sleep. She would assume a patient was calling.

As anxious as he was to call her, he decided to shower. Then he ordered dinner from an African restaurant. *In honor of Ruth.*

For the first time in a long time, he knelt on his plush living room rug, thanking God for reconciling his relationship with Ruth, for helping his business succeed. "Even when I'm unfaithful, You've been faithful to me, God."

A surge of peaceful assurance embraced him as he closed his eyes to meditate on the times God saved him from entangling with Crane, the conniving businessman. The time he'd come close to losing the only three resorts he'd had then. He'd met Eric at a business seminar then. His friendship and support had pulled Brady up from the dungeon. That could have been the time for him to stick closer to God, but he'd drifted further. The blessing of bringing Ruth into his life. "God, please bless her and her family. Her patients and the many people in the village who need healing."

When his food arrived, he ate the rice and beef stew with collard greens in a hurry before he brought out his laptop.

If he wanted to see Ruth and never be separated from her, he needed to get busy. So he spent the next hours browsing the internet for homes in Uganda.

Several beach properties were listed at far less than the price of his penthouse.

He could buy twenty of them if he sold this place. Perhaps he'd move to Uganda temporarily.

It would be nice for Ruth to try out this pool before I sell the penthouse. For tonight, his mind wandered to Uganda. He could move there until Ruth trained workers to take her place so they could move back to the States. He laughed at his plan. God had a good sense of humor. During his first week in the country, it was the last place he pictured himself staying long term.

Ruth seemed to have more to lose than him. Lots of people would lose a dedicated health care provider if she left. Yet, in her letter, she was open to the possibility of making that sacrifice. Perhaps they could alternate to live in both countries.

He stayed up late, counting down the minutes for Ugandan time and planning so they could talk for an hour or so before she opened the clinic. If he normally stayed up late working, he could manage to wait to call her at midnight New York time—eight a.m. Uganda time, especially since the love of his life was the reason.

Love of his life. Had he ever come to that conclusion with anyone before? He felt like he had red hearts floating over his head as Ruth consumed his mind.

CHAPTER 20

Ruth trekked the damp trail as she followed her younger sister's heels to hitch a taxi. The gray morning sky held the promise of more coming rain. October was almost over. After another month of rain, sunshine would take over.

"Thank you again for having me this week." Susan's bob danced above her shoulders when she wagged her head. "Even if you made me cook and wash your laundry! I will not hold that against you."

Ruth stifled a chuckle, breathing hard as she caught up when they made it to the roadside. Random taxis whizzed past. She needed to lay some ground rules after three years of her sister's drama.

"Next time you have your marital arguments, you better go home." Ruth pushed her single braided twists from her face. With the rainy season, she'd finally gotten her hair braided. She'd also had time to research American visas and knit scarves for Brady's family. "I can't be caught up in the middle of your fights every other month."

"I'm not going back home to be the village gossip."

"Go to Zakaria's." Ruth shrugged. With everything going on, she'd needed Susan's drama to distract from her own. However, if she kept welcoming her whenever she fought with her husband, she could be encouraging her to act this way forever. "Or go to any of our other sisters."

Susan gave her a look as if she wasn't being reasonable. "You don't have a husband or kids."

Letting her sister's point sink in, Ruth took in a deep breath. As usual, she had to play the big sister. She lifted one finger. "You knew the man had a wife before you married him." She lifted another finger, counting off on them. "He spends five nights at your house, sometimes the entire week." She shook her head and added a third finger. "You can't run away whenever he goes to stay one night or two with his other wife."

Susan crossed her arms over her chest, rolling her eyes. "Why do I sense judgment coming my way?"

Ruth had advised her not to marry a married man, but her sister always had her own mind. She was so beautiful, smart, and well-spoken, yet she took her gifts for granted. Always the kid who broke out of the dorms to go to nightclubs. Even after skipping her final year of secondary school, Susan could succeed at a vocational institute if she tried. "I'm the one still single, so why would I judge a married—"

Susan stamped her fancy blue sandal. "Just because you have a mzungu doesn't mean you can tell me how to live my life."

Wow. Ruth didn't see that coming. "Since when do I ever tell you what to do?"

She swallowed back the rising heat burning her throat. Her parents were so optimistic about Brady, they'd told all her siblings she was courting.

Taxis kept driving past without slowing. Every bit of her wished for an empty taxi so she could get back to her house and cry out to God.

She opened her mouth to respond, then clamped her lips and took a sharp intake of breath. A moment passed before she looked at her sister again, Susan's furrowed brows in a dare for argument. Nope, not today. Ruth forced a calm tone. "You're twenty-seven." She needed to act like an adult. "Your kids are watching the way you behave."

Feeling the urge to take off and leave Susan alone, Ruth pushed her flip-flops deeper on the muddy ground. She was only doing this because she was accountable to God for the way she behaved. And for herself so Susan's remark didn't ruin her day. *Lord, this isn't easy.*

Once upon a time, Ruth thought Susan shared her faith in Christ, but she got sidetracked.

"Susie, I'm sorry." It was a simple statement, but Susan's brows unfurrowed as her eyes softened.

"Sisters?" Susan uncrossed her arms and closed the gap between them to wrap her arms around Ruth. "I'm happy for you and your mzungu. At least, Dad got one kid who made his money worth the investment."

Ruth was yet to help out her family, and now that she'd messed up her chance with Brady, her parents would never get bridewealth. "Your husband already paid three cows."

"If I remember, Dad sold all of them to pay for your clinical trials or whatever."

Ruth winced. She'd used most of her dad's money, yet she was the only one who had barely offered help. Besides the groceries she took when she went to visit, she needed to build a house for her family someday, buy more cows for them to have milk daily. "I know my studying hasn't paid off yet."

Susan shrugged. "You get to use your English twenty-four-seven with your mzungu husband someday."

She couldn't tell Susan she'd messed up when she trusted a rumor on the internet. Unable to contain her tears, she'd hung up on him without listening to his side. She hoped the apology letter and package didn't get lost in the mail. She'd have to continue asking God for His help where Brady was concerned.

A horn tooted, and they both jerked to see the conductor lift his hand through the window, a way they asked if they should stop. Susan raised her hand, and the taxi slowed to a stop. "Bye, sis." She hugged Ruth one more time. Then she whispered in her ear, "Your advice always makes sense. That's why I get insulted."

Ruth chuckled and spoke over Susan's back. "Next time, bring the kids so they can see their auntie." She might as well get to spend time with her nieces and nephew while at it.

Susan turned and scrunched her face at Ruth before she got into the taxi.

And Ruth felt light as she walked back to the clinic, thanking God for the quick reconciliation with her sister.

Ivan's death discouraged her, and then Brady's picture with that woman racked her faith. Praying lately had been a dread as she questioned why God would answer her prayers if He already planned what He intended to do.

Except distancing herself from God kept her heart at war. She needed to trust He had a reason for everything, but she also needed to cry out to Him so He could fix her mess—the mess she'd created when she ended things with Brady.

A wave of panic coursed through her at the thought of not having Brady in her life. After she'd told Eunice about the internet picture, Eunice returned with two printed pages of the article—dated four years ago. How foolish she'd been to believe what she read—without even reading it fully enough to see how old it was! She'd never done something so stupid, and her actions may never have mattered more. She could only console herself that she'd been racing against her internet time running out.

She quickened her pace as she climbed the veranda stairs. Eunice arrived early today so she could beat the rain, and Ruth was going to carve out her morning to pray and reconcile things with God.

Saying she was sorry had smoothed things over with Susan so easily. Ruth needed to do the same with God and apologize for doubting Him. He knew what was best for every person He'd created. With Ivan's death, Paul's heart had softened toward God.

"Your sister needs to grow up." Eunice wiped the plates and stacked them in the basket. "When are you going to stop her from walking all over you?"

Yes, Susan needed to grow up, and yes, Ruth needed to stop letting some people take advantage of her. But talking about her sister wasn't going to help Susan's or Ruth's transformation.

"You didn't have to wash my dishes." Ruth took the dripping pan from the bucket. "I was going to do this after Susie left."

"You shouldn't have let her go until she washed the breakfast dishes."

"She cooked breakfast." Mainly because Susan was hungry. Ruth snagged the dishrag from Eunice and wiped the pan. "You know how I dislike cooking in the morning."

Eunice shrugged. She'd helped herself to porridge while Ruth escorted Susan to the taxi. "She makes good millet porridge. I'll give her that."

"Looks like it's going to rain again."

"One more month and we will be done with it." Eunice hung the damp dishrag by the jerry can next to the utility table.

September's constant downpour had rolled into October, keeping their clinic less busy and little money rolling in. Brady had left Ruth extra pocket money, but it was going fast when she had to pay Eunice and the rest of her bills.

Ruth walked back to the table and stacked her prayer journal onto the Bible before centering the vase. The fresh flowers filled the room with a sweet fragrance.

"Those lasted a while."

"They sure have." She reached for the note from her Bible. Brady's typed note had arrived with the flowers and chocolate last week. Even after the way she'd acted, he'd typed a sympathy note to comfort her in God's love. To remind her that her faith in God was stronger than any fierce circumstance. Her faith was one of the many reasons he'd fallen in love with her, and he was praying for her. Her heart squeezed. How blessed she was to have him. How was she going to make things right?

"Have you called Brady to thank him for the flowers and chocolate?" Eunice cleared her voice. "Did I say thank him? Apologize, I mean."

Ruth had been checking her texts and wanting to call him after he received her written apology. "I'm going to, soon." Maybe she shouldn't put it off any longer. The package could arrive one year from now. No joke—that could happen, and she couldn't wait another month or week, let alone a year.

"With all the rain we're having"—Eunice stared through the window, as drops hit the ground—"it's going to be another slow day. Call him."

Yes, today was a better day now that her sister was gone, except she needed to write her words first. "Maybe I'll wait... I don't know."

"Can I give you a bit of advice?" Eunice perched on the love seat and crossed one ankle over the other.

She was going to either way. "No."

"Sometimes no means yes." She pursed her painted lips and tapped a finger against her chin. "You know how people blame God for their mistakes?" She raised that finger, stopping Ruth from attempting to respond. "This is going to be one of those if you don't do anything."

"He hasn't called." He'd sent flowers, even after she'd broken up with him. He probably didn't get her text, or he would've responded.

"In this case, you owe him a call to apologize and thank him." Eunice was silent, now drumming her painted nails on her knee. "I agree with Brady. You do so much for everyone, and it's very easy to forget God is in control. That, and seriously, you trusted an article over his words. He said he loved you. Wouldn't he have confessed if he was dating someone?"

Ruth winced. She trusted him, but Ivan's death and her struggle to get in touch with Brady when she'd read the article had messed with her mind. She had more weaknesses than she knew. She plunked onto the other side of the love seat. "I'm learning, and thanks for the reminder. That's why I wrote him the letter."

Eunice stood. "I've said enough. I'll make myself scarce."

"Thanks," Ruth said so Eunice wouldn't feel she'd overstepped. She needed Eunice's bluntness sometimes.

Her cell phone rang, and she picked it up, looking at the screen. "I think it's Brady. It's a US number."

Eunice lifted both her hands in question. "Answer before it hangs up."

Why were her hands shaking all of a sudden? Ruth punched the green button. "Uh... Brady?" She wasn't sure if she whispered or spoke out loud.

"Ruthie!" His voice was soft. "I can't tell you how relieved I am to hear your voice."

He didn't sound as confident. Perhaps he thought she was going to dismiss his call. Starting with an apology was a good place. "I'm sorry, I—"

"I got your package." That explained why he called. "It's me who should be apologizing, for not understanding what you were going through, for not explaining about Violet, especially since I had an article written about me with her. I shouldn't have told you how to control your feelings about Ivan's death."

"Please..." She closed her eyes. Her chest constricted, and her stomach clenched as he took the blame. "Tell me any time. I lose patience all the time, but there's always something I can use to put blame to myself... and for Violet, sorry I didn't trust you."

"She and I were—"

"I don't want to talk about Violet anymore." The backs of her eyes heated, and she released a shaky breath, too joyous that he'd called and wasn't mad at her. "I just want to hear about you."

"I've missed you, Ruthie."

He had no idea. "Me the most."

She told him about the ongoing rain ever since he'd left, the chicken she was raising for him, her visit with Susan. "I just escorted her to the road."

"Is she your parents' fourth surviving child?"

Wow. He'd been paying attention. "You have such a great memory."

"Not always. I can't wait to meet all your siblings someday."

Someday—what a beautiful word! So there was still hope for them. "They'd love to meet you, too."

"I've been thinking... We need to figure out a better way to communicate, have video chats even. I'd like to see your beautiful face."

Such technology intimidated her—just look at her debacle at the internet café! But... "Seeing you would be amazing." Those blue eyes and pearly whites. She gave a firm nod, for herself because she knew he couldn't see her. "I'll do some research."

Speaking of research. "I looked up the type of visas. The fiancé visa requires us to be engaged, and the visit visa—"

"Requires I send an invite."

So he knew.

"I've been researching, too, but the process is longer than I want—six months."

Six months was a long time before seeing him, but it would be enough time for her to get three extra helpers for Eunice. "That's not too bad."

"I'm not a patient man."

"Is that so?" She lay down on her bed and fiddled with her braids.

"I want to see you much sooner than that... I'll think of something."

She didn't doubt he could accomplish anything he wanted to. And now he finally sounded relaxed, pleased.

"I'm sorry how I left things off last time." When she'd hung up on him.

"I'm glad you said something. Being miles apart, it's better for me to see how you feel than be left in the dark."

At least they'd solved that.

"Tell me about Ivan's funeral, how did it go?" So sweet that he asked.

"It was a blessing." She told him about her parents' willingness to have Ivan's grave in the family cemetery, how the villagers helped, and explained funeral rituals in Uganda. "Everyone comes and stays the night to comfort the person who lost a loved one."

"I love that ritual."

She kicked her feet. "I think it's very good, too." She smiled over Ivan's brother and giving him Ivan's hospital fund. "Paul's been asking questions about God and wants to move to our village soon."

"Maybe your dad can give him work to do."

"That's what Dad said, that he can work and live with them. He already has materials to build a hut for Paul on our land."

Brady was such a good listener Ruth felt almost self-centered talking about herself. Enough about her.

"What did you end up doing to the four resorts?" She hadn't bothered to browse the internet for his business updates.

"I ended up selling."

"Oooh..." Air slipped past her lips as she sat up. He'd wanted to keep those. "I'm so sorry."

"I'm sorry for those who lost their jobs, but I have some good news."

Her heart felt light. "I love good news."

"We got the Entebbe resort."

"What? How?"

"You prayed to God to move heaven and earth. That first day when I missed my flight and was lying down in your bed."

She rose, too pumped up to sit at such thrilling news. "That's amazing!"

"And that's not all—we're getting the Mabira Forest property too."

She jumped up and down. "How did you—?"

"I called to ask if the villagers could sell their items in the gift shop, one thing led to another, and I found out they were selling..." He spoke of calling the property lawyer who helped get the purchase. "I'm putting the forest property in your name."

Ruth's phone dropped. She stooped to pick it up. Her legs shook as she stood back up again. Good, she hadn't broken it or lost connection. "What do you mean? That doesn't make... That's your business."

"*Our* business." Confident and unwavering, his voice surrounded her like a hug. "It's going to be hard for you to get rid of me. I'm so in love with you, Ruthie."

Ruth closed her eyes, squeezing the phone tight to her ear, trying to let Brady's words sink in as he spoke of his plans for the resort and the forest property. The fundraiser he'd started so they could build a hospital in her village. "I'll add your name to the resort as well. Start thinking about a name for the village hospital."

Think? She had no idea what planet she was on, let alone how to think. "I want you to name it."

"How about House of Blessing Hospital?" he said without hesitation. "It represents your last name, but it's a blessing from God that the funds are available."

"God's blessings sound right."

Her knees buckled, and she sank to the floor. Overwhelmed that a man as handsome, kind, rich, and generous could be in love with a poor girl like her who had nothing to offer.

"Ruthie... You're still there?"

She cleared her throat to rid the thick lump that had taken it captive. "I'm..." She shook her head, not having a clue what to say. She exhaled and managed instead. "I love you."

A brief silence embraced them before he talked about her package and her note. "When I read the part where you've prayed for a white man—where you prayed for God to drop him on your lap again that morning when you found me on the side of the road—I had no doubt I'm that man. We belong together... I love you so much, Ruthie."

She lifted her head toward the ceiling, looking for the sky so she could say, "Thank You, Lord!" Moisture heated her eyes. Listening to Eunice talking to patients, Ruth knelt there, thankful she had this moment to herself, because she was in love with the most wonderful man and he was in love with her, too.

CHAPTER 21

Brady perused the cocktail tables in the back of the room as volunteers set up the wrapped gift baskets and display items for tonight's auction. As October shivered into November and December, he'd worked with his team to choose a few of the many applicants for his franchised resorts.

He'd also spent time learning how to run an international NGO. Ruth had been working with the Ugandan authorities getting approval to build the hospital on land her grandparents intended to donate. Brady insisted on paying them since he had the money, and her family could use it.

Being the main speakers for tonight's hospital event, Brady and Eric had flown in Eric's jet, making good time to Colorado before people arrived.

"I'm starving."

Brady spun toward Eric's voice.

Eric stood there staring at his watch. "We have enough time to grab a bite."

"Don't they serve dinner at the event?" Brady had dinner the last few years he'd attended.

"You should take my advice if you're the speaker." Eric motioned to the wide screen over the stage displaying slides of pictures Brady had set to the choreography Eric instructed. "You'll have people pulling you from one direction to another. By the time you're done answering questions, the servers will have the food and tables cleared."

He'd never thought of Eric missing his dinner whenever he'd attended the events. Even if he'd eaten some fruit on the airplane, in two hours he would be ready for a real meal. He adjusted his tie before retrieving his cell phone from his dress coat. "Let me see if there's a place to eat around here."

"I'll just talk to the event coordinator." Eric called one of the men dressed in black who was giving instructions to people draping white linens over the tables. "I hate to interfere with your plans, but I tend to go without my dinner. Any chance you can fix us something to eat before people arrive?"

The man bowed. "Anything for you, Mr. Stone." Apparently, Eric knew the guy after all. "Follow me."

They followed the dark-skinned man to a back room with a table setting for four and were served a steak dinner with roasted potatoes and asparagus.

By the time they returned to the event room, Christmas instrumentals and muted conversations drifted through the room. People stopped Eric and shook his hand. He introduced Brady to investors and executives from the most reputable businesses.

Shortly after several other gentlemen joined their circle, Brady excused himself and ambled toward his childhood friends.

"The two troublemakers." Draping his arms over their shoulders, he joined their circle. "Ryan Harper and Lucas Matthews!"

Beneath dark-blond hair slicked back, Lucas's brown eyes lit up. He slapped Brady on the back. "If it isn't the next billionaire."

"I wouldn't miss this event for anything." Ryan jostled him in a bear hug, shaking loose a shock of his thick hair. "Can't wait to hear you talk about medical stuff and charities."

Growing up next door to Ryan, Brady had dragged him to garage sales to get bargain items to resell for profit. "Surprised you didn't turn into a businessman."

Waiters passed shrimp cocktails, appetizers, and fluted champagne glasses. While Lucas snatched a meatball and slid it into his mouth, Brady declined, and so did Ryan.

"So who's the woman?" Ryan motioned to the screen showing a picture of Brady with Ruth tucked under his arm. Ruth had let one of the kids take their picture on the day she'd run out of medicine.

"You don't have to answer." Lucas crossed his arms over his chest. "That silence of you revisiting memory lane says it all."

Ryan's brow shot up. "I want to know."

"Ruth. I met her on my trip."

Lucas looked to the left, then to the right. "Is she here? Can't wait to meet her."

Brady wished she were here. He'd video called her before he left San Francisco. It had taken her two days to download the app on her phone. "She's still in Uganda. There's so much work for her to do before she can be in America." If he could get a lot done, he could go and be with her soon.

"Okay, I got everything you need." Destiny, Ryan's wife, joined them, a tray in hand. Realizing another person joined their group, she grinned. "Oh. Hi, Brady."

They'd met at Ryan's wedding and again when Brady had gone to see his mom in Virginia and Ryan and his family were visiting his parents. "I thought they have servers for that purpose."

She shrugged. "It's Ryan's and Lucas's fault." She handed Lucas a pastry plate. "Lucas wanted sparkling water and mincemeat pie, and Ryan wanted bacon-wrapped dates. I thought I'd save the servers some time and get them from the buffet myself."

"Thanks, honey." Ryan kissed the top of her head, sending vibrant hair bouncing over her shoulder before taking the tray.

"Let's go find our seats." She led them to their table and then looked at Brady. "Can I get you anything?"

"I'm good, thanks. Who's watching your kids while you're playing nanny to the guys?" Brady pulled out a chair. When Ryan became the legal guardian to his niece and three nephews, he'd hired Destiny as their nanny. Brady couldn't imagine a couple better suited to each other. Last he'd heard, she was pregnant. "You got five now?"

"Six." Lucas gulped water to wash down the bite of meat pie he'd just swallowed. "I'm the happy uncle."

He'd always thought Lucas would be the first of them to get married since he'd harbored feelings for one of the girls back home. "What happened to that girl you used to bring to our basketball shoots?" What was her name anyway? Cute kid with dimples that flashed whenever Lucas scored a basket. "Betty?"

"Brittney." Lucas's jaw clenched.

"Right... right." Brady pointed at Lucas. But he was gulping water nonstop, and Ryan's warning eyes were trained on Brady. Whoa, he could take a hint.

"Well, going home for Christmas?" That was surely a safer subject.

"The kids are so excited to see their grandparents." The light gave Destiny's amber skin a glow. Joy carried on in her voice. "Your mom is excited to see you, too, by the way."

Mom still lived in the house Brady had grown up in. Next door to Ryan's. "I'll be there."

The microphone crackled, and the emcee spoke, "Welcome to the fifteenth annual fundraiser..." She asked everyone to be silent as she prayed a blessing over the food.

When she finished, the servers in black approached with trays of food.

Brady pushed back his chair. He'd better go sit in his designated spot. He reached his hand out to Destiny. "So nice to see you again." Then, winking at her, he pointed to Ryan and Lucas. "Keep an eye on these two."

"Trust me, I have to." Ryan was already looking at his wife with longing. She hugged his arm to her. "Especially this guy."

After servers cleared the tables, Eric addressed the gathering and thanked them for their annual support. Then he introduced Brady. "He's the man of the hour, and as stated in the email, tonight's auction will be going toward his new project in Uganda. I'll let him tell us more about the House of Blessing Hospital."

The room vibrated as a thousand people began clapping. Keeping his head down, Brady took Eric's place at the podium. He spoke often, but this was different from a board meeting or press conference. He'd never talked about charity work. He closed his eyes briefly. *Help my words, Lord.*

"Uh... Yes, we're gathered here today for..." What was he supposed to call this again? Charity. "House of Blessing..." That wasn't the best intro. Something light was the way to go.

"God's sense of humor sometimes amazes me." Laughter carried through the banquet room when Brady talked about his accident and the beautiful nurse who rescued him. "When I missed my flight, I thought I could spend ten days vacationing in Uganda's best resorts and hotspots, but the woman I assumed would be my guide had plans to go to the village."

Focusing on Ruth eased his tension. He wasn't standing before a crowd of strangers anymore. No, he was sharing an amazing woman with fellow Christians—people who cared just as much as she did but may never have the opportunity to change lives the way she did. He described the village, the people, and the bike Ruth rode through cornfields to reach her patients.

He lifted both hands in question. "Who would've thought I'd throw myself in front of a cobra?" The choreographer put up a picture of the snake. Murmurs rose, and guests shuddered. "That's not the one we got out of someone's hut, but close enough. About ten feet long."

They deserved a glimpse of the dangers villagers faced.

"What if the snake had bitten Annie or a member of her family? How would they get medical attention?" He talked about Ruth's commitment and depleting her paycheck to treat people. "If one person can make a difference, how much more can ten people offer? I was burdened to do something about it..."

By the time he finalized his speech and the choreographer played the rest of the slides of malnutrition and cleft-lipped kids, plus the extremely thin women and men, several people were dabbing their eyes and sniffling.

The auction started, and people bid aggressively on the items available. Two people bid on the drums Brady had brought from Uganda. Thankfully, Ruth had talked him into carrying most of his gifts from the village.

"Ten thousand dollars for a set of djembe drums," the auctioneer chanted. "Going once, going twice, and the drums are sold."

"Ruthie." Brady breathed her name while the auctioneer continued chanting in a rhythmic monotone, sweeping people into a bidding war. She was probably sleeping right now. It must be four of five a.m. in Uganda. She should be here, witnessing God answering her prayers.

Building a hospital and placing doctors in it would mean Ruthie could take a break from time to time. He couldn't wait to video chat with her tomorrow from his mom's house.

ON CHRISTMAS EVE, BRADY centered his laptop on the kitchen island. He stifled a chuckle as Dad stiffened his shoulders while Mom fixed the brown scarf around his neck.

"Can I just lift up the scarf and show it to her?" Dad shook his head, jostling his graying hair trimmed and combed back the way he kept it all year long.

"No." Mom brushed loose hair from Dad's dark sweater. "She needs to see how good we look in our new scarves."

"Whatever Lisa says." Dad gave his ex a secretive smile before catching Brady's gaze. "Right, son?"

Brady could only shake his head. Dad and Mom adored each other, yet they couldn't work to mend their relationship. He glanced back at the screen. All he needed to do was press dial and pray Ruth would be available.

When Brady told Mom about calling Ruth on Christmas Eve, she'd called Dad and told him to show up with the scarf Ruth gave him.

"Your brother will have to meet Ruth next time."

"In person." Things had to work out for Ruth to come to the States soon. He'd even hired a lawyer to deal with the process. The lawyer thought three months instead of six. Which was still far too long. "I'll be going to Uganda at the end of January."

"You're moving there?" Mom's brows crinkled as she sat in the chair across from Dad. "I thought she's coming here."

Brady had made up his mind last night. He couldn't go on like this, thinking of Ruth and wanting nothing more than to be with her. "Until she gets her visa." And she had people working in her place. His fingers hovered over the laptop's keyboard. Her community would be more at a loss than if Brady had to leave New York. "Lots of people depend on her. She has so much compassion for hurting people—I can't imagine her engaged in any other type of work."

Mom folded her arms on the island. "You can't possibly leave your home."

Home. The house he returned home to each night. Lately, he'd just pictured Ruth walking around his house, him with Ruth in a jungle somewhere on an adventure. Ruth was home. "It's just a house."

"Your son is so much like you, Lisa." Dad's eyes softened. "Adventurous risk-takers."

Mom crossed her arms, and her blue eyes softened. "If I didn't know you well, I'd almost take it as a compliment."

The corners of Dad's lips lifted. A silence passed between them as if they'd forgotten Brady was in the room.

"Okay, you two." Brady looked at Mom, then to Dad. "You live like ten miles from each other, and you have to wait until Thanksgiving and Christmas to catch up."

Dad's face reddened, and he peered through the kitchen window as giant snowflakes floated to the ground.

"Dad, you need to stop by, instead of driving past. Mom, you need to go by his office, instead of looking at the law firm's website. Take each other out to lunch, guys."

Mom huffed. "I don't look at his website."

"It's okay." Dad took her hand. "I'd go to lunch with you any day."

Mom pulled her hand away and fumbled with her purple scarf. "Can we call? This scarf is getting too hot."

"Thought you'd never ask." Brady clicked the cursor to call. Having his parents reconciling in front of him… Well, that was awkward, yet it felt right.

His excitement rose as the first ring sounded and then the second, and then Ruth's face appeared on the screen.

She fumbled with her long braids. "Hi, sweetheart."

Those slinky braids falling over her shoulders—longer than her usual hair—framed her face. Man, she was gorgeous. "Did I say how much I like your hair?"

"Twice." She curled a braid around her finger. "I hope you remember these are extensions, not *my* hair."

He remembered. He'd never forget her spirally curls or the way they tickled his face when he kissed them. "I also like your regular hair."

She smiled and sank onto her bed. "Aren't you supposed to be at your parents' house today?"

She knew he celebrated Christmas with his mom and dad, but she'd had no idea he was calling today. He faced the computer toward Mom and Dad and stepped between them, placing one hand on each of their shoulders. "I am, and they'd like to meet you."

"Merry Christmas, Ruth." Mom touched her scarf. "I love my scarf."

Dad waved.

Ruth's face lit as she sat up straighter. "Brady said purple's your favorite color."

"I like mine, too." Dad patted his scarf. "It's perfect for a snowy day."

"Is it snowing right now?" Her eyes widened. "I still can't imagine what snow looks like."

"Brady will show you." Mom pointed toward the sliding screen door to the backyard.

Brady rose with the computer. "Ready to see what snow looks like?"

Her eager nod sent those braids twitching.

He walked through the screen door. Although Dad had wanted them to move to a fancier house, Mom clung to this place, claiming it had too many memories. Brady tipped the computer for Ruth to see giant snowflakes.

"That's amazing!" She pressed a hand to her mouth as if to hide her wide smile, but that smile that brought him joy peeked around the edges, warming his heart in the cold afternoon. "I can't believe something like our months of endless rain could turn into ice sometimes."

"I know, right?" He bent and scooped snow in a ball, wincing at the bitter coldness. It was worth it when he earned an extra smile. "This is what it looks like."

"Is it that soft to fold into a ball?"

He tilted the computer to show her while he chucked it over the fence. "If you were here, I'd have thrown that at you."

She twisted her face. "That's not nice."

Laughing, he walked back to the house and wiped his damp hand over his pants. "I'd be nice enough to teach you how to fight back."

"How kind of you."

"I can be kind sometimes." He passed his parents, who seemed not to notice as Mom laughed at something Dad was saying. "Why are you alone for Christmas?"

"I had a feeling you might call after the final fundraiser. I told my family I'd join them on Christmas Day."

"Looks like you can read my mind, I guess?"

"I was thinking of calling." She ducked her head, twisting a braid around her finger again. Her curly dark lashes hid her eyes from him. "But I didn't want to interfere with your family time."

He cradled the laptop with one arm, wishing he could hug her close instead. She was family, if not closer than anybody. "You can interfere with my events any time."

He grabbed a kitchen towel and wiped the dampness from the computer before heading upstairs to the library, his dad's former man cave. And while he walked, Ruth twisted onto her stomach on the familiar bed Brady had woken up in. Who knew he'd still remember the pink floral sheets he'd slept in for one night, the comforting scent that radiated from them. "Don't ever get rid of the pink bed sheets."

She lifted the corner of the Mickey Mouse blanket to reveal the sheets he had in mind. "Never. They're my favorites."

He settled into a plush leather armchair and stacked some sports magazines on the side table to get the laptop at the right height.

"By the way, I got the footballs." She bit her lower lip. "I'll pay Dongo to take them to the village after Christmas is over."

"We will need a van someday. It'll come in handy to deliver all those things."

"I hope you know I can't drive."

"*Yet*. I'll teach you." Or hire a teacher in Uganda to do so.

Ruth chuckled. "You mean to teach me through video calls?"

He twisted in his chair as his plans to arrive and set up temporary residence tried to wiggle out. It was Christmas Eve after all. Wouldn't that be a good time to surprise her? He shrugged. He could wait until he showed up in person. "Anything is possible, Ruthie."

"That's true." That priceless grin opened her full lips. "I still can't believe I get to see you while we talk! It was so special to get to see your mom and dad. What about your brother?"

"They're having Christmas with his in-laws."

She nodded, flicked a restless braid back over her shoulder, and then asked about the fundraiser.

"God has provided." They'd raised more than the startup costs for their goal. "People were so generous. Can you believe the two drums at the auction went for ten grand—I mean ten thousand dollars?"

"Wow! That will go a long way!" Her curly lashes wisped up as her eyes widened. "That will pay ten builders for one month's work."

"That's the cheapest thing on the auction..." He went through the items he could remember and the amounts paid. Plus, funds came from the three events before Colorado, and ongoing donors were willing to stand by them throughout their journey of running a hospital.

"No way!" She screeched, bounding from her bed. The screen spun, making him dizzy as she scooped up her phone and whirled around. "Brady Sharp, have I told you how much I love you?"

Pressure in his chest built up, needing release as Ruth's joy-filled face and tone overwhelmed him. "Not enough."

"You're such a tease." Her shoulders shook as she laughed and sank back on the bed. "And of course you're the godly man I prayed for." Her expression serious, she touched the screen where he imagined his image was and whispered, "You're the love of my life."

The pressure grew hard to breathe around as he, too, put his hand on the screen tracing the image of her soft-as-silk face. "I love you," he whispered, overcome by the urge to get on the next flight.

The big picture. Focus on the long term. "Next time I come, I won't leave without you."

She wiped at her eyes. He didn't blame her. His eyes were fogging up, too.

He'd work day and night to get everything in place for his business to thrive while he was abroad.

CHAPTER 22

Brady trudged through the tiny airport as he lugged his bags and almost tripped over someone in his way.

The direct flight from New York to Entebbe had taken longer than expected. Eighteen hours—which, with him anxious to get to the love of his life, felt like an eternity.

January had gone fast while he rearranged his business and trained a loyal manager to take his place in his absence.

Stepping out of the airport, Brady breathed in the fresh morning air of the land he'd missed. It felt like home.

"Brady!" Dongo called.

Brady squinted, peering over several heads before sighting Dongo's tall frame. Dongo's smile mirrored Brady's as he let go of his luggage to embrace him. "It feels like forever since I last saw you."

"Me, too." Stepping back, Dongo looked over Brady's attire. "Nice suit."

Brady brushed off the wrinkles. In less than two hours, when the sun hit, he wouldn't be needing it. "Thanks."

"Ready to go see Ruth?" Dongo walked toward the luggage.

"Yeah." Brady's stomach tightened, and his head pounded worse than after his accident as anxiety and something he couldn't pinpoint accosted him. He was too distracted to help Dongo with the bags as he scanned the parking lot. He'd said goodbye to Ruth right there. He could still see her standing there, her posture bearing up under pain.

Even though he knew she'd be at the clinic, he'd clarified her whereabouts when he'd called Dongo.

"You said something about pri... prisol?" Dongo strained his face as he started the car.

"A proposal." Brady fumbled with the velvet box in his dress coat. "It's when you ask a woman if she will marry you."

"Phew!" Dongo shook his head. "You mzungus have very complicated traditions. If you want to marry woman, go to her family and give them cows, goats, and food. Simple. You have your wife." He drove out of the parking lot.

"Without her consent?"

Dongo shrugged.

And Dongo thought Caucasians had complicated traditions? "So what's your plan to get Ruth?" Brady asked instead.

"I just tell her someone's injured."

Brady squirmed a bit. He winced, scratching his jaw. "I don't want to lie to her." But how else could he get her to meet him at the grassy place where she'd rescued him?

"It's not lying... You're injured."

Whoa! What was he planning? "What do you mean?"

Laughing, Dongo wagged a finger. "Your heart." He turned his gaze back to the road and placed both hands back on the steering wheel. "Love's the most dangerous disease a man can have."

Good point. Brady's lips lifted as he tried to relax in his seat. "I didn't know you have such a great sense of humor."

"I can be funny sometimes." Dongo grinned, obviously pleased to be right. "Trust I. When Ruth see you, she forget everything else."

Brady hoped so. Beyond the window, an amazing sky blanketed the incredible landscape, the hilly pastures and farms breathtaking as they glowed with golden and pink hues. How he'd missed this.

His heart raced when Dongo dropped him off the road. "I'll go fetch her."

His hands shaking, Brady lifted the handle to open the door and stepped out. The familiar sights of Kisubi—as well as knowing Ruth was walking on the same ground—consumed him as he trudged through the waving grass and started walking around in circles. If he could contain his heart racing, Ruth wouldn't have to find a collapsed man on the ground again.

Through his peripheral vision, he caught movement and turned. He sucked in a quick breath and held it when he saw Ruth marching along. With her hair braids gone, her natural hair clung to her forehead as if she'd just gotten out of the shower when Dongo told her of the "emergency."

She braced a hand to shield her eyes, then pressed it to her chest as recognition registered. She dropped her medical bag and broke into a sprint. "Brady!"

He strode forward to meet her. Their surroundings blurring, everything faded—everything but Ruth. Then his hands were cupping her face. Her skin was so soft, so perfect. "I'm home," he whispered, peering into the eyes he loved.

Home was with Ruth. Whether they were in a dungeon or a mansion, a village or a city. Lowering his head, he pressed his mouth to hers. Not calm and patient as he had before, but urgent. Hungry. Her hand gripped the front of his coat, the other pulling at his waist. She kissed him fervently, and they were both breathless when she stepped back. Her shock was tangible with eyes wide and hands trembling more than she probably realized.

"How?" She blinked glossy eyes. "Where did you...? Oh my!"

A gasp slipped from her lips as she edged back a step, and he found himself plunging a tear of joy.

"I want to be here. With you." He closed the slim gap between them again and wrapped his arms around her. Threading his hands through her damp hair, he kissed her head. She smelled like Ruth. Sweet and home. "From this day forward, I don't ever want to spend another day without you."

"Me, too."

He stepped back, retrieved the velvet box from his coat, and flipped it open as his knee sank into the dampened ground. "Ruth Kirabo, from the moment I met you, you turned my life around."

Both hands flew to her cheeks, and she gasped.

"You showed me there's more to life than chasing after wealth. There's joy in the simplicity. Your culture requires me to ask your parents first, but I fell in love with you first, not your parents..."

"Yes." She clasped her hands together, and her vibrant brown eyes sparkled to match her wide smile. She knelt across from him. "I speak for them. They will say yes."

He took her left hand in his and slid a princess cut solitaire diamond ring on her finger.

Lifting her hand, he kissed it and lingered with her soft skin against his lips. He closed his eyes for the briefest moment to double-check if he was dreaming. When he reopened them, Ruth was wiping away happy tears, and he stood, pulling her up with him and kissing her again. His hands wrapped around her waist, holding her and not wanting to let go. That pressure in his heart that he'd lived with in her absence released, love overflowing its bounds, sluicing sweet warmth through his veins.

"I'll call in another nurse today." Her breath warmed his chest. "We have some celebrating to do."

He hadn't thought past this moment. "I'm glad one of us is sane enough to make plans."

Ruth said yes!

Perhaps today was a better day to start making plans for their wedding. He was once young, and now was old enough to know what he wanted.

Whatever plans lay ahead for the day, he was confident that—no matter what they did—it was going to be one of the best days of his life.

EPILOGUE

EPILOGUE

Ten months later...

Perched on the most comfortable sofa, Ruth gripped the electrical blanket around her shoulders as her husband adjusted the fire to a low setting on the gas firepit. The Christmas lights strung from one corner to another gave Brady's rumpled hair a golden glow.

"I promise to keep you warm." He ambled back to the sofa and lifted the blanket from one shoulder before sliding his arm around her waist. "I can't believe you're cold even with the enclosed glass walls."

"Just because it's a rooftop doesn't mean we're inside the house." The terrace, with its stunning pool inlaid with glass and blue mosaic tiles, three seating areas, a bathroom, and an outdoor kitchen, almost felt like a house itself. She could easily sleep out here—if it wasn't frigid. "Okay, it feels like a house, but it's too cold."

"It won't be when we start roasting marshmallows."

S'mores fixings littered the table. She licked her lips. "I can't wait.
"

Brady's penthouse was like a fancy hotel. Not even close to the ones she'd walked past in Uganda. Those five bedrooms and four bathrooms were a huge contrast to where she'd lived. The beach house they bought in Entebbe was spacious, but not luxurious like this.

Since she hadn't made any friends in New York, she didn't want to stay at home alone in the big place, so she left with Brady on the days he went to his office. She helped his assistant with whatever extra work she could take on. Brady intended to put up his penthouse for rent when they returned to Uganda in March. His San Diego property would be their American home whenever they visited his country.

"It's not the typical outdoor experience, but you get to try the deliciousness." Hershey's chocolate wrappers crunched when Brady ripped open the package and started breaking candy bars in squares and layering them on top of the "Honey Maid Graham Crackers," as the blue box read.

After Brady proposed in January, they'd agreed to get married before the end of February. They did a traditional wedding, and Brady paid for bridewealth and wore the traditional long gown the men wore for the occasion.

His bridal wealth was more than Dad had ever dreamed. He paid to build her family a bigger house. Amazing what money could do! Because he paid cash, there were plenty of workers, and the house was built and ready to move into within four months.

With Brady's friend, Eric, promoting the hospital and the success of Sharp Resorts both in Uganda and in America, financial donors flooded the House of Blessing Hospital.

Although the main building was still under construction, they'd set up a temporary structure in the village with two doctors and six nurses on-site full time. The nurses lived in Ruth's childhood house, while the two doctors stayed with Ruth's parents until the charity could build a brick apartment for all the health care workers in the village.

Besides funding full-time doctors, Brady flew out a plastic surgeon from America. Zach Eron, a missionary doctor Eric had recommended, used to travel internationally, performing facial surgeries for kids with abnormalities. Zach stayed with Ruth's parents for two months while taking on the surgeries. He did a follow-up last month.

As for the city clinic, Ruth had rented a spacious building in September and given Eunice a raise. She'd also hired a doctor and five extra nurses. She still worked there whenever she wasn't overseeing the hospital's progress in the village.

At times, she went with Brady to the Sharp International Getaway in Mabira Forest, or the Sharp International Resort, formerly Entebbe Resort, to attend employee meetings at either site. The villagers were thrilled to have their items in the gift shops. Even though noncitizens couldn't buy a house or land for years, Brady was able to purchase both properties since he added Ruth's name to the title.

"Ready for the s'mores?" He jolted her from her thoughts and handed her a long metal stick with two white mushy objects. "Hold onto your skewer."

That's what the metal stick was called? She twisted a skewer in her hand. "How does it work?"

Leaning back on the sofa, he took the stick and snuggled her to his side, then kissed the top of her head. She was amazed by his ability to move when he lowered the skewer over the flames and began the roasting process.

She focused on the fire, the rotation of the skewer.

"It's all about having the right temperature and timing."

He was just the perfect temperature—she didn't even need a blanket anymore. She curled into him, snuggling and leaning her head against his shoulder. The feel of him close and secure made the new land less foreign. They sat there, letting the flames dance in front of them, as they fixated on the orange and blue heat sparking off the glass rocks.

A glance through the glass to the falling snow over Manhattan's stunning skyline reminded her of the upcoming Christmas at his parents' house in three weeks.

The texture of snow still amazed her. After two months in America, she'd seen far too many things, but snow was, by far, her favorite.

The first time it snowed for her was on Thanksgiving at Brady's childhood home.

Brady's dad, mom, and brother flew to Uganda to attend their traditional and church weddings. Brady's brother wasn't as warm as Brady, but not everyone had to be like Brady. If they were, the world would be a boring place.

Ruth had never feasted as much as she had on her in-laws' remarriage ceremony, and the food on Thanksgiving Day. She wished she could ship some to the kids in the village, but that was impossible. Though things tasted different and took some getting used to, she loved the variety America offered.

Whenever Brady took her out, Ruth ordered rice and chicken. Beef, chicken, and rice didn't taste as flavorful as her country's, but she appreciated Brady's effort's to have food delivered from an African restaurant every so often.

America was almost as good as she'd imagined. The big supermarkets like Costco and Walmart, and the glamorous shopping centers felt like a glimpse of a new planet. Seeing beggars in worn clothing when Brady took her to Brooklyn and Queens surprised her.

"You don't want it dark." His deep voice drew her eyes back to the fire, at the now-golden marshmallow. "It's all about patience. You roast with the inside out and aim to make the center gooey, so when you squeeze it between the grahams, you get oozing marshmallow over the sides."

"Is it ready yet?" She slid her arm around his waist.

"Yes, my love." He kissed her head again. "It will look like a sandwich."

She'd tried a sandwich twice last month, but she hadn't decided if she liked it or not. It might take a few more tries to decide.

"I finally found a church where they dance." He brought their marshmallows to the prepared grahams. He swiped marshmallows off the stick and collapsed them on the chocolate over the graham, before pressing another cracker on top. "You'll feel right at home."

Wow. He'd been researching the right church for her? "You're so good to me."

"So are you." He handed her the sandwiched cracker. "You attend an English-speaking service in Kampala, for my sake."

Even though New York proved to be surprisingly diverse, Ruth had felt out of place dancing for the Lord during worship time. The church they'd visited for the last five weeks seemed to stand still even during an upbeat worship song. She wasn't as good a dancer, but she looked forward to dancing for God.

"Take your first bite." Brady bit into one corner of his cracker, so she imitated him.

She paused to savor the test. The crackers reminded her of the biscuits in Uganda. "Hmm."

"What do you think?"

She already loved the chocolate part. Marshmallow? She wiped her mouth. "I love it."

She didn't like the marshmallow sticking to her mouth and her hand, but she licked the stickiness, imitating Brady.

Although Brady was wonderful, they'd both had some cultural differences to adjust to. She drove him mad whenever they went shopping or eating out and she compared item prices to Uganda.

"The standard of living is higher in America," he would say, and it may be so. But it didn't make it any easier to pay for fancy items.

She loved the unlimited soda she could drink, but couldn't bring herself to finish an entire can, and it bothered Brady if she kept a half-empty can in the fridge. He'd rather she toss whatever was left over so she could start with a fresh can.

They argued over him leaving his shoes all over the place. He hated when she moved his coat from the couch to the closet. He preferred having things a certain way, and so did she.

In Spite of their differences and minor disagreements, two things held them together—their faith in God, Who'd brought them together, and their love for each other.

-THE END-

If you've enjoyed Brady and Ruth's story, please share your review on Amazon, BookBub or Good reads

Read Ryan and Destiny's Story in Book 1

NEXT IN THE SERIES!-The Physician's Helper.

He was in love with his best friend, but she got engaged to his brother.

Just when Lucas Matthews was about to reveal his secret feelings for his best friend Britt, his brother beat him to the punch and proposed to her—forcing Lucas to take desperate measures.

Lucas rocked Brittney Young's world when he challenged the status of their friendship. Sealing his confession with a melting kiss, he left no room for confusion, but by the time Britt got over her doubts, Lucas had left town. Not only had she lost a best friend, but she also ended her engagement. The only thing she didn't lose was her job as his grandma's caregiver.

With each passing day, Britt realized that her feelings for Lucas went beyond friendship.

Seven years later, when Britt's ex-fiancé's wedding brings Lucas back into town, she's not prepared for the way her blood sizzles in his company.

Could this be a second chance to renew their friendship and find something more? Can Lucas risk giving his heart again to the woman who crushed it?

A NOTE FROM THE AUTHOR

Thank you for reading *The Entrepreneur's Nurse*. It's always a blessing to meet new readers. And to those who have read all my stories, thanks for giving me another chance and for your reviews and notes of encouragement.

My Dad and Mom (Both in heaven) were an inspiration behind this story. I can never forget to thank God who gives me the creativity to weave these stories.

You can connect with Rose on Facebook or email her at rjfresquez@gmail.com

ABOUT THE AUTHOR

Rose Fresquez is the author of the Buchanan -Firefighter series, The Eron Outsiders-Romance, The caregiver series, two short stories and two family devotionals.

She's married and is the proud mother of four amazing kids. She loves to sing praises to God. When she's not busy taking care of her family, she's writing.

OTHER BOOKS BY ROSE FRESQUEZ

The Buchanan Series

1. First Site
2. Something Right
3. New Light
4. Bright Side
5. Short Sighted

Romance in The Rockies

1. Complex
2. Choices
3. Beyond Repair
4. Stand Out
5. Crystal Clear

The Billionaires' Reunion

1. A Legitimate Date
2. A Sudden Romance
3. A Necessary Compromise
4. A Genuine Disguise
5. A Marriage of Convenience
6. A Surprise Rescue

The Caregiver Series

1. The Doctor's Nanny
2. The Entrepreneur's Nurse
3. The Physician's Helper
4. The CEO's Companion
5. The Investor's Wife
6. The Soldier's Trainer
7. The Realtor's Attendant